THE CIRCLE
BROKEN

by Richard Johnston

Order this book online at www.trafford.com
or email orders@trafford.com

Most Trafford titles are also available at major online book retailers.

Printed in Victoria, BC, Canada.

ISBN: 978-1-4269-1797-4 (sc)
ISBN: 978-1-4269-1798-1 (dj)

Library of Congress Control Number: 2009910349

Our mission is to efficiently provide the world's finest, most comprehensive book publishing service, enabling every author to experience success. To find out how to publish your book, your way, and have it available worldwide, visit us online at www.trafford.com

Trafford rev. 2/11/2009

 www.trafford.com

North America & international
toll-free: 1 888 232 4444 (USA & Canada)
phone: 250 383 6864 ♦ fax: 812 355 4082

Tika Dedication

I dedicate this novel to my wife Mary Alice Boyce Johnston, and family: Donald, Linda, Erika, Stephane, and Katia, whose tribal love and support are never in question.

I also thank my friends Judy Walden, Rick Thompson, and Mario Ivanoff who have read and responded to multiple versions of the manuscript, and acknowledge a special gratitude for my lovely daughter Linda Johnston who has been an inspiration for developing the character of Tikanaka in this novel.

THE SACRED CIRCLE OF LIFE

Disons simplement que le génie amérindien, parce qu'il reconnaît l'interdépendance universelle de tous les êtres... cherche par tous les moyens dont il dispose à établir entre ceux-ci... l'abondance, l'égalité et donc la paix. C'est le Cercle sacré de la vie qui s'oppose à la conception évolutionniste du monde selon laquelle les êtres sont inégaux, souvent méconnus, constamment bousculés et remplacés par d'autres qui semblent adaptés à "l' évolution."

Pour une histoire amérindienne de l'Amérique
Georges E. Sioui, Wendat historian
Les Presses de l'Université Laval, 1999

Let us say simply that the Amerindian genius, because it recognizes the universal interdependence of all beings...seeks by all means at its disposal to establish among them... abundance, equality and therefore peace. It is the Sacred Circle of Life that opposes the evolutionary concept of the world whereby these beings are unequal, often misunderstood, constantly under pressure and replaced by others who seem adapted to "evolution".

Translation by author

Notice: *The Circle Broken is a work of historical fiction, a story of romance and intrigue interwoven with selected actual historical persons and events in the life of the French explorer René-Robert Cavelier de La Salle. The romance of Remy and Tikanaka, along with other supporting characters—Native Americans and Europeans, is a creation of the author's imagination. (See Novel Notes in the back of this book).*

Chapter 1

THE GRIFFIN'S NEST

Sparkling embers shot into the air as smoke billowed toward the night sky. The stockade surrounding the worksite with its saw pits, piles of lumber and the massive Griffin swinging on its scaffolding, were all aflame, lighting up the forest. A warrior, eyes like black holes in his painted face, crouched behind a large bush, the sinews of his shoulders gleaming. He took aim and drew his bow.

Remy bolted upright in his bed of skins. By the fire's glow he thrust out his elbow to ward off the arrow. Unexpectedly the flaming battlefield disappeared. In the stillness a sound of rustling leaves floated up. Alert now and on his feet, Remy reached for his musket.

Rocks were skittering down the slope outside his cave. He pointed his weapon toward the entrance.

"*Qui passe?*"

"*Hallo. C'est moi,* Tonty," came a voice out of the blackness.

Remy lowered his weapon as a dark form scrambled into the cave.

"Sorry to awaken you at this hour, *mon ami,* but you are needed for guard duty."

"I thought Jean was on watch."

"At the moment he is missing. He was scouting the south perimeter and he should have been back two hours ago. I am worried."

"Do you believe they'll strike tonight?" Remy drew a deep breath. "In my sleep they were already here. Jean could be in danger?"

"I think not, but the men are frightened. There is evidence that the Iroquois are all around us. They are watching us build this monster vessel on their land. And they don't trust us."

"Strange. I was just dreaming that a Savage was drawing his bow from ten paces away. The Griffin was ablaze and twisting in the wind."

Tonty shook his head. "Remy, even those of us in command imagine things. But we have to remember our mission and hold out until our boat is finished. Most of all we must give courage to one another. "

He moved into the light of the smoldering coals.

"Let's cover this fire. You can smell it down wind and they might come from the south."

Pulling off his glove Henri de Tonty bent over and swept away the last live embers.

He looked down at his metal hand. "You can't believe how cold this gets."

Remy stared and nodded. He reached for his small pack containing a powder flask and musket balls.

Tonty peered into the darkness. "Do you really want to sleep here? You know there is a place for you in the stockade with the other men."

"My cave is comfortable and I enjoy the view of the river."

"We're not here for the scenery, young man." Tonty smiled. "By the way Remy, how old are you?"

"Seventeen, sir."

"I must admit that after only five weeks in the wilderness you've become a dependable *compagnon*. Well I suppose you have nothing to fear by sleeping in this place. We'll soon have the huts built for everyone."

"Until then I prefer staying here."

Remy was thinking about the rough language and teasing of the older men.

"The Sieur de La Salle would like to have our men together, but for the moment do as you wish. I'm off to find your friend Jean. Pray that no harm has come to him." Tonty slipped out into the night.

It may have been the howling of timber wolves that had announced the war cries of Remy's dream. Standing now at the mouth of his cave, he looked down upon rippling starlight on the

Niagara River. To the south he could make out the stockade extending into the dense forest. How different this was from the friendly hedgerows of France and his tiny village, a cluster of thatched stone houses surrounded by strips of oats, rye and wheat spreading across the land.

Right now he was curious to learn more about the aloof Sieur de La Salle, who having struck a bargain for his services, would control his life for the next two years. Perishing in an Indian attack, however, was not part of Remy's plan for finding freedom and adventure in the New World.

His cave was a short walk down to the stockade gate. To reach it he had to pass through heavy brush and trees. Vertical walls of limbs strung together and attached to the trunks of trees surrounded the work site. Remy could imagine that a few flaming arrows would mean disaster.

The Griffin was about half finished. A stout framework of timbers suspended the keel and ribs of the hull that under the tutelage of Henri Mollet had been shaped from raw lumber. When Jean did not return Henri had remained on duty. Remy found him peering around a pile of rocks.

"There have been no signs of attackers," he told Remy.

Night raids had cost them the loss of precious tools. Sections of fence had been knocked down in places before the sentry on duty could arrive.

"Tonty is looking for Jean on the western trail." Henri appeared uneasy. "Would you like company for a while?"

Remy shook his head. "You've already had a long watch. I'm worried though about Jean. We're close friends. We came over on the same ship."

"I understand. And I wouldn't want to lose such a skilled young carpenter." Henri departed.

Remy passed among piles of logs and the sawpits, savoring the aroma of fresh cut wood. He sat down for a while beneath a tall fir that sheltered the ship, thinking about Jean. Yesterday Tonty had related to Remy and Jean the tale of the Griffin, a mythical monster whose name the ship would bear. The creature was described as having the body of a lion with the head and legs of an eagle. It would put fear into all enemies.

He heard sounds near the entrance and hurried to investigate, musket at ready. As the big gate opened there came a creaking of wood.

"*Qui passe?*" Remy called into the darkness.

"*Hallo.* Lower your musket," a familiar voice responded.

With a rush of joy he saw Jean and Tonty approaching.

"What a relief." Remy embraced his friend. "I was afraid we had lost you."

"Not that easily, *mon ami.*" Jean dropped his musket and pack. He was still breathing hard from keeping pace with Tonty. He slid to the ground with his back against a tree. "Well, it all started as I was making my way south along the river. I heard something crashing through the woods, headed toward the shipyard. Then some animals came running past, probably elk. I thought they might have been frightened by warriors out for a night raid."

"Did you see anyone?"

"I followed a short distance certain that there was someone in the brush. Branches were swaying as I approached. Since I was alone I feared a trap so I turned back. Near the shipyard I heard twigs snapping and jumped behind some bushes. Who should be coming along but Monsieur Tonty."

Tonty laughed. "In the dark it's hard to tell a Frenchman from an Indian."

"So I can finish out the night." Jean rose to his feet and picked up his musket.

Tonty turned to Remy. "And now you can try to find some peaceful dreams."

Exhausted, Remy began to make his way back in the darkness eager to snuggle again into warm furs. Morning would come only too soon. He walked along thinking how fortunate he was to have such courageous friends. And he vowed to become a skillful woodsman like Henri de Tonty.

About half way through the thicket he sensed rather than saw movement in the bushes. He stepped behind a tree. A dark form was advancing into his line of sight. He pressed his body against the tree trunk, listening.

"Qui passe?"

Absolute silence. He raised his musket and fired into the darkness. The night visitor crashed into the bushes and disappeared.

The shot awakened the others. They gathered around their skeleton ship. Jean and Tonty had rushed over to learn what had happened. The Sieur de La Salle emerged from his hut, musket in hand. A head taller than any of his men, La Salle loomed even bigger in the darkness. He stood there in his linen nightshirt as if he had just stepped forth from his bedroom back in Rouen. He listened attentively to Remy's account of what had happened. Then with no comment the explorer turned on his heel and returned to his hut.

"*Merde.*" Remy glared at the departing figure. "Why didn't he say something?"

"You woke him up, *mon ami,*" Jean replied. "Maybe he was in the middle of a dream. Anyway, don't take it too seriously. The Sieur de La Salle is not known for his *politesse.*"

"To tell the truth when no one answered I was frightened and there was no time to aim carefully."

Without thinking he had jerked his musket to his shoulder and pointed it into the darkness of the night. This was his first wilderness lesson. Next time he would make certain of his target before firing.

As Remy returned to his cave, birdsong and the stirring of tree tops in the wind that came up with the sun seemed to make the forest a friendlier place. He hoped that the new day would be less eventful. Of course he had no way of knowing what lay in store for him.

By the day's early light he wrote in his Journal:

> *October 1680*
> *How stupid of me to shoot randomly into the darkness. I must watch how the Sieurs Tonty and La Salle do things. Can I ever gain their trust?*

Chapter 2

AN UNWONTED ENCOUNTER

The next morning a drowsy Remy was carrying planks over to the *Griffin* when he passed Tonty deep in conversation with Armand Brassart, director of the daily work schedule. Tonty motioned him over.

"The Sieur de La Salle is having some delay in his plans for the *Griffin*. This will give us more time to get ready for our expedition. Most of our men are not yet prepared for wilderness travel. "

Remy nodded. "Will we find more workers in Quebec Village?"

"Not until the boats from France come in the spring. We've decided to seek out an experienced woodsman to help train our work crew. Since Monsieur Brassart can't be spared to go on a mission at the moment I thought of a strong young man like you. Your task would be to locate a trader by the name of Pierre Chandavoine, who has been recommended to me. He is known for his skills in the forest and I want to get an impression of his character. Some *coureurs de bois* can be drunken troublemakers. We can't afford such a mistake. Do you suppose you could make a trip of three or four days alone?"

Remy's eyes opened wide. Would this be the adventure of his dreams? At the moment he felt inexperienced and uncertain. But Tonty had called him a dependable *compagnon*. The Sieur de Tonty kept looking at him. Remy could not deny the fear in his heart as he answered.

"I'll go."

"*Bravo, mon ami.* I knew I could count on you. Let me tell you what I know about this person. He lived for a time with the Algonquins.

6

He is of course a seasoned woodsman, also no novice in a canoe. If he's interested I would be pleased to have him come by for a visit early on. You can give us a brief account to let us know if you think he's reliable. Trappers passing by yesterday saw him recently along the River of White Waters to the west. This is his general location."

Tonty scratched a rough map in the dirt with a stick. "If you head one day northwest, the River of White Waters will be the second stream you encounter. It runs south toward Lake Erie, probably about two days time on foot from here. Turn left and follow that stream south. You should find him not far away, less than a day's march. I'll sketch a map for you." Tonty picked up a piece of bark.

Remy started off the next morning, relieved to be walking through the forest and not paddling all alone on rough waters. At this season the Niagara was icy. And it would be a pleasure to get away from the constant harassment directed his way at the shipyard. Big Jean Paul, the sawyer, whose skills did not include reading, had said, "Let's see our Latin scholar figure out which way this tree should fall."

It was true that in the dense forest Jean Paul could fell any tree with deadly accuracy.

Other men were friendly. Head carpenter Henri Mollet offered help. For the hull Henri was finishing boards that fit together so snugly that the joints were almost invisible. Yesterday he had watched Remy struggling to align two planks.

"There may be room enough here for a fish or two to wriggle through." Henri pointed out tiny gaps.

Remy glared at him. Henri laid his hand on the young man's shoulder. "*Ne te décourage pas.* These are better than the ones you did yesterday. Wood is a living thing, *mon ami.* To master it takes years of practice."

Tonty helped Remy assemble his pack: a buckskin cover, a wool blanket, tin cup, plate, and tiny iron cooking pot. He added a chip of flint, an iron striking strip, and crushed charcoal, plus dried corn, smoked venison, and some bread sticks of twisted dough that Barbier, the cook, had baked on a hot stone. All this was wrapped in an oilskin that would serve also as a ground sheet or as a rain cover. Tonty demonstrated the way to fold the edges and roll it into a tight bundle. Then they both leaned over the birch bark map.

"Bears have a keen sense of smell," Tonty told him. "If you take small game, eat what you can, then bury the rest. Advance a good distance to sleep."

With water in a moose bladder, musket, and hunting knife Remy was ready. Grateful for the help, he dreaded disappointing the Sieur de Tonty. Remy was still remembering his inept performance with his musket.

He set forth that morning on his first wilderness mission. A parting slap on the shoulder sent him on his way. Tonty and Brassart watched the boy stride out of sight.

"It may be a mistake to send him into the forest with so little preparation," Tonty pointed toward the departing figure, "but we don't have much choice."

"He asks questions and learns quickly," Brassart observed, "but he has a streak of independence that may get him into trouble."

"La Salle is aware of that and doesn't like him sleeping alone in his cave. However the boy may be useful if he can handle such missions and write up accounts."

Meanwhile for some strange reason Remy began to think about Le Coquin, his faithful Paris friend. If he could learn to be as clever in the forest as Le Coquin had been in the city, diverting the attention of street merchants while snatching food or coins in *la grande ville,* they would be a formidable pair. The defiant urchin, abandoned by his mother, had survived by sheer determination. His struggle to stay alive in the city explained his irreverence and Remy understood. The memory of his valiant friend gave him renewed courage.

As he made his way into a thick stand of pines he reviewed what he had learned about the forest. Tonty had explained that a tree in a clearing is as good as a sundial. Trees can tell you direction. Limbs are generally bigger on the south side and any moss on them is softer and darker. On the north moss is clean and dry. Then, too, if you find the highest points of the area traversed by the trail you can determine in which direction streams are flowing. *C'est très logique.*

Night and day in this wilderness depend not only upon the path of the sun but also the density of tree growth. Light ranges from twilight to darkness. How do you keep a sense of direction if you cannot see ahead? Well, you have to stop until your sight adapts.

For several hours Remy pressed ahead, pausing now and then to drink water from his moose-bladder. Emerging from a dark stretch of forest he stopped and blinked to let his eyes greet the sunlight. With a feeling of relief he spied one of his landmarks, a cockscomb of scraggly trees along the highest ridge of an otherwise barren mountaintop to the northwest.

Before him lay the lightly wooded slope of a shallow valley. There, not more than a bowshot away, he saw a figure moving along the bank of a stream. Remy started diagonally across the hillside to remain screened by the trees and to get a better view. At closer range he saw that it was a woman, a Savage bathing in the river, first swimming into view then disappearing behind a steep bank.

In a thicket of heavy brush he paused to rest for a moment, then mounted a boulder to get a better view. The swimmer seemed to be alone. After a time he crept to the rim of the riverbank clutching pack and weapon. Unable to hear her splashes he peeked over the bank. No one. He stood up and walked cautiously along the rim, peering down the bank.

Without warning he was struck from behind. Over the river's bank he plunged through the air into shallow ripples along the stream's edge. His musket flew from his hands to lodge in sandy mud on the riverbank. As he struggled to his knees icy water filled his boots and rose up his leggings, oozing into his jerkin. For a moment he could not get his breath.

Dazed, Remy dragged himself from the stream and frantically cast about to retrieve his musket that was now jammed with wet earth. Hearing a noise he whirled around. Less than a canoe's length above, a girl was looking down at him and laughing. She was young, maybe about his age. Her wet hair was plastered to her head.

A sleeveless deerskin robe came down to her knees. The few Indian women he had seen in Quebec Village wore long buckskin dresses. This one with bare arms and legs was more exposed than the street women of Paris.

Furious, he scrambled up the bank and lunged at her. She danced lightly away. He hesitated. Were there others from her tribe hiding in the bushes? Realizing the musket was his best security, he grabbed up the weapon, broke off a twig to start picking out the mud. Then he felt taken by a sudden chill. His hands shook as he fingered the barrel. His soaked leather clothing bound him like chains. Only his pack was dry.

To his amazement the girl squatted between two nearby rocks. She did not seem afraid. She took out a piece of wood full of little round holes, into which she inserted a stick and spun it round and round between her palms over a small pile of twigs. Within minutes tiny flames appeared. He watched, fascinated. Why would a woman alone in the woods need to carry fire-making tools? That explained the quiver on her belt. There were no arrows or bow in sight. He wondered again if friends of hers were watching all this.

Across the rocks she wedged two lengths of broken limbs and motioned for him to toss over his clothing. Still trembling from the cold Remy began to revive. Removing his jerkin he approached close enough to grab her. She snatched his icy garments. When he reached out she threatened to throw them back into the stream.

He seated himself on a log while she stretched his shirt, jerkin, breeches and leggings on some branches above the fire. In agony he finally gave up his frigid breechcloth then hid himself with the pack. He had never felt more ridiculous.

He kept his eyes on the woman, watching for any movement indicating that she was waiting for men from her tribe, wondering what he could do if they came. Knowing this might be Iroquois hunting ground, he hoped no warriors were near. They would not hesitate to kill him.

As he rubbed his arms and body she motioned him closer to the fire. She retreated but remained nearby with an expression of curious but wary amusement, making it clear she did not want him closer to her.

Meanwhile, stooping behind a small bush, he cleaned his muzzle-loading musket with its St. Etienne seamless barrel more than a pace long. He reloaded it with powder from his pack that had remained dry. The weapon should enable him to overwhelm this woman. Of course taking prisoners was not part of his mission. Anger began to subside as he pondered his choices.

Pointing to his chest he said—"Remy... Remy... Remy."

She looked puzzled. Then, nodding, she answered something that sounded like "Wendat".

He considered the possible absurdity of being captured on his first mission. He could only speculate about what the men at the shipyard would say if they knew he had been pushed into a river by a girl.

"Will your Indian friend wash your wand for wampum?" He could hear Big Jean Paul.

Remy was puzzled. Her eyes above high cheekbones regarded him in a gaze more curious than fearful. He found her prettier than Odette, the girl on the ship coming from France. Even in his anger he had admired the grace of this native girl as she was building a fire.

She appeared not to notice Remy's naked body but stared at his face. Was it the anger in his eyes, he wondered, that held her interest. Meanwhile she busied herself picking up sticks for the fire as if this were an everyday task. She gathered pine nuts for a chipmunk that kept scurrying back for more. Sweeping up a frog that ventured near she held it up to her face pursing her lips as she talked to it. The creature would jump out of her hand, hop around, and then return to her.

Remy, an interested but reluctant observant, watched her while trying to understand how he had managed to get himself into such a predicament. Further attempts to talk with the girl elicited nothing but silence and quizzical expressions.

Piece by piece she tossed him his garments. It had taken some time for the leather to dry. The sun was moving to the west. Fully dressed once again he slung on his pack and started backing away. She beckoned him to come with her, crossing the small valley and climbing a steep slope on the far side. His musket at ready he followed silently.

From the brow of the ridge he could see in all directions across a valley of birch trees. No danger of ambush. With the sun's rays caressing his back and tinting leaves gold he had a strange desire to linger a while. Fleetingly this scene recalled his favorite Paris church, *l'église Saint-Germain l'Auxerrois* bathed in afternoon light through stained glass windows.

They stood there in silence before starting back down the hill. He slid on ahead over loose rocks. Intent on keeping his balance he laughed at his own clumsiness. Then he looked back.

She was gone. Remy could not believe it. Scrambling up again to the crown of the ridge, he combed the area trying to find a trace of any movement. Darkness was coming on and he had already lost a good half-day.

His thoughts were in disarray. Why had she led him up the ridge to share that beautiful valley of birches? But why then had she attacked him with no provocation? He was angry with her while feeling a strange attraction. How had she disappeared so suddenly? Did he really encounter an Indian girl, or was it his imagination?

Returning to the riverbank he found the ashes of her fire. Clearly she had been no illusion. He emptied dried mud from his boots before chewing on some smoked venison. Spreading out his deerskin bedding he thought of the words he would write in his journal.

What nerve it was for that Savage to stare at his nakedness as he waited for his clothes to dry. Remembering his discomfort under her scrutiny he had to smile. In the fading light he wiped the nib of the pen that Brassart had cut for him from a wild turkey feather. To protect the precious paper in his journal he washed his hands. The bound book was a parting gift from Father Bernard in Paris. Remy searched in his pack for the tiny container of lampblack ink to scratch out:

October 1680
I guess I don't know anything about women.
I never had a personal talk with a woman.
Should I tell Tonty about this? Maybe not.

After packing away his writing materials Remy carefully placed his musket alongside his blanket. He went to sleep wondering if warriors from the girl's tribe might find him during the night.

Chapter 3
PIERRE CHANDAVOINE

What really happened yesterday? On the next day of his mission Remy set out into the forest puzzling over his encounter with the Indian girl. Pushing him off the riverbank was a cruel trick. But drying his clothes was a friendly thing to do. He was intrigued by her apparent lack of fear. Yet he was tantalized by her desire to share with him the magic valley of birches, a spellbinding moment he would not forget.

He squinted at Tonty's simple map. It helped with general directions but how could he judge distance? Surely Tonty would cover more ground than he could in a day. Remy's apprehension grew knowing that a wrong decision could lead to disaster.

The second stream he came upon looked as if it might be the one sketched on the map except that it seemed to be flowing more toward the west than to the south. He followed it into a deep canyon under a clouded sky. There were no shadows to tell direction and he was feeling disoriented. He sat on a rock to eat Barbier's last bread stick and chew on more venison. Sighting a distant rocky slope he decided that if he were still in doubt at that point he would backtrack.

Fortunately the stream did turn sharply southward so he continued on until nightfall. It was a full two days before he located the trappers. However, their camp was so well hidden that he passed right by. Then a wisp of smoke drew his attention and he retraced his steps.

"Hello. Are you lost?" A voice came from the forest. "Stop and rest a bit."

Peering through the underbrush Remy saw two men standing among the trees. One was tall and redheaded while his companion of powerful build had a dark complexion.

"*Bonjour messieurs.* My name is Remy Moisson and I am looking for a person called Pierre Chandavoine."

The stocky man stepped forward. "At your service, and this is my *compagnon* Camille. We saw you hurrying past and thought perhaps you were gathering herbs for your dinner." Pierre smiled as he put out a welcome hand.

"I have a message for you, *monsieur,* from the Sieur de Tonty down on the Niagara River."

"*Bien.* Come visit our camp."

In a clearing back from the stream they stood around a campfire. *Bien sûr* Pierre had heard of the famed Henri de Tonty, and he knew also of Cavalier de La Salle's plans to explore the wilderness to the south. With arms crossed and feet firmly planted he replied to Remy's message.

"I will have to think about that proposition. Training men for travel into new territory might be an amusing task. I'm not certain, however, that I would want to help build a French empire by taking more land away from the Indian people."

"But I assure you monsieur, that is not at all what the Sieur de La Salle has in mind." Remy's face revealed his amazement. "The expedition can be a great adventure of discovery and at the same time helpful to the natives."

Camille listened attentively as he folded pelts.

"Do your pelts go to France?" Remy inquired.

"Not immediately. It is in summer that beaver pelts are best. At that time the animals are plump and well fed. But their fur must first be processed. A whole family of natives will season these choice pelts for you."

"How do they do that?

"They rub them with bone marrow and wear them around their bodies."

"Then they smell like Indians." Camille sniffed.

Pierre looked at him. "In the wilderness our unwashed countrymen don't smell much sweeter."

"So how do you catch the beavers?" Remy asked.

"Camille and I trap a few just for amusement, then exchange with our Indian friends for buckskin and tobacco. They laugh at us because we don't have their skill. Natives capture the beavers right in their dams, ensnaring them with nets. However, out of respect for the animals Indians have no right to destroy their homes."

"What do you mean by that?"

Camille cut in quickly, "These crazy Savages believe they're related to wild animals and even to trees."

Pierre turned to Remy. "Camille can't get used to their thinking."

These exchanges between the two traders, uttered with a certain bite, revealed real differences of opinion, Remy observed, but his hosts obviously enjoyed their verbal fencing. They listened as Remy related his first trip alone into the wilderness. He did not go into detail concerning his river adventure, although he mentioned casually, "On the way I happened upon a lone Indian woman who said her name was Wendat or something like that."

Pierre laughed. "That is not her name. She's a Huron and that's her tribe. They call themselves Wendats. Huron is our French name for them because the warriors dress their hair in a tuft. Unfortunately there are not many of the tribe left. The Iroquois have destroyed their villages and slaughtered hundreds of them."

"I thought she might be Iroquois. They're so hostile, and some have guns." Remy looked at Pierre. "Why can't we all agree to stop selling arms to the Indians?"

Camille was quick to agree. "We should have done that from the beginning. All we need is a little brandy or colored beads to get them to part with their furs."

"Why should we not sell arms to the Indians?" Pierre addressed Remy. "They can use them for hunting."

"And to kill us," added Camille.

"So it's all right for us to kill them with guns and wrong for them to kill us in the same manner?"

What an idea! Remy shook his head.

"But why are the Iroquois so violent?"

"That's a long story." Pierre looked up from slicing a portion of venison off the carcass hanging in a tree. Gathering handfuls of green birch leaves he wrapped them gently around the meat. Then he enclosed the package in wet clay scooped up from the riverbank.

"Fortunately, along this stream we can find patches of fine clay that holds together in a cooking fire."

Remy watched in wonder. He was beginning to think that Pierre was almost as skilled as Tonty.

"Let's put this to roast." Camille had gouged out a hole in their fire and covered the packed clay with live coals.

"About the Iroquois," Remy reminded Pierre, "Where's their main tribe located?"

"The Iroquois aren't a tribe. They are a league of five nations: the Mohawk, Seneca, Onondaga, Oneida—" Pierre paused.

"And Cayuga," Camille finished.

"Why are they all against us?" Remy wanted to know.

"That probably started when our celebrated Jacques Cartier arrived about 150 years ago. You may have heard of him."

"In school Father Foignet told us about a French navigator named Cartier. I've always wanted to know more about him."

"He discovered the Saint Lawrence river. Several of his men were dying from the sickness of sailors. The Indians saved the lives of the survivors by giving them tea brewed from spruce bark. Cartier invited Donnacona, the greatest Iroquois leader, and four other tribal chiefs to the French fort at *Stadaconé*. When they arrived, French sailors seized them and forced them on board ship. Then off they sailed to France. Their families never saw them again."

"They may have liked living in France," Camille suggested.

Pierre shook his head. "I just can't believe that. It's said that Cartier wanted to present some Savages to the King for the amusement of the court. At any rate, none of them lived to see their native land again."

"How do you know all of that?"

"I lived for a while with an Algonquin family upriver from Quebec. They still tell about these white-faced strangers who first appeared in their rivers. They had never seen huge boats propelled by white sheets nor watched anyone behave as the French sailors did scampering up the ropes like squirrels in the trees."

"They tell those stories to their children?"

"Yes, I remember sitting by the fire and hearing something like:

> *Over the waters*
> *on wings of wind*
> *came a hairy-faced demon*
> *spiriting away our men*
> *leaving no bones*
> *for a good death.*

Remy listened, wide-eyed. Pierre wasted no words on the foolishness of La Salle's boat-building project.

"Why build such a big ship to carry supplies when canoes are faster and can navigate in shallow water?"

"But the *Griffin* is only for trade on the inland seas. Tonty said we will travel in canoes when we explore the rivers."

As the sun dipped behind treetops Camille scooped the lump of clay from the glowing coals. It had baked hard enough for him to crack it open with a sharp rock. The meat came out pink in the middle. Remy remembered that he hadn't eaten since early morning. Pierre reached into his sack for a lump of salt. Seasoned with a few chipped grains the juicy morsels were shared by three hungry men.

From a pewter flagon they sipped red wine that Camille claimed had been saved for a special occasion. In the crisp evening air Remy felt certain that no chateau could serve better fare. Of course he had never been invited to dine in a chateau. But he felt honored that these traders had brought out their precious wine to share with him.

Pierre turned to Remy. "Training men for wilderness travel would be a tempting challenge for me, but I love the freedom of the forest. And I sometimes feel more comfortable with the natives than with my own countrymen."

Camille shrugged. "That is probably why we earn less than the *voyageurs.*"

"Who are they?" Remy asked.

Pierre thought a moment. "Actually we're illegal traders. The *voyageurs,* skilled boatmen, are given licenses by the government. But in reality they are only hired help and possess neither canoes nor merchandise. On the other hand the merchants often become wealthy."

"The *voyageurs* travel alone?"

"*Mais non.*" Pierre stirred the fire. "Eight or more men are required to paddle their large Montreal canoes. They transport wampum beads, iron tools, guns and brandy to the north country, stopping at trading posts where the goods of their *patron* are exchanged for furs."

Sitting around the fire before slipping into their warm furs for the night they sang some *voyageur* songs. It was the first time Remy had heard this music. Pierre's baritone and Camille's tenor blended and quivered in the popular *A La Claire Fontaine, Alouette,* and *En Roulant Ma Boule.* Remy was surprised at the heartiness and sometimes tenderness of the voices of these rough men. He could tell that this was one of their great pleasures. They encouraged Remy to join in.

Next morning Pierre promised to come to the shipyard and speak with Tonty, but he was uncertain about the notion of training men for an expedition. Remy liked this new friend and was prepared to recommend him for the task. He would bring valuable skills to the shipyard. Disappointed by Pierre's hesitation, Remy set out with some cornmeal and dried meat that the trader had slipped into his pack. He followed Pierre to the riverbank where they reviewed Tonty's birch-bark map. Remy was reassured. Perhaps he could cut a day's time out of his return journey.

Remy held out his hand. "*Merci bien.* May God be with you."

"God is hardly my favorite *compagnon,*" Pierre replied with a smile, "but if you find Him of use so much the better. *Bon voyage, mon ami.*"

Reluctant to leave on that exchange Remy stood there for a moment.

"Don't take offense." Pierre pointed beyond the river. "I have my own deities out here. They guard me well."

"I was told our God took care of everybody."

"You have a right to your own God as do the Savages and everybody else."

"I have been wanting to ask Father Hennepin why *le Bon Dieu* doesn't make himself known to the natives."

"Perhaps they don't need Him."

The two traders watched their visitor out of sight in the woods.

Deep in thought about Pierre's words Remy worked his way back, determined not to lose his direction. Passing the night alone in the thick forest was somehow not so threatening on this journey. When the howling of wolves sounded close he rolled up tighter in his bed of skins, making certain that his musket was at hand. The excitement of fear was not entirely unpleasant. This was why he came to Canada.

In heavily wooded areas he sometimes heard large animals crashing through the bush and felt their eyes upon him as he followed the trail. There were squirrels and rabbits, and a few immense snowshoe hares with their brownish coats blending into the brush. Tonty had told him they would turn white in winter. The white-tailed deer and spotted fawns did not seem to mind the young traveler's intrusion.

A raven swooped down onto a low branch over the trail ahead announcing Remy's presence to the distant meadow: kwak, kwak, kwak. Then came a soft birdcall, perhaps the "Alouette" Pierre and Camille sang about last night. They would no doubt recognize its song.

Remy began imagining himself as a *coureur de bois,* making his way in the world, subject to the authority of neither La Salle nor any priest from the monastery. Quickening his pace he started to sing a verse he remembered from last night:

> *A la claire fontaine*
> *M'en allant promener...*

Then he realized it might not be wise to attract the attention of curious animals or hostile Indians. He found the trail he had followed before, reaching late one afternoon the site of his river adventure. The ashes of the Wendat's fire were still there. He circled the area, scrambling up the slope to the ridge that overlooked that magic valley of birches. Bathed once again in the sun's warmth he felt a pang of loneliness.

How had that Indian girl disappeared so suddenly? Was her village nearby? He looked around, half hoping to catch a glimpse of her before descending the slope. The only sound he heard was the crunch of rocks under his feet as he skidded downward.

After some hesitation he decided to spend the night there again. It would be only a short day back to the shipyard. By late afternoon shafts of sunlight he wrote in his Journal:

> *October 1680*
> *I am not the same person who started into the wilderness one week ago. I would not be afraid to go on another mission. I like Pierre. How can he think the way he does? What would he say about my life in Les Rapides de Moulin?*

Chapter 4

FATHER LAURENT

Returning from his first mission Remy reported on his meeting with Pierre Chandavoine describing the traders' camp. Then he ventured an opinion. "Pierre knows the forest. He could inspire our men. I hope you can persuade him to work with us."

Tonty smiled as he read the text.

"That was a rough first assignment," he told Brassart. "The boy is to be encouraged."

Remy took pride in what he had done. Yet he felt a strange anxiety. Was he now committed to being French or Canadian? He would never forget his adventures in the streets of Paris.

The mild winters in France were in his memory as his numb fingers strove to control the frozen lumber. With fewer daylight hours the pace of work slowed and a deep cold settled in. Even with a crackling fire, men on guard moved about constantly stamping their feet. Fortunately there had been no more night incidents with hostile Indians.

Remy's lonely mission into the forest seemed long ago now that winter prevailed at the work site, blanketing the woods in white. The Sieur de La Salle was rumored to be having increasing trouble with his creditors in Quebec Village.

Tonty chose Remy to be one of a group accompanying the Sieur de La Motte on a mission for La Salle. They were to visit an Iroquois village. La Motte and his men were to assure the Indians of French friendship and calm their fears about the construction of the monstrous *Griffin*. Armand Brassart and Father Hennepin were members of the party.

"Why must we keep trying to convince the Indians of our good intentions when in reality we are working to improve their lives?" Remy wanted to know. "Don't they believe us?"

"Our treaty with the Iroquois grants us the right to inhabit the area together in peace," Father Hennepin replied, "but they don't hesitate to attack our forts and to kill our men in isolated incidents. So we need to constantly remind them of their obligations. They fear that we wish to take away their land."

Remy remembered the day long ago in France when the Sieur de Senlis repossessed some of their land strips. How helpless his papa had felt to lose his best wheat land.

Father Hennepin, a Franciscan *Récollet* who had come over on the same ship as La Salle, was versed in the language of the Iroquois and in other native dialects as well. He was to serve the mission as interpreter. Observant of native ways, Hennepin seemed friendly and responsive to Remy's litany of questions.

Seven men undertook the march in deep snow through heavily wooded country. They wore webbed *raquettes*, thin ash-wood frames strung across with strips of leather called *babiches*.

"Moose hide," Father Hennepin informed Remy, "is believed to make the best *babiches*."

Awkward to manage at first, these large flat shoes made walking on top of snow possible even with a heavy burden. Gradually Remy's pace quickened and his stride lengthened.

Their packs were stuffed with deerskin covers and trail supplies. Staple food always included dried Indian corn and bear grease in leather bags. Remy remembered hearing of these delectables back in Paris, a tale he did not believe at the time. Of course they hoped to supplement the dried corn with tender squirrel or rabbit, or—best of all—deer.

They made their way among low-hanging trees, loosening showers of heavy snow on their shoulders. Early on the second day they descried four Indian hunters approaching. They appeared to be friendly and Father Hennepin bartered with them the exchange of an iron hatchet for chunks of venison and five black squirrels. They all parted content with the transaction.

The first night Remy noticed Brassart blowing on his hands then striking flint to steel starting a fire with a tinder of charcoal and dry twigs in a space hollowed out of the snow. As he watched, Remy re-

membered the Wendat whirling her stick. Could she make a fire like
that, he wondered, in a snowbound forest? If ever he saw her again
he would ask.

After five days of steady walking La Motte and his men came out
of a driving snowstorm into a larger than expected native settlement.
The village of Tegarondies spread out along the edge of the wilderness. Offering gifts of blankets and knives, the visitors were well
received and escorted to the cabin of chief Sawida. The women and
children gathered around, not unfriendly but excited to see such
strange beings.

At close range the Indian women who crowded the cabin stared
unabashedly into these bearded faces. Remy did not mind the curious eyes and chatter of the children and returned the gaze of the
women with a smile. The Iroquois children wanted to touch their
visitors' clothing. One child laughed in delight when permitted to
pull on Brassart's beard.

The Sieur de La Motte informed his French companions that it
was the Saint-Sylvestre, eve of the New Year 1681. It was their good
fortune to arrive at a friendly place on this *jour de fête*. Remy recalled
the traditional New Year's Eve service in the monastery chapel.

Early next day Father Hennepin offered a special mass and
sermon for La Motte and his compatriots after which about forty
Iroquois elders wrapped in robes of beaver and wolf skins invited
them to their Council for a peace pipe ritual. Father Hennepin and
Brassart interpreted the greetings and responses with bows and
smiles.

The Frenchmen were surprised to find in the village a Jesuit
priest who entered the bark hut with the chief for the welcoming
ceremony.

"*Bonjour, messieurs.*" He gave the visitors a brief nod. "I am Father
Laurent."

After the chief bowed and bade them to seat themselves the Sieur
de La Motte remained standing.

"Are you a representative of Bishop Laval?" he asked the priest.

"*Non, monsieur*, I am a visitor on my own initiative."

La Motte turned to Father Hennepin.

"Please inform the chief that we cannot speak with the Council
until this unauthorized person is removed."

The elders regarded their guests in puzzlement. Father Hennepin looked uncomfortable.

"The Black Robe who is your guest is not an official member of our delegation," he told chief Sawida in Iroquois.

Father Laurent rose to his feet. Bowing to the chief, he touched him lightly on the shoulder and withdrew from the hut.

Father Hennepin, sitting next to Remy, seemed agitated by La Motte's action and whispered to him that forcing Father Laurent's departure was an unwise thing for their leader to do. Then he arose to follow his fellow priest from the chief's cabin.

An awkward pause interrupted the meeting. The Récollets and the Jesuits were fierce competitors in Canada. Ignorant of La Motte's reasons Remy judged it generous of Hennepin to support a fellow priest.

Brassart, Tonty's faithful aide, stepped forward to act as interpreter. He knew the language as well as Hennepin. The discussion could continue under his direction. A handsome man, and always neatly groomed, Brassart commanded attention. His blue eyes fixed directly upon each speaker.

The Iroquois appeared to enjoy hearing La Salle's message of friendship and talk of trading for iron tools. There was an exchange of words that brought smiles and nods of approval from the elders.

Next day, before La Motte and his party were ready to leave, Chief Sawida apologized to Brassart, saying that a customary dance honoring his guests' departure was not possible outside in the deep snow. He invited the visitors into his shelter, wherein a circle was formed and the stone peace pipe passed from one to another. A young boy in feathered headdress performed a graceful dance to the rhythm of drumming.

Then a dozen young warriors lined their path as they departed and again everyone exchanged expressions of friendship. For Remy it appeared to be a successful mission. Brassart said they would have to wait and see.

"You never know by their faces what the Indians are thinking. They will agree with almost any statement you make. They will answer 'Niaova,' meaning 'That is right my brother. You are right'. Perhaps they just don't like arguments."

"I don't understand all this." Remy strove to catch up to Father Hennepin. "What do you think?"

The priest responded, "The Savages are men who have *ny roi, ny loi, ny foi* (neither king, nor law, nor faith). However, we must always remember they are our brothers, descended from Adam and Noah."

"Why did Sieur de La Motte insist that Father Laurent leave the meeting?" Remy wanted to know.

"La Motte does not like the Jesuits, but he should not have shown such anger at a fellow Frenchman before the Savages. Men of the cloth especially must support each other."

"Did you speak with Father Laurent last night?"

"Yes. He told me he was born at Aridieux near Limoges. His merchant father moved the family to Paris, where he grew up in a comfortable home. Right now he is overwhelmed by the difficulty of life in this wilderness."

"Why was he here at Tegarondies?"

"He is waiting to be assigned a mission and wishes to learn the language and more about native ways."

"What sort of man is he?"

"I would say he is a devout person and ambitious. He wants to gather the Savages into church communities like those in France."

"You believe he can do that?"

"I doubt it. But he appears to be a man of strong conviction. His enthusiasm is quite engaging."

"Are the Jesuits not evil men when they try to stop us from building the *Griffin* and having trading relations with the Indians?"

"Men of the cloth cannot be evil," Father Hennepin replied, "but their plans to gain power in the New World are not always wise. Their ambition tricks them into doing harmful things."

Remy was not sure he understood this reasoning, but Father Hennepin said it with a gentle finality.

When La Motte's party returned to the shipyard, Remy wrote in his journal:

> *January 1681*
> *I must write to Father Foignet to tell him and papa about visiting this Iroquois village. I am glad to be here but sometimes I miss France and often think about my friend Le Coquin in Paris.*

Chapter 5

REMY

From the earliest time he could remember Remy was angry with God.

"Where is my mother?" he would ask his papa.

"God took her away before you were two," Martin Moisson told his son.

"Why did He do that?"

"I do not know."

When he asked the village priest, Father Foignet could only reply that we cannot always understand the acts of God and we must not question His judgment.

Each year on All Saints Day Remy's father led the little boy and his sister Monique to place chrysanthemums around their mother's grave marked by a simple wooden cross:

COLETTE MOISSON
1636–1665

Remy would close his eyes and try to picture her deep in the wet earth. Sometimes he made little graves in the dirt to bury dead mice he found in the fields.

When Monique, six years older than he, was sent to a convent school upon the priest's recommendation, Remy was furious. He fought constantly with his father who tried to make him wash his own clothes and help with the housekeeping.

At age seventeen when he returned to *Les Rapides du Moulin* from six years of study in a monastery boarding school, Remy's most important questions remained unresolved. He had come to visit his papa before departing across the sea. Martin Moisson rushed to embrace his son.

"You are a real scholar now."

Remy had to smile as he remembered his angry departure from the village.

"Why not study to become a priest here?"

"Papa, in Canada I can get land for both of us. We could work our fields together."

"My son, I would never leave this village."

"You want to be near my mother."

The old man nodded.

"Do you think the Nuns will let me tell my sister Monique goodbye? I wonder if she looks like *maman*."

"I don't know." Martin looked at his son, already taller than himself, broad-shouldered and muscular. "It is now ten years that she has been away."

"That must be a terrible life, shut away from the world. Always praying. I will never forgive God for taking Mama before I even knew her."

"You must never have such sinful thoughts." The old man crossed himself.

"Well Papa, God has not been good to you."

Remy had kept in touch with home through the village priest who brought his letters over and read them aloud to his father. Now Father Foignet offered his friendship.

"I feel sad about leaving Papa once again," Remy told the priest when he stopped by the church. "He still misses Mama and refuses to talk about her."

"Our missionaries report that Canada is a wild place. You will find use for your education perhaps among those Savages. Your father will be lonesome but you can send him letters through me. Of course it will be a long time between ships."

At age six in Father Foignet's catechism class Remy frequently whispered to his classmates or interrupted with questions. But he was also the first to learn his letters. Most of the boys merely memorized their responses but Remy could actually read and print out words. Curious about things beyond his understanding he would ask troublesome questions like "Why did God give the Sieur de Senlis more land than my papa has? Why must my father bow to him?"

Remy could not forget the day the Sieur de Senlis appeared at their door to announce that he was taking back two strips of their land.

He dug into the dirt with his staff. "This soil is packed and not ploughed deep enough to drain properly. Since you lost your woman, Moisson, you have more land than you can work."

"That is not fair, *Mon Sieur*. This is my home. My papa worked this land."

"*Vous ne voulez pas semer la discorde* (don't make trouble), Moisson. We can perhaps reduce a little the Censitaire you pay each year."

The seigneur signaled to his driver, climbed into his carriage and they pulled away.

"My best wheat land. *Quel injustice*." Martin stamped his heels into the ground. "He already owns half of the village. May God strike him dead."

For weeks Martin Moisson was in a foul temper. Remy would waken in the middle of the night, hearing his papa stalk out into his fields.

The priest knew that Remy was lonely and unhappy and that the boy had once told a young friend, "Father Foignet had God take away my mother because her flowers are prettier than the ones in the churchyard."

How could such a capable student be so rebellious? Was he a wicked boy?

Several days later Remy panicked the seigneur's horses into a run. The careening carriage bed threw the Sieur de Senlis to the floor. His lady's nose bled as her face smashed against the front seat. The next day the coachman recognized the culprit playing by the river. He jumped down from his seat to accost the boy.

"You little rock-throwing devil, I'll pound some sense into you." He shook Remy and struck a hard blow to his head.

"Let me go." Remy struggled and kicked the shins of his assailant.

"If you scare my horses again my team will drag you on a rope all the way to the watermill." The coachman pushed the boy to the ground and walked away.

Remy saw a chance to revenge his smoldering rage soon after this encounter when he noticed the carriage parked on the bank of the river while the horses were in their barn. His weight on a spoke as he climbed up started a wheel to turning. With great persistence he could make the carriage move. On a slope toward the water the vehicle picked up speed rolling backward to plummet into the river. Dashing home Remy could not suppress a little smile.

Father Foignet accompanied Martin Moisson when the seigneur came to demand a reckoning for his damaged carriage.

"Moisson," he said, "that boy of yours is a menace to all of us. He must be taught how to behave with his superiors. He should be given a good thrashing."

Father Foignet spoke up. "I condemn Remy's actions. But remember that there is no mother in the house. He is intelligent, the best student in my catechism class. I am willing to help his father correct him."

"I will hold you to that, Father. A carriage can be repaired but in repayment you, Martin Moisson, will perform extra labor for your annual *corvée*."

"*Oui, mon Sieur.*" Martin bowed and touched the brim of his cap.

"Your son must learn to obey or villagers may punish him," the priest told Martin after the Sieur de Senlis departed.

"What can I do? He is no angel at home either."

"Remy needs to be in a place that demands obedience. Laon has an excellent school at Saint Martin's monastery. There he could learn to listen to others. I am sure that the principal, a classmate of mine at the seminary, will admit the boy."

"I have to think about this, Father. He is almost eleven and is getting big enough to work with me in the fields. He does some chores around our house. I can use some help."

"Remy has a fine mind, but that boy holds a lot of anger in him and he is a liar. He cannot continue to misbehave here. For his own good he must go."

"Well, I will talk to him, Father."

Remy had just returned from a visit to his mother's grave when his father announced that he would be sending him to a new school.

"What do they do there? Is that like the convent for Monique? I don't like that. Do I have to go, Papa?"

"Yes, son. Father Foignet thinks they can teach you to be a good boy."

"I don't think they can."

Chapter 6

CARRYING GOD

Father Laurent's experience at the Iroquois village of Tegarondies and visiting the area around Quebec Village had not prepared him for the hardships of reaching his first missionary post in Huron territory.

However, his journey to Montreal sailing in a launch included a pleasant two-day stopover with colleagues in *Trois Rivières*, a fortified post serving as an important fur-trading center. There he visited with old friends and made the acquaintance of two recently arrived Jesuit colleagues, Fathers Nicholas and Drapeaux. Then, traveling in a brigantine along the north shore of Lake Ontario, he had arranged a stop at Fort Frontenac, hoping to have a talk there with the Sieur Robert Cavelier de La Salle.

Finding that the explorer was away at his shipbuilding site, the priest met with the six Huron warriors who were to transport him to his final destination. With some difficulty he made them understand that they were to pass by La Salle's work location on the Niagara River. The interpreter named Ouentono was a broadshouldered man whose skill with a canoe far exceeded his ability in the French language.

The priest struggled in vain to communicate with his traveling companions. During the long days passed in silence he thought out carefully what he wanted to say to the Sieur de La Salle.

Squatting on their haunches for hours the Huron warriors saved their energy for paddling. They rose at dawn and heated a clay pot of water into which they stirred coarsely ground corn, sometimes containing bits of bark, ashes, and whatever else had fallen into it as it was pounded into flour.

When the mixture became a watery gruel it was poured into bark bowls. The priest carried his tin cup and partook of the repast with as much grace as he could muster. After a night of sleeping among snoring Indians and battling the mosquitoes and deer flies that seemed not to bother the natives, he found the cornmeal scant fare to prepare him for each day.

At the shipyard a surprised Father Hennepin greeted Father Laurent cordially. His Jesuit guest savored meals of roast venison and wild turkey served to the workers in a rude dining shelter with tables of hewn lumber, pottery plates and metal tableware. In his honor Barbier, the cook, even put wild lilies in a cooking-pot vase on the center table. Sleeping in Father Hennepin's bark chapel was a comfort the Jesuit had almost forgotten. But Father Laurent waited with growing impatience to see La Salle, still occupied with completing the ship's hull.

They met eye to eye at last in La Salle's dimly lit hut and seated themselves on a pair of stumps. Although the priest had no official mandate, his conversations with Bishop Laval had led him to believe that he represented all the Jesuits.

"Sieur de La Salle," the priest began, "we have come to believe that your trade with the Indians exchanging brandy and guns for furs is in conflict with our efforts to convert the natives."

La Salle removed his broad-brimmed hat and placed it on his knee.

"Commerce is the most effective way to establish connections with the natives," La Salle replied. "All can benefit from the exchange of goods."

"But, Sieur, the brandy often incites them to violence, and in the end these very guns may well be used against us."

"Excessive use of brandy is beneficial neither to them nor to us, but they will eventually adapt to its use. We Frenchmen should discourage excess by example. Metal tools are received gratefully and make their lives easier. Guns are valuable for hunting."

"But hunting for game and furs encourages their nomadic ways. It reduces them to the level of animals constantly roaming the forest to find their daily food. We must gather them into stable communities established around churches."

Both men looked up when Brassart appeared at the entrance.

"Sieur, sorry to disturb you but the tripods and rope slings are not strong enough to mount the cannons on deck."

"Tell Tonty to take Big John Paul and Crevel to see if we can mount them on an inclined plane of peeled logs. I will be out shortly."

"*Très bien*. We can give that a try."

"Please pardon the interruption, *mon Père*." La Salle turned to Father Laurent. "You were saying—?"

"You are fitting your ship with heavy guns?" The priest sat up straight. "This will motivate them to possess more arms and to trust you even less. How can you do that?"

"The ship's guns will be used both to protect trade to benefit us and our native friends. With commerce firmly established, the Indians may ultimately see that permanent settlements will be to their advantage. However at the moment fixed communities are not suitable for them. It will take time for their thinking to adapt to a less eventful way of living in nature."

"But Monsieur La Salle we strongly believe that our immediate mission is to replace their ignorance and superstition with Christianity and a civilized culture."

"I have no quarrel with that. Perhaps we can best succeed in such a task by both teaching and learning. Do you not think they have something to offer us? I believe that we can learn from them. These Savages have already developed great skill in wresting a living from the wilderness. We must gain respect from them for our teaching by showing appreciation for what they have accomplished."

"But *mon cher monsieur*, they starve or feast according to caprices of weather and the hunt. Their souls are as yet untouched by divine grace. Moreover they worship nature."

"I would judge they are not yet ready for prayer and our fashion of worship."

La Salle stood and replaced his hat. He reached for an object hanging on the wall of his hut. It was a stout stick split at the end to insert a chipped stone wedge larger than an arrowhead.

"Do you know what that is, Father?"

"*Bon Dieu*, what a terrible weapon."

"It's a tool for planting corn. Our immediate priority should be to teach them how to improve their agriculture, and how to construct shelters of bark and skin by using metal tools."

"Don't you realize that your use of trading posts places the gains of trade above the imperatives of salvation?"

"My dedication to exploring a new continent for France clearly demonstrates my priorities. To secure this continent for the motherland provides an opportunity to advance *la civilisation française*."

"*Mon cher* Sieur de La Salle, I must warn you that we may feel obligated to oppose your trading plans with all the resources at our command. Bishop Laval has already expressed his concern in this matter."

"Father Laurent, do you not risk straying from your Order's commitments?"

"The battlefields of the Lord know no boundaries. Prayer and devotion to the Holy Bible are at the heart of our civilization. They are the *raison d'être* of Jesuit teaching. I must say in addition that I regret your having abandoned our Order."

"Father Laurent, I haven't abandoned my faith. I, in turn, regret that our Order has departed from the principles we once shared. It would behoove you to review those ideals. I am proud of the colleges we have established. But the Jesuit politics in Rome and at the French court are less than admirable. And now I must attend to urgent affairs at Fort Frontenac. Good day, *mon père*."

La Salle concluded the meeting with a handshake. The priest hurried out to tell Ouentono that they must prepare to leave immediately. After collecting his belongings and thanking Father Hennepin for his hospitality Father Laurent departed in late afternoon accompanied by his Huron crew who were reluctant to resume their journey so late in the day.

Reaching their destination required several portages, one of more than two leagues. By woodland custom each traveler carried his own luggage. Boatmen portaged their canoes, paddles and packs.

Father Laurent carried with him wine for Mass, altar breads, and a Mass kit containing vestments and utensils. In addition he had been advised to lay in knives and hatchets for gifts and trading. At their first portage Ouentono stared at the pile of equipment.

"You carry God?"

The priest smiled. His interpreter squatted and hoisted a bundle of the priest's supplies onto his shoulders.

A weary Father Laurent reached Manera Springs, the Wendat hunting camp, to be greeted by barking dogs and shouting children. He was led to the bark hut reserved for his use. A tall native woman presently brought him a bowl of cornmeal with chunks of cooked fish. Ouentono informed him that Chief Owassoni would welcome the new priest on the morrow. Father Laurent fell asleep that night reflecting upon the responsibility for carrying God to "his people."

Chapter 7

TIKANAKA

"Remy, *regardez* those trees, a spectacle of nature." Brassart pointed skyward.

"What are they?"

"Norway pine, spruce and fir. Some of them are more than thirty paces tall. There's enough wood for masts to fit out a fleet of ocean-going vessels."

Tonty had selected Remy to accompany Brassart on another mission for La Salle. The young man welcomed the chance to learn about the forest from such a wise gentleman. In this calm unassuming man there was a quiet strength like a strong undertow in a placid stream. The shipyard workers respected Armand Brassart but were curious about him because he kept to himself and confided in no one. His manner of speaking suggested a titled family. Had he been banned from France for political reasons?

After three years in Canada he was reputed to be one of the most exacting French interpreters of the Wendat and Algonquin dialects. He seized every occasion to converse with the natives. At the visit to Tegarondies he had inspired a spirited discussion in the Iroquois language. Remy soon found him to be a fascinating companion and knowledgeable about the lore of *La Nouvelle France*.

"Why are we taking time for this mission to visit the Hurons?" Remy wanted to know, "when we are in such a hurry to finish the *Griffin?*"

"Well, The Hurons were the first people Sieur Samuel de Champlain befriended when he arrived about a hundred years ago. They became important allies. He persuaded them to take up arms

34

to help him against the powerful Iroquois tribes whose cornfields he destroyed by fire."

"Pierre did tell me that it was Champlain's plan to exterminate them. But that was long ago. They still remember?"

"Indeed they do. In their eyes the Hurons, by hunting to supply us with game and working at the shipyard, are still French follow-ers determined to annihilate them. That's why we must keep reas-suring the Hurons that we will protect them from the Iroquois."

"But we've just told the Iroquois at Tegarondies that we are their friends."

"That's a problem for La Salle." Brassart smiled. "Courting the Iroquois as friends while supporting their enemies the Hurons, is called diplomacy."

"What do the Indians get in return for letting us settle in their country?"

"Well, by treaty we protect the natives and help them develop their land and food gathering."

"Protect them from what?"

"From the the Dutch, the English, the Spanish, and from each other."

"But we don't pay them anything?"

"Only in exchange for furs."

Remy was beginning to believe that there must be a better way to live in friendship with the Savages. Would the Hurons welcome him and Brassart with their message from the Sieur de La Salle?

The morning of their third day on the trail they located Manera Springs, the Huron hunting camp. The Indians occupied a shal-low dip where a stream below and the fountainhead above pro-vided water. As the Frenchmen drew near a foul odor assailed their nostrils.

"What is that smell!"

Brassart breathed in. "They must be tanning hides. They make a paste of deer brains placed in the sun to ferment."

They stopped to watch a woman with a wedge of flint scraping the inside of a hide stretched across a peeled log. Nearby a girl with a stout stick was flailing a hide suspended from a branch.

"Looks like hard work. Why does she do that?"

"If she just let them dry in the sun, they would be too stiff. Now when smoked over rotten wood they become soft and pliable." Brassart tugged at Remy's sleeve. "Let's keep moving."

Other women were spreading the paste on the flesh side of the hides with flat wood chips, rubbing it in with their fingers. The visitors kept their distance.

As they quickened their pace, one of the women from the group started toward their visitors. As she drew near Remy's heart jumped. It was the Wendat of his icy river bath. He automatically grasped her outstretched hands, then pulled back. His hands were smeared with the sticky brain paste. She laughed and turned to Brassart.

"*Bonjour, mes amis.* Father Laurent teach me French."

"What! Is that priest here?" Remy's eyes opened wide. He was trying to scrub away the paste with dirt. "We saw him not long ago in an Iroquois settlement."

"*Le Père Laurent* nice man, très gentil," the girl replied. "Tell me stories from book."

She swept up sweet ferns for Remy to clean his hands. Then she led them into camp where Onendo, the medicine man, bowed in welcome. He informed Brassart that Chief Owassoni would receive them soon. Remy turned to speak to the girl. With Brassart's help he learned she was the chief's daughter, that she was named Tikanaka.

"What age are you?" Remy asked.

She gave him a blank stare.

Pointing to himself and counting slowly on his fingers he repeated the question saying "seventeen".

Her face lighted up. "*Sootahrehscarreh.*"

"What?"

She called over to Brassart.

"Tell him what mean "*Sootahrehscarreh*".

"She said she has seventeen years."

Then she asked to hear the words again coming close as she watched his mouth. After a few attempts she repeated a "seventeen" he could understand and he nodded approval. Brassart moved away with Onendo. She wanted to continue the word game with Remy as they walked from the clearing into the woods. From time to time she would point up to the sky (*caghronniate*) and wait for him to say the French name which she would then sound out. *Yearonta* was the word for "tree". He found the Wendat words soft and musical but too long to remember. Excited, she studied his face as he spoke. Later she recited several of the French words.

On a flat stretch of trail she challenged him to a race. Surprised, he dug in his toes and dashed away. In minutes he found himself watching her back as she passed him by.

They returned to camp laughing to meet Brassart who was irritated because the chief had been kept waiting. But Tikanaka's father beamed when they arrived. The girl remained a few minutes, interrupting him to explain some French words. The chief listened to his daughter proudly. Brassart was obviously uneasy with her brashness.

The visitors' gifts of cooking pots were received with bows and nods. Some Elders at the chief's hut had joined the visitors for the welcoming ceremony. Sitting beside the chief Remy had his second experience smoking a calumet. As he drew in deeply on the stone pipe his nostrils filled with smoke and—as before—tears came to his eyes.

After the calumet had gone full circle, the moment arrived for La Salle's message. Presenting it in two languages, they decided, would be more respectful of Huron ceremonies. After Remy pronounced the words in French Brassart interpreted for the Elders who nodded in pleasure.

"The Sieur de La Salle would have approved of your oratory." Brassart seemed pleased with the meeting.

Remy laughed. "At least the Elders are courteous listeners."

Onendo accompanied them to the hut where they would sleep. Interlaced fir boughs made a thick mat on the ground to provide comfort and warmth. The chief had invited them to share dinner with his family and several Elders.

Tika, as Remy began to call her, beckoned him to follow her. They clambered up the hill into a grove of birches on a rise overlooking the camp. In a clearing at the top was a fire pit lined with rocks. Nearby stood a post bearing a sculpted bird painted ochre and blue.

Tika said nothing for a time. Then he asked what it was for.

"I make you see."

She stood tall and started to chant from deep in her throat. Raising her knees in full stride she danced around the fire circle swinging her arms with clenched fists in rhythm with her steps. Then she moved to the edge of the hill, looking toward the sky. She stretched both arms high above her head, holding still for several moments.

At a narrow passage in their return trail Remy stumbled over roots and bumped into Tika knocking her off balance. She laughed and held onto to him for a moment starting a playful jousting and pushing game as they walked along. When they separated back in camp she surprised Remy with a quick parting hug.

Speeches followed the evening meal in the chief's hut. Brassart directed Remy to tell their hosts about the Great White Father in France, friend and protector of their native brothers, and his emissary the Sieur de La Salle. Once again he interpreted. The Elders smiled and nodded in appreciation. Even though Tika sat beside Remy the meal was an ordeal.

They shared a common earthenware pot using their fingers, a spoon of carved wood, and a bark plate. Hunks of meat had been boiled in water with crushed corn. Remy longed for a few grains of salt. Dried blueberries completed the meal.

Lying on his bed of boughs that night Remy was thinking of words to ask Tika if they might meet again. He would write about her in his journal by daylight. His attempts to speak with her at the river meeting had produced no results. Now the memory of Tika's brief embrace, the scent of her hair and the contact of her body, brought a tingling to his loins.

The following morning the visitors were hardly surprised to be presented with *sagamité* (boiled cornmeal and dried blueberries). As they prepared to take their leave Tika was nowhere to be seen. Remy delayed getting his blanket roll and musket together. Finally Brassart became impatient and they departed.

Remy kept looking back.

"I noticed that the chief was polite but had little to say," he told Brassart. "I'm not certain he likes us. He kept asking how far away our soldiers are. He doesn't seem to trust us."

"Chief Owassoni does not lack intelligence and he has reason to be skeptical." Brassart paused. "As to the chief, how did his daughter know you?"

Remy tried to think of a way to describe their first encounter that did not make him look foolish, but decided to tell it as it happened.

Brassart laughed. "You were lucky. You could have had an arrow in your back."

"I was angry, you know."

"She's a clever girl. I'll wager she gets plenty of wampum from the young bucks."

"What do you mean?"

"These native girls, especially the Hurons, receive wampum from the young men when they lie with them in their furs. Even when they settle for a time with one youth the girl can change mates if she wishes. It's a point of pride to collect wampum. That girl is a daughter of the chief and a *coquette*, probably not lacking young warriors."

Remy stared at his companion. "Do you believe this to be true?"

"*Mon ami*, their ways are quite different. Selecting a mate for long term, as far as I have learned, is a free choice for both men and women."

"Well, do they have a ceremony?"

"Oh yes. There is a calumet dance for a wedding and sometimes a ritual with each one holding the end of a stick as they stand on a mat. It is a joyful occasion."

"In what way?"

"Marriage for them is a personal choice Remy, not a religious contract, no promises to remain together *toujours*. They are free to mate with somebody and can leave when they choose."

"What if the girl has a baby while collecting wampum?"

"The child will probably belong to her family. She might invite the father to live with them. Whatever property they have, the mother owns. There are no arranged marriages as we have for all but peasant families in France."

"They can change mates at any time?"

"I believe so, but after they have a few babies most of the women become fat squaws that nobody thinks are worth much wampum."

Remy closed his eyes. He could not imagine Tika as a fat squaw.

Brassart had taken an interest in the way Indians use wampum, those strings of beads desired for their beauty. Like French money, they were offered in exchange for something of value. But the transaction was not the same thing as a sale in France.

"They have different ideas," he said, "about private ownership of property, especially of land."

"What do they call a young woman who accepts different partners each night? Like *une putain*?" Remy wanted to know.

"I doubt that they have any such word and certainly they have no need for prostitutes."

The thought of Tika collecting wampum was unsettling and Remy moved the conversation to yesterday's dinner.

"That food had a strange taste."

"Do you know what we were eating last night?" Brassart asked.

"Well, it was not particularly tasty."

"With our cornmeal we were eating dog."

Remy was silent while digesting that piece of information. Along the trail back to the shipyard Tika and the canine stew remained in his thoughts. With Brassart's help he reviewed his scant Wendat vocabulary and vowed to keep learning.

The next day as Remy was working on the *Griffin* Tonty spoke to him.

"The Sieur de La Salle is concerned about Brassart's report of your meeting with the Huron's Council of Elders. What was your impression?"

"I think the Wendats fear that we are too far away to defend them. But I could not understand every word."

"You know the Indians are more clever than we sometimes think. They like to keep us guessing. Watch Brassart. You can learn a lot on missions like this."

Remy could, in fact, better understand the difficulties of getting along with the natives, but at the moment he was more occupied trying to fathom the motives of one young Savage. In his journal he wrote:

> *April 1681*
> *Why did Tika not say goodbye? She seems to vanish like magic.*
> *Anyway, I will probably never see her again.*
> *A girl like Odette on the ship from France might be a better companion.*

Chapter 8

SMALL BEGINNINGS

Before going to sleep in his cave Remy would sometimes reflect upon his early days back in France. He wished he had written to his father more often through Father Foignet. The village priest had actually done him an immense favor by forcing him to go to school. Remy wondered what would his wise friend Father Bernard back in Paris think of the way the French treat the Indians, calling them Savages and taking their land?

His first two years back at Saint Martin's Monastery School had been a nightmare of trouble, punishment by canings and once being locked into a dark closet. Then one day Father Bernard arrived at the school. He was the new principal and a teacher of Latin poetry. He introduced the poetry of *Quintus Horatius Flaccus* to the older boys.

Remy was enthralled by his strange manner of reading and speaking. The words looked somewhat similar to French but quite incomprehensible to his ears, a secret way of thinking. He looked forward to each lesson and spent many hours with his books. He made an uneasy peace with Brother Couperin who had seemed to enjoy caning him: for fighting, for insolent language with teachers and for blaming God's judgment in taking away his mother.

"I'm pleased that you like learning Latin," Father Bernard told Remy. "You could perhaps continue in a Jesuit college some day."

In time Remy came to trust the man and he had the good fortune to be under his guidance for another three years. He was sad when one day his mentor was transferred to a college in Paris. His replacement, the unsmiling Father Darien was not popular with

41

the students. Shortly after his arrival he told Remy, now sixteen, that he had outgrown the school and would be wise to leave.

When Remy closed that big front door upon six years of monastery life his mind was made up. He would never choose to work in the fields with his father. He hoped to locate Father Bernard in Paris where he might find work and continue his studies. Father Bernard was now principal of *le College de Boncoeur*.

The Paris school term had already started and the priest recognized that his former student could profit from a bit more preparation for college. He sent him with a note of introduction to one of the diocesan offices not far from the prison of *Châtelet* near the river Seine. There, Remy was offered employment as a messenger boy.

In a dormitory attached to the school he found a place to sleep. He felt honored when Father Bernard offered to give him Latin instruction two evenings each week. Remy soon began to sneak out at night to explore the city. When he returned with a bruised cheek and black eye from fighting with a drunk who had offended him in the street, the *surveillant* of student housing told him to leave the dormitory. He gathered his meager belongings into a sack.

"You have much yet to learn about directing your life," Father Bernard told him, "However I will continue your Latin instruction if you wish."

Remy, although angry at his dismissal, agreed to continue with the lessons. He found lodging in a room over some stables on the *quai des Celestins*. He could come and go as he pleased. After soup and bread in his landlady's kitchen Remy on his free evenings would cross to the Left Bank and walk downriver along *le Quai de la Tournelle* to mount a slope called *le Mont Sainte Geneviève* in the Latin Quarter popular with the students. There he encountered a new world. A carved bird hanging above the door on *la rue Guerlande* drew attention to a tavern called *le Corbeau*.

Wearing a cape and a black band across his eyes, a man called Farouche perched on a stool at the entrance.

"I don't know you." He stretched out his cane.

"*Vrai, monsieur.*"

"And pray tell me what is your business?"

"My name is Remy and I work for the diocesan office *Quai de l'Hôtel de Ville.*"

"From the Holy Offices indeed. And do you drink wine, Church Boy?"

"Only for the sacraments, monsieur."

"Well now, Church Boy, you must try the wine of Gonzo. Not the blood of Christ, mind you, but from oak barrels and very good."

Remy did try the wine and found it to his taste. He watched with amusement as Gonzo and Farouche joked with the customers. There was laughter and singing. Students from the Sorbonne would dispute with townsmen and render drinking songs like *Les Moines de Saint Bernardin* with much fervor and a good deal of quaffing. Remy learned to his surprise that the Church was of little interest to *citoyens* like Gonzo and Farouche, dealers in goods of uncertain origin.

An urchin, a bit younger than Remy, called Le Coquin who frequented *le Corbeau* was immediately hostile to this strange newcomer. He wanted to have nothing to do with the Church Boy.

One night, however, in a lane called *la rue Coupe-Gueule* (Cut-Throat Street) a bellicose young petitioner drew a knife when Remy refused his request for coins. Remy grabbed the man's weapon arm and delivered a blow to the side of his head. The assailant thrust his knee into Remy's groin.

Le Coquin happened to be passing by at the time and he came to Remy's aid.

The two of them wrested the knife from the attacker, who fled. The young men faced each other.

"You are a fighter," Le Coquin rewarded the Church Boy with a look of approval.

"And you, monsieur, came to my rescue." Remy extended his hand. "Shall we be friends?"

Le Coquin, already wise to the ways of the street, agreed and he set out to reveal the pleasures of the Latin Quarter to his new friend.

Several nights later Remy was surprised to see Le Coquin rushing down Cut-Throat Street clutching a leather bag in his hand. He had snatched it from a lady as she stepped from her carriage. Her coachman in hot pursuit was gaining ground when the urchin turned sharply left and slipped into a side street.

"Which way did he go?" the coachman demanded.

Remy, coming up *la rue Coupe-Gueule* pointed to the right.

"That way."

Without a word the coachman dashed away.

"*Bravo*," said Le Coquin when the two were together again at *le Corbeau*, "you're a good friend. I'll split the purse with you."

Remy shook his head. "Stealing can get you into a lot of trouble. We can talk about that later."

"Well, I offered to hold her horses for a coin. She ordered her coachman to whip me." Le Coquin looked Remy in the eye. "She's an evil woman."

Remy did accept a glass of Gonzo's wine from his companion.

Le Coquin then confided to him that his mother had abandoned him long ago. He claimed in fact that he didn't remember what she looked like.

Remy replied, "My mother left me, too. She died. I don't remember her at all. I believe *Le Bon Dieu* could have saved her."

"I have nothing to do with *le Bon Dieu*." Le Coquin's face brightened. "Let's visit a red-lamp house. I know of one that has a back entrance."

Remy hesitated, unwilling to admit his inexperience. He had been fascinated by the women smiling from doorways at the passing world and sometimes pulling their skirts up above their ankles. Except for his young sister he had never ever talked to a woman. Now he feared he would not know how to approach one of those *prostituées*. Le Coquin opened the door to the dimly lighted building and they mounted a stairway smelling of perfume. At the top a stout woman walked down the hallway in house robe and curlers.

"What are you boys doing here?"

"We hear you have some pretty girls." Le Coquin answered.

"What are you saying? The King's Archers will close my house down if I start taking in *les enfants*. You boys had best be out of here *tout de suite*."

"We are not boys. We are gentlemen of distinction." Le Coquin pressed forward.

"Back to your châteaux, *messieurs*, ere I pierce your vital parts."

"What does she mean calling us children," Le Coquin grumbled when they were out again on the street. "She was laughing at us."

Remy told himself it was wrong for his friend to steal but there were many things in the city—like blind beggars and old people sleeping under bridges—that were wrong. Would his father have to live like that if the Sieur de Senlis took all his land strips?

The two friends walked along the *berges* of the Seine watching women kneeling near the bank washing clothes, slapping them against rocks to get them clean and sometimes singing. Some were quite young. When Le Coquin teased them they would laugh and splash water at the boys.

And so it was with life in *la Grande Ville*. Meanwhile Remy, although he still enjoyed his evening lessons with Father Bernard, wanted for himself a life more exciting than carrying messages to churches. Good fortune came his way one day when a gentleman sitting on a bench in *le Jardin des Tuileries* told him that the French court was seeking young men to settle across the sea in Canada. Remy hurried to get the advice of Father Bernard.

"Remy, at your age I was a bit of a rebel myself. Some of my colleagues still disapprove of my attachment to pagan poetry. Yes, it is indeed true that we have missions in New France and this may be an excellent opportunity for you. Our Jesuit Order publishes a series of reports called *Les Relations de La Nouvelle France*. Rumor has it that Canadian land for farming and hunting is free."

"That would be a great adventure, Father. How could I pay for my journey?"

"I'm told that young men can work as sailors for passage. You can inquire at *le Ministère de la Marine*."

"Do you really think that would be possible, Father Bernard?"

"Well, you have a fine mind and may be a leader some day." The priest paused for a moment. "I've come to realize that you do not have the spirit of faith a cleric must have."

"Is that bad?"

"No. You can find many ways to serve God and your fellow man."

"Father, how do you advise me to keep learning in a far-away land?"

"When you see a book, examine it. To discipline your thinking write down each day ideas or events that are important to you. This can be brief." Father Bernard shuffled through some volumes on his desk.

"Take these." He held out a copy of Horace's *Ars Poetica* and a bound journal of blank pages. "We will inquire for you at the *Ministère de la Marine* about how to apply for passage."

"*Merci mille fois.* I will treasure these, Father." Remy placed the books under his arm.

"Go to mass and read when you can." The priest placed his hand on the boy's shoulder. "I will pray for you. Faith and learning are your best friends."

Remy knew all the churches in Paris. *Saint-Germain-l'Auxerrois* for him was a special place where a vast stillness encompassed aromas of burning tapers and parchment prayer scrolls. He headed there now with his new books. Afternoon sun filtering through the tall stained-glass windows painted the stones of the floor with patterns of blues and reds.

Remy tried to collect his thoughts. Looking at a statue of the Virgin Mary cushioning the infant Jesus, he thought about his own mother. Did she hold him with such gentleness? Why do Farouche and Le Coquin and others at *Le Corbeau* not care about the Church and even make jokes about it, singing with more merriment than anyone ever did at the monastery?

Before leaving France Remy was determined to see his sister Monique. His request to visit her was at first refused. Thanks to the help of Father Bernard he finally obtained permission to be with her for one half hour.

At the convent Remy pulled a bell-rope over the entrance and waited, pulling the cord again before the door cracked opened. He thought it was perhaps the prioress her self. A voice was heard from the robed figure.

"One moment," it said.

Monique emerged, her face covered by a veil. She pressed his hand quickly and led him over to the bench beneath a large sycamore tree.

"You're very tall, Remy. I still think of you as a little boy. You were full of questions and mischief. When you were a baby *Maman* was so proud of you, even putting fresh flowers by your bed. She thought you might grow up to be a priest and could never bear to punish you."

"Did she punish me?"

"You were very little. It was mostly Papa. How is he? Is he well?"

"Papa moves slowly now and his hair is white. He works the land as always."

Monique turned toward him and Remy moved closer on the bench. "Tell me, Monique, about *Maman*. Why did she go away?"

"It was a sickness in the chest. When she spit up blood I was frightened. She comforted me, told me how to help Papa and care for you when she was gone."

As she spoke Monique lifted her veil. Looking into her face Remy found her beautiful. Could that be an image of his mother when she was young?

"Are you happy here, Monique?"

"When I was twelve Father Foignet recommended that I be sent here. You were only five. I didn't want to leave you and wept. But now I have to believe that the love of Christ I share with my sisters is everything I can desire from life."

A voice from the convent called out. Monique took his hand and squeezed it hard. After she disappeared into seclusion Remy went back over every word she had spoken. Why did he not think to embrace her?

Walking along the tree-lined lane leaving the convent Remy tried to recall what his papa and Monique had told him about his mother. Bright poppies along the way brought a memory of her name on a wooden marker in the churchyard.

He had little notion of the distance across the ocean, but knew that it was far. That night he made his first journal entry:

May 1680
Will I ever see Monique and Papa again?
How can I make my fortune in the New
World?

Chapter 9

JESUIT LETTER

My Reverend Father Nicholas
The Peace Of Our Lord
March 1681

I trust you will remember me, Father Maurice Laurent, from our brief time together at *Trois Rivières. I* am happy to hear that you are now assigned to a mission at *Sault Sainte-Marie.* Isolation from colleagues in this forgotten part of God's earth renders our task more difficult and I welcome the opportunity to share common experiences.

What success are you having with your Indians? I have learned that fifty years ago a certain Father Brébeuf on Georgian Bay achieved remarkable results evangelizing the natives. Do you have any remaining Christian congregations?

My mission is at the Huron's settlement of Manera Springs, location of their winter hunting site two or three days west of the Niagara River. To my knowledge there have been no previous efforts to convert these Hurons.

En route to this settlement we passed an immense *seigneurie* on the shores of Lake Ontario, where the Sieur Robert Cavelier de La Salle has built a great stone structure that he calls Fort Frontenac. In order to meet with him I was obliged to travel south to the work site, where he is constructing a large ship called the *Griffin* to promote trade with the Indians on the inland seas.

Some time ago an emissary of La Salle, the Sieur de La Motte, in a chance encounter at the Iroquois village of Tegarondies, treated me with disrespect before my native hosts. I was hoping that this might be a caprice of the Sieur de La Motte's character rather than an indication of La Salle's *modus operandi.*

During two full days La Salle was too occupied to see me. When at last I was ushered into his hut he received me with courteous condescension. He is a tall man with a commanding presence and wears a wide-brimmed hat. But he could not accept my protestations about his trading activities.

"The Indians will have to adapt to the use of brandy," he said. And finally he intimated that I "risked straying from our Order's commitments."

After our less than friendly exchange he dismissed me and returned to his shipbuilding. The *Griffin* will be equipped with canon. He believes that gaining the friendship of these natives is more important than saving their souls. Such arrogance borders on evil. We must stop him.

I am asking God to forgive the anger in my heart. The rebuff was not only to myself, which in truth is a personal problem, but also to the dedication of our Society in New France.

Disheartened, I proceeded to my new mission with the Huron tribe. The chief did receive me with some courtesy but does not appear curious about our teaching.

I remember reading at the college in Rouen an account by André Thévenot, an early French traveler in Canada. "The Savages," he wrote, "are living like unreasoning beasts, just as nature produced them."

So strange they are, these natives, possessing many skills yet existing without knowledge of God, without law, and without written language. Still we must note that during the past centuries official Bulls issued by three of our Holy Fathers in Rome ruled that these Savages are "veritable thinking people capable of receiving divine grace."

They do exhibit energy and enthusiasm in celebrating native rites. I must admit to a reaction of excitement listening to the beat of their drums, and I find a certain grace in their dancing.

The Hurons who transported me from Quebec did not respond to my attempts to communicate at any time during the journey. When a canoe almost capsized, one could read neither fear nor anger in their eyes. They were, however, most helpful with carrying my belongings on portages.

How difficult it is to find a pathway to their souls. In a land of people who cannot produce bread or wine for the Eucharist, our task becomes more burdensome. I sometimes feel that we are trying to commune with wild animals in these dense forests. With only our faith and Bibles we are not yet capable of explaining our message to creatures who cannot grasp the truth of our words. While living among such unfamiliar beings we must constantly remind ourselves to exemplify our faith.

When I was a child in Paris our coachman would take my father and me to a market called *Les Halles*. The big sweaty men who unloaded the carts frightened me with their rough talk and loud laughs. I did not want them near me.

I asked my father if those men were Christians. He said that they probably profess faith but do not know what the words really mean. If some of our own countrymen cannot understand our teaching, how much more difficult it will be to reach the Savages with our message. As a child I wondered how those workers in Paris could learn the true meaning of Jesus Christ. Papa said that was a task for the priests. Then I had no idea I would be playing that role some day.

My Hurons are still in their winter camp. They arrived in late autumn and waited for deep snow. I am told that bull elk, which Indians call *wapiti*, stand taller than an adult man and weigh as much as a full-grown ox. Long-legged elk and deer are easier to hunt as they flounder in the tall drifts.

If only we can teach them to apply such clever thinking to producing food on plots of land large enough to harvest. It would be a blessing for their bodies and their souls were they to remain in one place. It is true that they do now plant small plots of corn, squash, beans, and tobacco. But they have no idea of using an axe to clear the land. Permanent villages around a church with cultivated fields would supplement their precarious food supply.

I often think of the Apostles who carried the word of our Savior to fishermen, herdsmen, and tillers of the soil in the ancient world. How can we build a common faith with natives such as these who are always going off into the wilderness? We must attract them into Church communities.

At powwows La Salle promises the Hurons that French soldiers from Fort Frontenac will protect them. Although some Hurons are helping to supply shipyard workers with food and buckskin I think they have doubts that he will keep his word. I too have doubts. We must build upon that.

Unfortunately the small supply of paper and lack of leisure compel me to say in a few words what could fill volumes. In reports to my superiors I will include as much information as possible, passing on accumulated knowledge of this land to advance the work of our beloved Society of Jesus. Do you also keep a journal?

I have wondered about the soothsayers in this region, called *arendiouane,* who use their magic for causing rain to fall or for predicting future events. They make visits to treat the sick and claim to cure their diseases. We know of course that secrets are revealed to them by the Devil but are related with so much ceremony and obscurity that one can never prove them to be false. Have you observed such pagan rites?

My friend Father Dolet in Montreal writes, "The Savages are exceedingly independent; they have neither civility nor conversation with the French; the oils with which they smear their bodies offend the nostrils, and the poverty of their clothing and their cabins offends the sight. Only the pure grace given by God renders them lovable."

Although this echoes my own thinking, I wonder if we are being too harsh. Does our God distribute his grace in a random fashion? And, most important, will they one day desire to follow our way to salvation?

These Savages—even the gentle Hurons—become madmen when intoxicated. They fall upon one another brandishing their knives, mutilating friends and family.

It is rare that a native will ask a question about our world. I would welcome any curiosity as a sign of friendship and intelligence. However a daughter of Chief Owassoni recently made known to me that she would like to learn our language. The interpreter called her Tikanaka. She is said to be a willful young woman who seeks adventure by herself in the forest.

Is her request serious or some sort of ruse? We shall see. If I could work with but one such person it would be a promising beginning. She has appeared several times for lessons and remembers what I tell her. One difficulty is my lack of knowledge of her language. It is a challenge I will accept with pleasure.

Kindly let me know what success you are having with your Hurons.

IN UNION WITH YOUR HOLY SACRIFICE, I REMAIN,
FATHER MAURICE LAURENT, S.J.

Chapter 10

THE MAGIC OF WORDS

Could anything be more exhilarating than leaping from a rocky height into clear flowing water? Tikanaka thought not. The ecstasy of plunging into an icy stream was irresistible. Following a trail through the forest to find such a spot was part of the joy.

Now she was discovering the path leading to an excitement she had never before experienced, hearing her self speak in a strange language and listening to others in conversation. Far more complicated than making her way around trees and rocks, this adventure was both confusing and a challenge. Father Laurent was opening up new ways for her to look at the world.

The beginning was far from easy. She found the black-robed priest an odd figure and did not like the smell of his body when he came too close. But his manner of speaking and the gestures that accompanied those strange sounds intrigued her.

He reminded her of the youth she had met at the river: the same pale skin without paint or adornment, and the mobility of eyes and hands. She had been fascinated by that young Frenchman, the pale clear-cut features of his face and especially the expression of rage in his eyes. Her curiosity continued after a second encounter with him and his friend Brassart at the Wendat hunting camp.

When first she inquired about learning his language, she liked the way Father Laurent looked directly into her face and gave his full attention to her presence. And then it made her feel important when he called her "*Mademoiselle.*"

"I learn to talk like you?" she inquired through Chaweda, the Petun interpreter who was helping Father Laurent at the moment.

Father Laurent asked Chaweda to tell the Wendat girl "yes" while informing her that it would require patience and much effort.

Tikanaka was soon spending many hours in study, finding it more thrilling than seeking new swimming places. Remembering the sound of words and phrases was for her the easiest part. Father Laurent was surprised at how quickly she managed to form the letters of the alphabet. She was learning printed letters. (Manuscripts might come much later.)

Within a square of smooth sand from the stream outside his chapel the priest would scratch large letters. The girl then made smaller copies with a charcoal stick on birch bark. She drew them with skill and was proud of her little pictures. She loved to form the letter "O," which for her represented the Sacred Circle of Life. Matching these drawings with the sounds was like a game.

Even more difficult was combining these letters and their sounds to compose entire words and sentences. She was bedeviled by the fact that the same letter could have different sounds. Yet she would sometimes repeat sentences without knowing the meaning.

Meanwhile Father Laurent lent an eager ear to the Wendat dialect. He could soon comprehend enough to carry on simple conversations. But explaining the idea of "God" in either language proved to be the greatest challenge.

Little by little he and his student began to have discussions that enabled them to reach mutual understanding. This took many weeks.

"Who make God?" she inquired one day.

"God was always there, my dear. The whole world and everything in existence comes from Him."

The girl struggled with that idea.

"Why," she asked, "God make Adam first? Is not earth the mother of all things?"

"You will come to realize that our earth and everything upon it is the creation of God. He needed Adam to begin his plan."

"God only one on earth?"

Father Laurent paused a moment. "Yes. I believe so."

"Why God not make Eve first? He could amuse Himself with her as man with woman."

"Mademoiselle, God is not exactly a man..." The priest gulped and reached for words. "He is a Superior Being, and—besides—amusing ourselves is not the sole reason for our existence on earth. Man and woman are here to plant seeds and continue the tribe so they can do God's work by helping each other."

"But can they have what you call 'joy' together?"

"Joy—deep contentment—is what comes to a person whose heart is filled with the love of God."

"Your magic strange. Not way to be happy," she concluded.

Later, reading letter by letter and word by word "In the beginning was the word and the word was with God and the word was God," she struggled to find meaning.

"No words before God?"

"No. This means that God was the manifestation of the Divine message of creation." The priest could find no better way to simplify this idea.

She shook her head. "If no words how God speak to angels?"

"You will come to understand more about prayer and God's silent messages."

"If not for Devil," she continued, "God have nothing to do. Why God let Devil make trouble?"

"The Devil represents evil. Good and evil are part of God's plan of creation. We must learn to accept the good and reject evil, thus supporting God's eventual triumph."

"If my father powerful like God, he kill Iroquois for what they do. So we all be happy."

"But then," the priest told her, "your people would never seek grace and God's forgiveness."

"Forgive mean not do anything, like not happen?"

"It is more complicated but that is the main idea."

"If I God," she said, "never forgive the Iroquois."

"Then it is my duty to teach you how to accept God and the practice of forgiveness."

She spent many hours reading and repeating the words, capable of imitating them often knowing the sound if not the meaning. The priest's own study of the Wendat dialect sharpened his awareness of the girl's difficulties. He admired her determination.

Chaweda, the interpreter, had to return to his Petun tribe so the priest and his student were obliged to depend upon their own abilities. Tikanaka was now spending time with Father Laurent every day helping prepare simple stories in Wendat for the children. They enjoyed the attention. How much they understood was uncertain.

Moon Cloud became concerned that her daughter spent too much time in study with the priest. Tika was neglecting her obligation to help the tribe prepare deer hides for tanning. And talking in a strange way while waving her hands about made her appear different from her friends.

"There are so many words, Mama, a big book of them."

"We have enough words here." Moon Cloud pointed to her head. "Mokanoa can tell stories of our people from all of our ancestors."

"But these are words of many tribes everywhere. Is new kind of magic."

Chief Owassoni listened to his daughter.

"May be bad medicine. White man's magic brings guns," he said. "That's why Iroquois are so powerful."

"Magic of stories in big book not bad. I learn to read little pictures, can speak with paleface tribes of many moons ago, "Tikanaka told her parents.

She observed that the priest spent hours in prayer and meditation each day in his chapel. Why did he not go out into the woods?

"We walk?" Tikanaka looked at Father Laurent. "Show you forest."

It was clearly an invitation, one that the priest did not relish at the moment. But he did not wish to restrain his student's enthusiasm for learning.

"Maybe tomorrow," he answered.

The following day he accompanied her up a slope from their stream to the beginning of a steep trail.

"I show you how river come to us." She pointed to a rocky ridge that gave her favorite view of the valley.

Raising his knees high under his robes for each step he struggled along to a wall of stones. He stumbled as small pebbles rolled away under his feet. Grasping the top of a rough rock he pulled with all his might, ignoring the helping hand his guide held down from above.

"How much higher must we go?" He pointed toward the top of the ridge.

Tika stopped to survey the trail.

"Maybe we go to spring." She watched Father Laurent wipe the perspiration from his face with bruised hands. "Is better."

She led him to a spring in a nearby glade where they sat on a log to let him rest. In the small clearing of grass and flowers, away from sounds of the village, he slowly said the Lord's Prayer, facing his student and waited, line by line, for her to repeat the words.

They then explored a pond by the spring frightening away a pair of black ducks. Tikanaka spotted and gathered ripe wild strawberries nestling in the grass. They sat again on the log to savor the sweetness.

She was surprised when Father Laurent turned to her and said, "You have nothing to gain by seeing the young Frenchman who visited our camp recently. Some of my countrymen cannot be trusted. You could keep studying, perhaps in a convent, and help your people by giving your heart to Jesus."

Her eyes opened wide. "Will think about."

"You and your people do well to respect the calm and beauty of this place." The priest surveyed the wild roses and lilies of the glade. "But we must remember that this is the handiwork and the gift of God."

As they prepared to leave, Tikanaka dropped to her knees and drank from the spring, inviting her companion to do the same. Leaning over the water on hands and knees, Father Laurent, saw his reflection. Could that gaunt face be his, the features of a man looking more than his forty-five years? The image unexpectedly evoked recollections of a young boy drinking from the stream near his home in Arideux. What had he done with so much of his life?

In silence he walked beside his student as they returned to the village. He cherished the opportunity to rest again in his chapel.

Tikanaka told Moon Cloud that evening, "I think Father Laurent happy here."

Chapter 11

FOR THE LOVE OF GOD

"Boast not thyself of tomorrow," Brother Messionnier would tell his students at the monastery school, "for thou knowest not what a day may bring forth."

Remy had occasion to remember those words in the Canadian wilderness. Fearing attacks at the shipyard, the small crew of Frenchmen kept guards posted at all hours. But in the woods it was hard to remember that they were under an ever-present threat.

He and Jean had been accompanying the Sieur de Tonty and a small party of workmen the previous day exploring the Niagara River where the *Griffin* would be navigating to reach the inland sea. Springtime buds festooned the birch trees and even Tonty seemed in a jolly mood. They were proceeding at a leisurely pace when without warning an arrow slit Jean's sleeve.

"Down," Tonty cried out.

Everyone dropped to the ground. In an instant the Iroquois seemed to be everywhere. Clasping his musket Remy rolled into the nearby bushes. Jean had already fired at an attacker. When Remy raised his head he saw a Savage spring from the bushes, drawing his bow not more than three paces from Jean's back. Remy's weapon exploded without his being conscious of firing. For a moment he thought he had missed. Then the warrior took another step before crumbling almost on top of Jean.

Keeping low Remy reloaded and crawled out toward his friend. Jean had whirled about to fire at an advancing Iroquois who dropped out of sight. They both backed into the heavy brush beside the trail and lay waiting. Then there followed an eerie silence.

For a time they remained in place, until Tonty signaled them together. At first they thought all the men were there and looked at each other in relief. But after a brief moment Tonty asked, "Where is Henri?"

The men spread out through the trees to search for their comrade. Remy was the first to discover him.

Henri Mollet lay on his back, head turned to one side and legs spread wide. One arrow had struck near his heart and another below the throat. The blood was still fresh. Remy dropped to his knees and gently felt the face of his friend. There was no breath. Remy arose and leaned against a tree until his dizziness passed.

Finally he called out to his companions, "Henri is over here."

They gathered around the fallen man.

"Not even a war whoop," Big Jean Paul cried out, clenching his fists. "We hardly had a chance to defend ourselves."

"I wish we could kill the whole band." Gaston grasped his musket. "But why did it happen to Henri?"

"He was my best friend. I'm glad we got two of those devils anyway." Big Jean Paul, his eyes misted with rage and sorrow, laid his arm across Remy's shoulders in a rough half-embrace. "Good work, *mon ami*."

"Fortunately these Iroquois didn't have guns. I think I counted eight of them but can't be sure," Tonty said. "This band of hunters dared to attack with bows and spears because we were careless and a tempting ambush in the thicket. That should be a lesson. Always have an advance scout and the rear guard must be off the trail."

They stood together in silence a few moments. Removing his *veston* Tonty spread it out over Henri's chest, pulling it up over the dead man's face. Then he started cutting down saplings for a stretcher to carry him home.

Glancing around Tonty caught a glimpse of Remy staring down at the warrior he had killed. The young Iroquois had turned his face in the direction of the shot as he fell. His mouth remained slightly open, a look of wonder on his face as if he had been awakened suddenly from sleep. Blood was dripping from mangled flesh and buckskin. Tonty watched Remy grimace and place a hand on his stomach.

Before they headed back Crevel started stripping a beaded belt from one of the slain warriors. Tonty stopped him, "They care for their own dead. We do not take trophies."

This angered some of the men and they grumbled as they made their way home. They thought Tonty was too strict. It was true that he did drive the men hard, but he was fair and slow to anger. Now for the first time Remy heard remarks about being under Tonty's "iron hand."

Father Hennepin had told Remy that Tonty lost his right hand— blown off by a grenade—when he was fighting for France in Sicily.

They shared the task of carrying Henri. In steep places that sometimes required all hands. Advancing slowly they kept their muskets at ready. By now everyone was silent.

Back at the shipyard all of the men stopped work as they chose a site to dig a grave on a grassy rise of ground some fifteen paces from the *Griffin*. A grim-faced Big Jean Paul leaned on his shovel.

"Here he can overlook our work on his precious boat."

After a long consultation in La Salle's hut Tonty called the men together. "Our leader is furious," he told them, "So much for our treaty. The government in Quebec will hear about this. It is probably an isolated incident but we can't assume that. We must be prepared for more trouble."

Father Hennepin suggested building a fire and keeping watch over Henri's body. The priest would say a funeral mass in the morning

Midnight found only three men around the firelight. Father Hennepin and Remy sat on sawed-off logs while Henri lay encased in a box made from the same boards he had so skillfully prepared the previous day. Remy recalled him laughing as he joked with Big Jean Paul at breakfast.

Remy watched flames flickering, casting shadows on the coffin. What really takes place when life ends? Is it different for the French and the natives? Pierre had said Indians don't need the French God. But how can they find salvation? Remy asked Father Hennepin.

The priest replied that since the man Remy killed had never been baptized, of course he could not enter into heaven. Remy rolled his log around to face Father Hennepin.

"Father, I can't forget the expression on the face of that young warrior. Why, if God is all powerful, does he let us kill each other like this?"

Father Hennepin stirred the coals of the fire as darkness closed in around them. Remy piled on more wood. For a time they watched flames coming to life before the priest answered.

"Remy, I was at the battle of Seneff in Belgium, where the Prince de Condé defeated William of Orange. Many perished by fire and steel. I administered the sacraments to more than three thousand wounded and to hundreds of dying soldiers. I told myself that God envisaged a peaceful life one day for all of his children. But we must offer something in return. That's a *quid pro quo* for redemption."

"We have to kill each other to have peace?"

"My son, the best support to help the Church in spreading the word of Christ, God's messenger, comes from the great kingdoms of Europe. We must risk something to build His church under their protection. The glory of France has been built on war."

"Father, if long ago the Sieur de Champlain killed many Savages and burned their crops, why was it wrong for them to defend themselves?"

"They have no reason to kill people who want to help them. The Sieur de Champlain, acting for France, was bringing them civilization to improve their lives."

If an Iroquois warrior, never baptized, could be denied entry into heaven, so could a Wendat maiden. As Remy pondered upon that fact, images of the dead warrior and the provocative Tika were mixed in a most disturbing way. The night wind whooshing through the branches accompanied his thoughts.

"Father Hennepin, if the Indians cannot enter into the kingdom of heaven, that is not fair. How can we ever believe in a loving God?"

"That's a dangerous way to think. You risk the damnation of disbelief."

"I suppose I still believe in God, Father, but I cannot look at the world and have confidence that He's all powerful."

"You need to pray, my son, that faith will lead you to a better understanding of your religion."

Then as the two mourners fell silent Remy thought about his gentle friend in the box by the fire. Recently Henri had suggested to Tonty that Remy and Jean work closely with him in finishing boards for the hull. Since they were young and willing to learn that might speed up the project. Both men were eager to profit from the opportunity.

"You are struggling against the wood," Henri had told Remy. "Try to imagine that these planks want to be shaped and will work with you."

Other than Brassart, Henri was the one Remy had told about Tika.

"Mixing with Indians may not be wise," Henri had said, "but don't take a hasty decision about your future."

In truth Remy thought about Tika every day. He told Henri, "I spent a delightful day with Tika. You think I should try to see her again? Their camp is far from our work site."

"I hesitate to say. People are like wood. We need to be seasoned then act according to our natural grain, not against it. If I had done that I might still have a house and a pretty wife in Alsace."

"You had a wife?"

"Some day I'll tell you the story."

Now Remy would never know. After bidding Father Hennepin goodnight shortly before daybreak, he passed the remaining hours of darkness in thought.

He could understand Indian anger about losing control of their country. But why then should Henri die for a problem not of his making? Until his father lost land strips to the village nobleman, the Sieur de Senlis, Remy had never thought about such problems. He could hear his father's voice, "How can he take my best strips? He already owns half of the village. May God strike him dead."

And why can't an Indian— even Tika—go to heaven when they had no way of knowing about the church? Remy sat in the cave's entrance looking at glowing stars. Was anybody really up there? Sleep would not come.

By the first light of morning he picked up his journal to write:

May 1681
Yesterday my musket killed a man about my age. Is building the Griffin worth what we are going through? Henri will never see his work afloat.

Chapter 12

JESUIT LETTER

MY REVEREND FATHER LAURENT
THE PEACE OF OUR LORD
MAY 1681

Quelle bonne surprise. I am delighted, my dear Maurice, to have news from you. By notions of distance in this vast wilderness we are neighbors and what is more, both working with Hurons.

I regret that the Sieur de La Salle would not consider our objections to his way of dealing with the Savages. The evil commerce in alcohol he abides will doubtless continue under our new *Intendant* and will have the approval of Governor Louis de Buade, Count Frontenac. I am told he is engaged in this trade himself. Do not suffer unduly, *mon cher collègue*, from your anger in this regard. Remember that Jesus, undoubtedly in righteous indignation, overturned moneychangers' tables and drove cattle dealers from the Temple.

In answer to your inquiry, my Savages may be more familiar with our ways than those in your region. Given our proximity to Michilimackinac and active trade on the inland seas they have had a better opportunity to acquire iron tools and guns.

Our natives also live with an uncertain food supply. Corn does not grow well in the soil here. However, our inland sea teems with white fish of excellent quality, and the Indians with their sharpened sticks have developed great skill in spearing them even quite deep into the waters. Close to their longhouses our Hurons grow some squash and beans. Unfortunately, they have no notion of clearing and tilling larger fields as we do in Europe. Yet they are robust and vigorous. These natives who love to feast when food is available can go two or three days without eating while continuing their work, whether engaged in hunting or fishing or erecting shelters.

To answer your question, memories of our illustrious Father Jean de Brébeuf remain with some of our elder natives whose parents knew him. But in the intervening thirty some years since he was martyred, two generations of Hurons have strayed from the teaching and good works he established amongst them.

In the shadow of this giant evangelizer I am striving to establish strict observance of our faith. Natives can readily use distorted versions of our teachings to combine with their Great Spirit and animistic notions of nature gods.

Last week in a cabin of bark slabs I had our natives pray to God, all on their knees for many hours. Finally, there or in my chapel open to the weather I, myself, caught a severe cold.

Since others were so afflicted I passed by to visit several suffering persons. Indians are gravely affected by this malady and were happy just to have survived. They recognized that their prayers had enabled them to continue life. I asked one man what he did with the rosary I had placed around his neck. He told me he gave it to his son, who was ill with fever. Soon after the father attached the beads around the boy's neck he was healed.

This is how we offer the catechism. We sound a little hand bell to assemble them in the fashion in which village Elders meet in Council. I don surplice and biretta adding a certain dignity to this ceremony. Kneeling we chant the *Pater Noster* together, rendered in Huron by our interpreter. Then we chant it once again, after which I arise and make the sign of the cross. We then review the previous lesson. If certain children answer well, we place in their palms a little bead of glass or porcelain.

We repeat endlessly in these meetings the Truth that their souls are immortal and they all go either to Heaven or to the fires of Hell. The children receive this with interest but often I am obliged to conclude by talking only with the old men, elders who make me listen to their beliefs.

I pray that the young daughter of your chief proves willing to accept the truth of Jesus. You speak of her intelligence and I agree that confirmation of such a person could be of enormous help to our Huron missions. But I urge the utmost caution in placing trust in what may indeed be a whim or even a ruse. If she continues to study I entreat you to keep me informed of her progress.

These Savages do have qualities of generosity and hospitality with one another. But as you mention they become unreasoning beasts when intoxicated. And they can be liars, pernicious beggars and often thieves.

You speak of your journey by canoe from Quebec. When I arrived at the Sault my Indians from a mission on Georgian Bay forgot the kindness I had lavished upon them in their sickness. Despite their fair words and promises to me, having landed me with Church equipment and a few necessities, they departed leaving me there quite alone with no shelter. Without a backward glance they resumed the journey to their village.

Although some of my supplies were stolen, I must say the Hurons welcomed me. They even provided a bark hut. From the beginning I have tried to grasp their language. The complexity of their vocabulary, with no written grammar for guidance makes this an awesome task. That I may converse with the Indians in their dialect I pray God to grant me patience for a long period of learning.

The Hurons were fascinated by some of the objects that serve our daily needs. They watched us using a hand mill and poked at the fine grains in delight. The magic of a magnet attracting bits of iron will hold their attention for many repetitions. And our small clock—well they thought it was alive! They gather to hear it strike and do not hesitate to enter our habitation without knocking.

For a joke, after the clock struck four times I called out to it, "That is enough. Speak no more."

The Savages asked what the clock had said. We told them it commanded them to go away and close our door, which they promptly did.

Unfortunately their curiosity about these strange devices does not extend to spiritual teachings. You have no doubt noticed that it is difficult to convey the idea of only one God ruling the world. I give thanks to the Holy Scripture for guiding us in this task. It will be a comfort to work with a colleague in addressing these challenges. If you have any instances of success in these matters I pray you to share them with me.

Coming from a city like Paris you must find this wilderness fearsome indeed. The lack of civilized amenities and a spiritual community are truly a test of our determination to bring the Kingdom of God to these Savages.

I was born in the mountains of Auvergne (*le pays de Dôme*). Thanks to a local priest I was sponsored by my parish as a student at the Jesuit College in Clermont Ferrand. Having grown up in a climate of rigorous weather and general poverty I am not shocked by the meager existence of these native peoples.

You mention a certain excitement in observing ceremonial dancing and drumming. Frankly, their wild abandon during native rites gives me a fright. This brings to mind my youth, when peasants celebrated the end of grape harvest with drunken dancing and loose behavior between men and women.

Nevertheless the native's capacity for emotional excess opens opportunities to use prayer and song to celebrate the rites of the Holy Roman Church. We must also insist upon at least an elemental grasp of what our faith demands: one God, one wife, one path leading to salvation, and punishment after death for sins against the Church.

You inquire whether I keep a journal. I do indeed write reports on a regular basis to Father Drapeaux, our spiritual advisor. Attempts to record my thoughts and meditations have been sporadic and not particularly satisfying. It is for dying children that native mothers are most willing to accept baptism. Only then, looking into their faces, do I truly feel a spiritual kinship with these Savages, sensing the depth of their love and suffering. Such moments I cannot capture in words.

On other occasions I search into the eyes of these people, who are often quite handsome, and find absolutely no change of expression while we talk. What, I ask myself, are they feeling? Do they really have a soul?

I look forward to exchanging accounts of our experiences in bringing the gospel to the Huron people. Thus can we support our friendship and share the mission of our beloved Society in New France. Can we ever convert these natives?

IN UNION WITH YOUR HOLY SACRIFICE, I REMAIN
FATHER R. NICHOLAS, S.J.

Chapter 13

MANNA IN THE WILDERNESS

More alert after the Iroquois attack where Henri was killed, Remy walked ahead of his companion constantly scanning the dense tree growth for signs of movement. A squirrel jumping from branch to branch would often bring him to an abrupt halt. And he was wondering what the Wendats might think of that Iroquois attack. Would they approve?

Once again he was *en route* with Brassart to inform the Wendats that the Sieur de La Salle would soon set sail for a long expedition. How would they receive La Salle's message?

If the Indians had all moved from winter camp, Tika would no doubt be once again at the longhouse village. Brassart had probably been right about Tika, Remy reflected. *Quelle flirteuse* she had been, first pretending to enjoy being with him and then not having the courtesy to say goodbye.

La Salle's messengers arrived at the longhouses to find that Chief Owassoni would reserve a bark cabin for them. He proposed that his visitors wait until the next day for an official welcome from tribal elders. Small bands of Iroquoi warriors had recently been reported in the area. Brassart suspected that the chief was eager to discuss help in case of an attack.

As they proceeded to their hut someone approached from behind. They turned to see Tika who held out her hands. Brassart greeted her and then walked on. Remy stood there determined to keep his distance.

"Seeing you make forest sing. You not happy for me?"

Straightening pack and weapon he bided his time before answering.

"I don't know."

"Since last visit I think of you."

"You missed me?"

"Why you ask?"

"I thought you had no interest. When we left you did not say goodbye. "

"You know I must go to women's hut."

"Could you not even say goodbye?"

"It was time of moon for me. Not allowed with men."

He wondered if she were telling the truth. Then he realized with a start that they were talking with less difficulty. Tika was speaking in French mixed with native words.

After placing pack and musket into the shelter he walked into the woods with her while Brassart and Onendo were visiting. Peaceful it was to be making their way with no fear of enemies.

Tika remained silent for a time before she asked, "Why you come?"

"We bring a message for Chief Owassoni."

All afternoon Remy alternated between thinking about the dangers of the expedition south and the carefree moments of being with Tika. Returning to the hut he found Brassart asleep. Later when Tika called them to dinner the trouble in his mind was matched by a tremor of uneasiness in his stomach anticipating what they might have to eat.

The evening fare happened to be fish grilled over coals. It was appetizing but with a bit of salt it would have been even better. Boiled dried corn cooked with a sweet green herb made this more delectable than their previous meal with these natives.

From where they sat on skins around a cooking fire the visitors could see platforms of limbs scarcely more than head high piled with baskets of corn, drums, and buckskin garments. Rows of elm wood poles formed the walls of this longhouse about ten paces wide. At the top, crowns of saplings joined with bark cordage left slits for smoke to escape. Slabs of seasoned elm-wood bark covered the outside of the building.

Floor level sleeping compartments were divided by woven mats. Some had hides to screen the space from the center passageway.

Drying herbs hung above the beds. Stacked firewood covered both ends of the interior.

Fires were blazing at intervals along the central passageway stretching fifty paces to the end. Tika explained that two families, one on each side, shared one cooking pit.

Chief Owassoni's place near the entrance admitted fresh air, giving relief from smoke-laden cooking odors. After several days in the open the two Frenchmen found the smell of dogs and sweating bodies difficult to ignore.

For the evening repast Onendo placed Brassart at his side. Remy was seated between Tika and Mokanoa, the storyteller of the tribe. Encouraged by Chief Owassoni he began to relate the Wendat account of the creation of the world.

From Brassart and Tika's translation Remy could follow the gist of this story:

> One day many moons ago a woman named Aataentsic descended from the sky on the back of the Great Turtle. Immediately she ordered the animals, all of them water creatures, to gather bits of earth from the bottom of the sea. The toad, most humble of these, dived deep gathering sand to spread on the Great Turtle's shell. The pile grew and grew.

Mokanoa's eyes shone in the firelight:

> The silt became the island where our people were to make their home. In a tiny house on this new land lived an old woman. Calling her Shutai (grandmother), Aataentsic found there a shelter for herself and the daughter she was carrying.

> This child was born and grew to be a beautiful young woman. Several male spirits vied for her attention. Upon her mother's advice the daughter chose a Turtle Spirit. By placing an arrow beside her while she slept he impregnated her.

> After a time this daughter gave birth to twin boys. But how different they were! Gentle Tsetah wanted the world to be a perfect place. The other twin Tawiskaron (man of flint) endeavored to create pitfalls and dangers in the world about him. Then, more evil yet, Tawiskaron had refused to follow a natu-

Richard Johnston

ral birth path. He carved his way out of his mother's body through her armpit, causing her death.

Tsetah, first to enter the world, set about creating parallel rivers for comings and goings without need for portages. Huge berries and luscious fruits became plentiful. Trees were endowed with sweet sap for making syrup. He provided abundant grasses to feed succulent animals that had no fear of arrows.

Tawiskaron believed his brother's work made life too easy. Finally he reversed or vandalized Tsetah's creations.

Eventually the brothers fought a duel and the wicked Tawiskaron was slain. However, his malevolent spirit survived and continued to visit his grandmother. The Earth Mother understood why this had happened. The brothers represented the two forces of creation. She realized that from death and suffering comes the need for all of the people to care about and help one another. This must guide them in all they do. They are part of a family that includes all living creatures and all that grows upon the soil of their island.

This is the Sacred Circle of Life.

So saying Mokanoa clasped his hands together and made a circle with his arms. By this time most of the people in the longhouse had gone to bed as their cooking fires smoldered out. Now Brassart wanted to retire for the night.

Remy suggested to Tika that they go for a walk.

By the light of a half moon they drank in the fresh air and walked along in silence. Emerging from the longhouse that night Tika blended with the evening freshness. Her hair gave off "a fragrance of damp moss" Remy later wrote in his journal.

When they returned to the barking of village dogs Remy stood with her at the entrance, not knowing how to bid her goodnight. Woven rush mats hanging over the opening served as doors.

"Come." She tugged at his arm.

He pushed the mats aside and entered with her. Tika found a place to pile furs and hang skins on each side of them for an illusion of privacy. Soft buckskin hides had a faintly smoky odor.

For a moment Remy lay quietly. Then he reached out to Tika and she turned to press herself against him. As they groped around on their bed of skins he found the warmth of her body. She helped him to undress. Her moist skin under his hands was a new sensation. Reacting to his touch her breasts became erect pressing their nipples into the palm of his hand. When Tika turned to press herself against him in a warm embrace Remy pulled her firmly against his throbbing body.

As if floating in a sky filled with sunlit birches, they found each other in mutual delight—oblivious to snoring Indians, restless dogs, and wakeful cries of children.

Next morning Remy's savoring of his exhilarating experience was interrupted. Brassart asked his young aide to deliver La Salle's message in French to the Council of Wendat Elders while Brassart interpreted. When they arrived the calumet was unwrapped and tobacco from a skin bag pressed into the bowl. A sprig of burning sage lighted the pipe. Remy had not yet learned to enjoy this taste but drew in bravely, taking care not to fill his chest. Somehow it did not taste as strong as the last time.

La Salle's message explained to the tribe that he would soon be departing to explore the great river to the south encouraging more trade with the Louisiana territory for the benefit all the natives. He assured his Huron friends and allies that he would return soon and remain in the area to help and protect them.

The elders replied that they wanted to live in friendship with Onontio. That was their name for the governor in Quebec. One elder urged the French to make peace with the Iroquois. He pointed out that the Wendats lacked muskets to face an attack and wondered if La Salle would provide the Hurons with arms before he left?

Brassart assured the Elders that their remarks would be relayed to the Sieur de La Salle. The Indians clearly wanted to know what guarantees of protection he could promise. It was past noon when the ceremony ended.

The chief and Onendo offered to show their visitors certain sacred sites so Brassart decided to stay on another day.

"You need not feel obligated to go with us this afternoon," Brassart informed Remy, "if you want to spend more time with your woman."

Remy and Tika took dried fish for a long afternoon walk to a small waterfall in a grove of birch trees near the crest of a hill similar to the one they had seen at their first meeting. She said that the spot reminded her of him.

They were glad to rest near the stream talking and sometimes just holding hands. The cool air of evening reminded them to return. They arrived in the dark after the Chief, Moon Cloud, and Brassart had finished the evening meal. Remy and Tika ate more dried fish and went outside to escape the smoky air.

She took him to a bark shelter where she had told Bible stories to the children. Furs were spread on the floor and a bench of branches held some printed manuscripts Father Laurent had given her along with a rough slate and chalk.

She built a small fire and then she queried Remy about his family. He told of his mother's death and described his papa and sister Monique. Tika struggled to understand. With the help of repetition and gestures, she could grasp much of the story.

As he recounted for the second time his visit with Monique at her convent Tika's face flushed and her eyes lighted up.

"Why they no let you see sister?"

"Because she is married to Christ and kept away from family and friends."

She could not understand why his sister should be shut away in a big stone building.

"Father Laurent say convent good place to learn. Would be for me like your sister?"

"*En France? Oui.*"

"I stay here."

Again they lay together, this time in delightful privacy. Midst a tangle of furs they fell asleep wrapped in each other's arms. They awoke before dawn and sat together bundled in buckskin wraps against the morning chill.

Remy asked Tika if she would like to see more of Canada beyond the woods and live in a settlement of houses.

"You know enough of our language to make yourself understood in a French village," he assured her.

"I am happy here but like to see new place."

"The village of Quebec is beautiful."

"Where is?"

"Far away on a great river near mountains."

"What tribe there?"

"Mostly French people in stone or wood houses."

"I would have fear."

"Why?"

"Your people. Sometimes they kill us."

"Tika, that is because of war. Your tribes go to battle against each other. No French person would harm you."

"When I am small I see our people attacked. Women and children. Villages burned. Even the dogs they kill."

"But that was the Iroquois."

"Yes. That was what they do." She shook her head. "But your soldiers kill. Maybe us."

She sat in the chill dawn rigid as a totem pole. Remy put his arm around her as they listened to morning sounds of the village. They returned to the longhouse in time for boiled cornmeal.

Again Brassart had plans for the day with Onendo.

"I am learning much about this tribe," he told Remy. "Fear of the Iroquois makes them doubt that they can defend themselves. They need support but at the same time are suspicious of our intentions. La Salle will want to hear about this."

Tika took Remy to meet Father Laurent in a larger bark hut used solely as a chapel. "Father, this my friend Remy."

The priest acknowledged the introduction with a stiff bow. Then he stepped back.

"What brings you here, monsieur?"

"I am on a mission for the Sieur de La Salle."

"Do you have brandy or firearms?"

"No, Father. I am not a trader."

"Do you approve of such commerce?"

"I have spoken with Father Hennepin about that and agree that it can be harmful."

"Then why do you work with men like La Salle? They are corrupting the people of Mademoiselle Tikanaka and other natives."

"In truth, Father, the Sieur de La Salle is trying to help the Indians. He speaks several of their languages and he has gained their respect. Myself, I feel fortunate to be learning how to live in this wilderness. Then too he paid for my passage."

Remy almost said he wanted to be a fur trader but thought better of it.

"You have much to confess, my son."

Remy wanted to get away but Tika kept talking. He could see that her teasing surprised the priest and that he liked her attention, even when she put her hand on his shoulder.

"Would you believe, monsieur, that she has studied French for less than one year?"

"She knows many words," Remy answered.

"You have profited from Catholic teaching," Father Laurent told Remy as they were leaving his chapel. "Now you have an obligation to set an example for your countrymen and for the natives by observing the practice of confession and praying to find a better way to serve your country than you are now doing."

The air of hostility between them Tika could sense but not understand. For a time they walked in silence absorbed in their thoughts. Then they both forgot their problems at the prospect of a day together. As they left the camp she introduced Remy to Little Eagle, a young warrior who often spoke to her in a familiar way. He greeted the visitor with an obvious lack of enthusiasm.

"Who is he?"

"He is friend."

"You like him?"

"He teases me but really kind. Is good friend."

"Perhaps he would like to marry you."

"Oh no." Tika laughed. "We are both of Wendat tribe and of Cord clan. Clan is like family. No marry each other."

"Have you coupled in your bed with another man?" Remy asked.

"Oh yes.

"How many?"

"Two."

"How many times?"

"Once with Kitisaga, who is my age."

"Were you in love with him?"

"What that mean?"

"Did you like him more than anybody else and want to be with him for many moons?"

"No."

"Then why did you lie in furs with him?"

"Is kind boy and give me present of wampum."

"And the other man. How many times?"

"Maybe three." She counted on her fingers.

"You are still doing that?"

"Oh no. Spear Thrower is warrior. He not speak with me, even when we together. With him, no magic. Like mending his moccasins."

"When you get married how will your mate know that you will not continue taking wampum from other men?"

"Because I choose only him. If you married as you say and want to be with other woman who make you more happy, you go with her?"

"Of course not."

"Even if you want to be with her?"

"Probably not."

"Because married?"

"Yes."

"If two people must be always together when one no longer wants, why stay? Like slave."

"When you share your life with somebody you have to be able to depend upon that person," Remy replied.

"I like better our way."

Again they enjoyed a night in her bark shelter. At last she had time to talk about her own life. Her mother was part Mohawk from a grandmother in that tribe who married a Wendat. Being of mixed blood caused some to look upon her with suspicion.

Tika's tribe, having fewer warriors and a smaller fur-gathering area, was weak compared with their nearest neighbors the Petuns. They were in constant fear of the Iroquois, who in the lifetime of her father had massacred almost half of the Huron population.

Tika was intrigued by hearing about Remy's family and enjoyed speaking with him about her own. She moved her hands about and laughed over this new experience. It was a different kind of storytelling that set her to thinking.

"I like Father Laurent and what he tell me of Bible, his magic." She paused to form words. "Learning stories about your strange spirits make me want to know more."

They spent hours around a small fire in each other's arms kissing in a manner she found strange and at first did not like. Remy didn't know whether the French way was different or if it was his lack of experience with women. But such details became less important than the joy of just being together.

Tika reached out to the brass medallion Remy still wore around his neck.

"What magic?" She rubbed the polished metal against her cheek.

"The magic of friendship, I guess." Remy took it off so she could examine it. "My companion Le Coquin gave me this in Paris. I will tell you about him sometime."

In the early dawn Tika asked, "You come back soon?"

"Bien sûr."

Brassart was anxious to let La Salle know that the Hurons were asking questions reflecting distrust of the French presence. It was the first time the Indians had openly expressed such concern. He was not particularly pleased when Tika set out to accompany them. But for more than a half hour she kept pace. He did embrace her in parting. She kissed Remy and watched them disappear down the trail.

"Mokanoa's story sounded a little bit like the Bible. Could that have been copied?" Remy asked. "The twins resembled Cain and Abel."

"I believe not. Remember these people were around long before we invaded their territory. I am aware that girl you call Tika makes progress learning French."

"I just cannot understand how those people think." Remy shook his head. "Tika is intelligent and amusing but she seems to have no understanding of what it means to be loyal to one person. How could you depend on somebody like that?"

"I have seen mixed marriages," Brassart answered, "and they are not always happy. I doubt that you or I could live as they do. Dried corn and dog meat are not my favorite repast."

"She wants to see me again, but I want to get started on our expedition." Remy pulled up beside his companion.

"You won't have long to wait. The ship may be ready two months after La Salle gets back with the rigging and other supplies."

As they continued on the trail Remy was thinking about how freely Tika gave her favors to two other men. How could she recount something so sinful with no regret? *Une Fille du Roi* like Odette might give him less worry.

Yet Remy wrote in his journal:

July 1681
For the first time I have known a woman.
Was that a sin for me? For her, if she is not
Christian? She may think I am just another
man. But with Tika I have experienced an
indescribable joy.

14

JESUIT LETTER

My Reverend Father Nicholas,
The Peace of our Lord
July 1681

In his epistles to the Galatians, Paul counsels them to "Bear ye one another's burdens, and so fulfill the law of Christ." It is heartening to have your news from the Sault and share our task of bringing Christ to these Savages. I am pleased that the services rendered by Father Brébeuf still live in the memory of some Hurons.

We have learned that La Salle's ship is almost ready for launching into the Niagara River. They say it can carry a large load of brandy and muskets that will certainly increase the quantity of furs traded. This is not only counter to good sense, but also a threat to the Holy Church and dishonor to our King and nation. We can only hope his plans do not come to fruition.

I share your disappointment that these natives who can be so curious about the novelty of our mechanical devices yet have no interest in exploring the spiritual realms we could open for them. In some aspects of their daily behavior the Hurons exhibit traits that are not far from the virtues of the Christianity we wish to teach them. As you mention in your letter, they love their children and strive to protect them.

I find also that the Hurons share their space and food with visiting Petun neighbors who are welcome to stay as long as they like. In hunting or battle they are brave in the face of danger. Then too,

if our young Mademoiselle Tikanaka ever forgot to help with catechism class she would never lie or make excuses.

However, I have learned that their customs permit them to
change mates at will. Young boys and girls can couple before marriage without shame. Nor do they understand the value of respect-
ing private property. And at times they trust dreams and omens
more than the reality of everyday experience.

This is how I am endeavoring to learn their language. Using
birch-bark scrolls I write down according to sounds as many useful Huron words as possible. But conveying the Bible's message is
not easy. Perhaps that is why they prefer their own religion.

Now I have a new appreciation of Mademoiselle Tikanaka, who
makes amazing progress in our language. She also helps me to understand her dialect. That gives me satisfaction and even personal
pleasure. Of course she can be of no assistance in writing. I am
sometimes amused by her questions and find it difficult to choose
the words that can satisfy her curiosity.

Our martyred Father Brébeuf at the Sault made a diligent effort
to get some of their language into transcription. But their speech is
both prolific and imprecise so the task is, as you have no doubt observed, formidable. One cannot find a name for God that they can
understand. We call Him the great Chief, or Captain of all men.

A notion of mystery and miracles they do have but they attribute
these things to such a variety of objects and natural forces that the
true meaning of an all-powerful Being eludes them. Worldly learning and scholarship are not what we need. Rather patience, humil-
ity, and apostolic charity may eventually win the souls of these
poor Savages.

With my tiny group as the center of a future church, I decided to start celebrating some of our festivals. For the *Saint Jean*
on the 23rd of June we built a bonfire and conducted a service.
Mademoiselle Tikanaka asked her people to help and there was
great enthusiasm.

They gathered a huge pile of wood that I feared might set the
whole forest aflame. She invited her father, Chief Owasonni, to
light the fire. He proudly carried a flaming torch on high from
the longhouse adding a dramatic touch to the ceremony. The entire village was there. I sang the *ut queant laxis*, the *benedictus* and

St. John's prayer; the *domini salvum fac regum,* and a prayer for our King, all this without surplice.

Afterward the Hurons wanted to start drumming and dancing, which at first I opposed. Mademoiselle Tikanaka suggested that was one way to combine our teaching and the traditions of the tribe. With apprehension I consented. Now I believe it was worthwhile. Do you have an opinion about this?

In my disapproval of the projects of the Sieur de La Salle and his henchmen my mind turns to the martyrdom of our brothers. We have shed so much blood to promote the noble work of salvation despite the corrupting influence of our countrymen who would sacrifice these souls to the profits of commerce.

The emissaries of these venal pursuits include a young Frenchman named Remy Moisson, who seems already to be a spokesman for La Salle. Unfortunately he has attracted the attention of Mademoiselle Tikanaka, who takes an interest in him. I must make her understand the danger of becoming attached to such a person. Apparently this young man will go with La Salle on his exploration to the south. One can hope he will find other adventures to keep him occupied elsewhere.

Mademoiselle Tikanaka must be protected. She can read our language well enough to advance in instruction but is yet a combination of youthful energy and daring that is difficult to direct, not only for me but for her parents as well. She wanders by herself in the forest and seeks adventure more eagerly than most boys. Water has a great attraction for her, reputedly impelling her to leap from rocky heights into a stream. She does not hesitate to swim by herself, which I understand is the way she encountered this fellow Remy.

What a tragedy if he succeeds in using this woman for his pleasure. I must admit to some bitterness that these traders not only corrupt entire communities of natives but also harm individuals who might lead their people toward salvation.

Mademoiselle is beginning to be conversant enough in French to receive religious instruction. She could be trained to be a Sister, the first native one in New France.

Though not always correct, her speech is excellent for an Indian who has studied the language for only one year. She spends much of her time reading and repeating the words. With a discriminative sense of hearing she imitates them without always knowing what they mean. I am in awe of her ability to remember.

I call her Mademoiselle Tikanaka and insist that she call me Father Laurent to give her a sense of dignity and discipline. Sometimes she shocks me deeply, but I must be mindful of my mission. She is my God-given chance to do His work.

She wants to teach the native children French but she is not yet qualified. She does try to tell them Bible stories in their own language, which I approve. She seems to have no trouble holding their interest. Gathered around her they listen attentively and sometimes nod and break out in laughter.

The thought that Mademoiselle Tikanaka could one day help bring the story of our Savior to her people gives me new hope. It bolsters my faith in what our beloved Society is doing.

In the midst of this terrible wilderness attacked by swarms of mosquitoes—these tiny flies which are troublesome in the extreme—and eating revolting food, I have found my *raison d'être* here in Canada and what my mission is to be. I count myself one of the happiest men on earth.

IN UNION WITH YOUR HOLY SACRIFICE, I REMAIN,
FATHER M. LAURENT, S.J

Chapter 15

NIAGARA FALLS

"*Attention!*" Remy's voice rang out.

Only then they heard the rattle.

Jean grabbed a stick and probed behind a rock. His eyes followed the path of the reptile uncoiling and gliding into tall grass at the trail's edge. The two friends looked at each other in horror.

They had received permission to visit the great falls for a few days when work on the Griffin slackened. La Salle was still in trouble with his creditors. Tonty had given Remy and Jean directions to the trail, adding that a shelter they would find there was the remains of a fort La Salle had once started to build.

To reach the falls was an easy day of walking. From a supply of smoked fish in camp along with a bag of ground corn, they had brought enough food for the journey. Both were looking forward to time away from work and especially a chance to be together.

Father Hennepin called the great falls an awe-inspiring prodigy of nature. "You must see them," he told the two young men, "but keep your eyes open for serpents. I have heard that the Iroquois who once lived near the falls abandoned the entire area to be free from these venomous reptiles."

Tonty related to Remy that once when the Sieur de La Salle was climbing over a rock near the falling water he encountered three snakes about two paces long and as big around as a man's arm. It so unnerved him that he had a fever that lasted for several days.

That vision slithered through Remy's imagination while they were making their way along the trail.

"I wonder why God made such frightful creatures." Jean was watching where he placed each foot as he walked through the undergrowth.

"I don't like them either and I'm glad the Iroquois have departed. I keep thinking of Henri."

Jean slapped his friend on the shoulder. "But for you I might have been a second victim. I really miss him. He showed me how to make mortise and tendon joints. I may someday be that skillful but meanwhile I am going to use everything he taught me at the worksite. And I feel fortunate to be right here in Canada."

Remy agreed. "More than anything I'm eager to get started on our great adventure to the south. Later perhaps I will learn the fur trade. What will you do when we've paid our passage?"

"If I can earn enough as an independent woodworker I dream of bringing my sisters to New France," Jean answered.

"Where are they now?"

"They are both in Paris." Jean stopped to examine a prickly branch. "Look here. Blackberries. They will grow to be big and sweet. *Maman* used to put them in a bowl with a little red wine and sprinkled sugar on top."

Remy laughed. "We had wild blackberries too. When I was little I picked some and brought them home in my pockets. What a mess that was. Papa didn't see the humor and wanted to whip me. But Monique just laughed and stopped him. He made me wash out the stains in our stream."

At dusk they came upon the source of the roaring sound they had been following. A breeze ruffled patches of mist under an otherwise clear sky. From the top of the falls they could feel the force of this swift, upended river plunging into a rocky pit.

Approaching the brink, flowing waters parted around an island in the center. Two separate sheets of river glided over this lip of the falls to hit the bottom with a roaring boom.

Jean and Remy stood there long moments before the wet and cold impelled them to continue.

About a hundred paces from the river they caught sight of a partly finished log structure, doubtless the fort mentioned by Tonty. La Salle had decided that a location this near the falls was not a suitable place to build the *Griffin*. After inspecting all the dark corners Remy agreed with Jean that the shelter might be safer than sleeping in the open. Night was descending so here they made camp before eating their smoked fish and falling asleep.

Remy awoke with somebody shaking him.

Jean was excited. "You must come out and see this."

An almost full moon rising above the horizon cast a golden halo over the falls as they edged their way along the precipice. Clouds of mist captured and magnified the glow.

"Do rattlesnakes come out in the moonlight?" Jean was feeling his way forward.

"I think they prefer warm sunshine."

"I hope so. Anyway let's wait until tomorrow to look around."

Back at the shelter they built a small fire and watched the moon's path across the sky. It was late morning when they set out to explore the top of the falls.

"I wonder why the land drops off so suddenly?" Jean shouted above the roar of the falls. "This must drop at least a hundred paces. Shall we climb down?"

They descended in zigzag fashion clinging to the slippery, moss-covered rocks.

"Look what happens here." Jean had reached the bottom.

With clouds of spray and foam the two cascades came together and shot into a narrow canyon. Before the two explorers started upward they watched the turbulent waters become a powerful rapids.

At the top of the falls the land surface of the island covered with cedar and spruce, did not appear much more elevated than the two banks of the river. The two friends were fascinated to watch how quickly the Niagara current increased in speed along the west branch on their side of the island. No craft could survive such a powerful current.

After a day of climbing around they returned to their campsite. By then the mist was turning into rain as clouds moved in overhead. Starting a fire was a challenge. Chipping off wood splinters with their knives and striking sparks with flint on ground charcoal finally kindled sparks. Soon a blazing fire was giving off heat and they both stripped down to dry their clothes.

Hanging his garments on limbs Jean had arranged close to the fire Remy started to laugh. He was remembering of course his first meeting with Tika and the anxious moments fearing the arrival of ferocious Iroquois warriors.

"What's so amusing about getting wet?"

Picturing Tika atop that riverbank looking down and laughing at him, Remy began to recount his river adventure with the impertinent young Savage.

Jean looked up from behind the branches where he was stretching his clothing.

"How could you talk with her?"

"Excellent question. I couldn't speak her language. Also I was cold and raging mad. Finally we tried to exchange a couple of words. Anyway, she built a fire and dried my clothes. And I have seen her since. She is learning French from a priest."

"I can't imagine being with an Indian woman. Do you know her family?"

"Just a little. Chief Owasonni, her father, doesn't talk much. I cannot tell what he is really thinking. Moon Cloud, the mother, seems to approve of me."

"How is that?"

"Well, she makes certain I have enough to eat and greets me in a friendly way. She even smiles and nods when I try to say a Wendat word. She is very much in charge of the household."

"What is the girl like?"

"Tika is beautiful and exciting. But these Savages do have strange ways. You can never be certain an Indian woman will stay with you. They change mates easily."

"That would not be amusing and are you really interested in her?"

"I'm not certain. I thought at first that I could enjoy helping her learn French. Anyway I'll probably never see her again."

"It would be pleasant to have women around for a change. I miss my sisters." Jean fed the fire." One of the girls on the ship was pretty and I hoped to meet her when we arrived."

"Which one?"

"She had auburn hair and smiled at me. Of course I didn't know her name."

Remy laughed. "That was Odette. I had an eye on her and even talked to her a wee bit."

"Let's go to Quebec next summer when the next boat load of women arrives. We should be back from our expedition by then."

"I'll go if you do." Remy took up a gourd of water. "Let's drink to that."

They agreed gleefully to a joint search for beautiful young women.

As they sat by the fire Remy thought a while about the lovely Tika. But he went to sleep anticipating how exciting it would be to sail on the Griffin, confident now that he would be chosen for the expedition.

They had planned on their last day to hike up river toward the sea. But the sun was out as they awoke. A faint rainbow crowned the falls as if to bid them farewell. Finally they scaled the rocks to the landing below the falls, stopping to sit in the sunlight with no further thought of serpents. A foaming crescendo of falling water and shimmering stretch of river reminded them of the precious spectacle they were enjoying.

Starting home the next day they walked in silence. As the sound of falling water dimmed each of them kept turning to look back. By late afternoon they were once again at the shipyard. Passing by the work site they noticed that the hull of the Griffin was almost completed.

"How long will it be?" they asked Tonty.

"I would judge less than two months." Tonty stroked the hull.

"So we should be launching soon."

"Unfortunately that's not possible. While you were away at the big falls the Sieur de La Salle was summoned to Quebec where creditors had seized much of his property."

"So we'll be waiting once again?" Remy looked at Jean and shook his head. "How much time?"

"Work will slow down a bit. We will be delayed perhaps two months."

"Sieur de Tonty I would like to visit my Wendat friend at her longhouse village. Would that be possible while we're waiting?"

"Let's consider that." Tonty paused in thought. "You would have to return no later than three weeks from this date. You will be needed when the rigging begins."

"Thank you. I shall return on time."

Remy wrote that afternoon in his journal:

September 1681
I know I must see Tika again. The Griffin
is only a small ship. I hope I can remem-
ber what I learned crossing the Atlantic on
L'Esprit de France.

Chapter 16
RITES OF PASSAGE

Looking at the hull of the Griffon evoked in Remy's memory his strange feeling of unsteady gait upon landing after a sea voyage of ten weeks. For a whole day and during his first night in crowded sleeping quarters of a room in Quebec village his body was rocking to the earth's undulation as if he were still on the deck of *l'Esprit de France*. He realized how small the handcrafted Griffin was in comparison with a seaworthy ship. He hoped it would it be easier to manage.

He had been eager for the adventure of a sea voyage but all the same the parting with his sister Monique at her convent had made his leaving more difficult.

Back in Paris his decision to emigrate had not been greeted with a cheer. Offended when he learned of Remy's plans to leave Paris, his friend Le Coquin announced that people who left the city were either cowards or peasants. But at the last minute he came around to say goodbye. He handed Remy a small brass medallion on a loop of cord.

"Gonzo gave it to me. This will bring you good fortune and you must wear it always." "Thank you, *Mon ami*." Remy thumbed the worn metal with its illegible inscription. "But you should keep it for yourself."

"You need it more going away to a strange country with dangerous animals and wild people. Besides I know you will come back. You are the only friend I have ever had. Together we can make our fortunes in the Latin Quarter."

So saying he gave Remy a sharp punch on the shoulder before turning abruptly to walk away.

Now in a completely different setting Remy had a new appreciation of what his departure must have meant to his friend. Le Coquin's fearlessness had been an encouraging memory for Remy in the Canadian wilderness. His companion of the Paris streets along with patrons of *Le Corbeau* remained a stronger element of his recollections than all of his time at the Monastery school.

Farouche at *Le Corbeau* had advised Remy in parting, "Always drink the best wine and never trust a man who tells you he is honest."

With the wisdom of Father Bernard and Farouche in mind Remy boarded a coach for La Rochelle carrying two small sea bags. Destined for the same ship, *l'Esprit de France*, the passengers looked around at each other. Remy noticed a muscular young man with a pleasant smile who introduced himself as Jean Fauvet and said he was a carpenter hoping to find work in the New World.

Julien, the coachman, held the travelers' papers and money for lodging. His dark beard and mustache veiled a gap left by missing front teeth. The pride of his life was a long willow rod attached to a strip of leather splayed into three strands at the end. At first the passengers pitied the horses under that relentless whip until they discovered something. Jean was the first to notice.

"Just watch him," he said. "Keep your eyes on that weapon."

The flying strands never touched the horses.

Magnificent chateaus appeared at intervals along the banks of the Loire River south of Orleans. Julien told his passengers these great stone mansions were guarded by the King's archers. Hatless in rain and wind he sat on the coachman's throne wielding his whip. Once, in a lightning storm, they pleaded with him to find shelter. He laughed.

"The Lord has his arms around me."

Looking through windows as the coach passed along the river valley they could see vineyards loaded with ripening grapes and patches of wheat, rye, and oats. Whole fields of sunflowers always turned toward the sun.

The passengers shared rooms at the inns. More than once all seven slept shoulder to shoulder on straw mats covering the floor of one small chamber.

Julien would spread his blanket in the stable loft over the stalls or sleep outside near the horses. Up at dawn before his passengers arose he would swallow his wine (*un coup de rouge*) and *une tartine* before harnessing the team. Each morning he would stand in front of the carriage, holding the lead horses by their bits and pulling down their noses while he prayed.

The travelers would take along three loaves of bread and two bottles of wine plus some rich yellow regional cheeses. These they consumed in the carriage or standing outside when Julien stopped to rest and water the horses. The trip seemed to be taking forever.

"I had no idea France was so big." Jean traced the horizon with a sweep of his arm.

"Nor I." Remy was looking across the plains along the Clain River near Poitier. "Julian said there were Roman ruins here but of course we will not stop to see them."

"He's afraid we'll miss the ship," Jean said.

The port of La Rochelle was basking in a mid-June sun as their carriage rattled into town. Julien drove through streets bustling with carts of fish and wagons loaded with freight for the ships. The surging sea entered the port between two tall stone structures called *la Tour Saint-Nicholas* and *la Tour de la Chaine*. Several sailing vessels were docked or riding at anchor. After twelve days in a cramped carriage the men leapt down to stretch their legs.

In a waterfront shed clerks recorded the travelers' names and processed the papers that Julien handed them. Just as they were boarding the ship something whistled past Remy's ear. He ducked and looked back. At the edge of the dock Julien had snapped his whip over their heads, calling out the name of Saint Antoine by way of bidding them *adieu. Au revoir amis. Au revoir à la France.*

Remy and Jean looked at the great wooden masts reaching up into the sky. *L'Esprit de France* was a square-rigged *barque* of more than 600 tons. This immense ship was to be a new home. Working as partial payment for their passage the two boys would be learning a new, nautical language. The tilting deck and briny smell promised adventure.

Heavy ropes called shrouds were strung from masts to terminals mounted on the starboard rail. Horizontally across these shrouds tarred ropes called ratlines stretched like rungs of a ladder. Remy and Jean watched in wonder as barefooted sailors scurried up the rigging to balance on cross beams like birds on a willow branch.

When, after introducing working passengers to the crew, First Mate Bobbet barked out orders he didn't understand, Remy listened with unpleasant memories of the monastery school. He did not like it. But later, when the Bobbet found out that Remy already knew how to write, he instructed him in the uses of the compass and astrolabe, a privilege for a novice. Moreover he was assigned to keeping an inventory of the ship's supplies during the voyage, recording day-to-day reserves of food and water. Dried peas and fish along with salted meat and sea biscuits were their usual fare. The fresh-water supply was measured out daily in small portions.

In stormy seas all hands helped with ropes and canvas on slippery decks. The ship looming so large at the dock seemed tiny in the towering waves tossing it about in the ocean. Everyone had visions of being washed overboard. And the sailors thought of the women huddling down in the hold.

The ship's officers slept in bunks. A part of the hold was partitioned off for a dozen young women called *Les Filles du Roi* (daughters of the King) being transported to become brides in New France. These young women from orphanages and Catholic shelters would be available to be courted by men who desired brides.

The other passengers were crowded into the steerage, some sleeping in hammocks and others on mats. Remy was fortunate to have a hammock. At first he liked the rocking motion of his bed. But the air soon became foul. The stench of bilge water and seasickness enveloped his sleeping space. So he spent as much time as possible on deck. In clear weather the night skies were velvet black with stars so bright they seemed to bring the heavens within reach.

Remy wrote in his journal:
June 1680.
On a ship we live at the mercy of the wind.
In the sea and sky is a vast loneliness. How I
wish Monique could be with me now.

When not working, Jean Fauvet often joined Remy at night on deck. They would gaze for hours at the stars over the endless water. What if *l'Esprit de France* should go down out there?

The sailors took an interest in the young women aboard but *les demoiselles* were kept apart. They looked younger than the street women Remy had seen in Paris. Whenever they came on deck he always felt a certain excitement and a pang of sadness. The young women reminded him of his sister Monique. Their brief farewell meeting lingered in his memory. There had been so little time to learn more of his mother. She would have probably been younger when she died than the woman in charge of these girls.

Madame Lambert, their chaperone, well aware that her nubile charges would be cooped up with sex-starved sailors for nine to twelve weeks, was determined to keep them distant. Ever vigilant, she foiled all attempts of males to contact the women.

One of the girls Remy found *très jolie* and noted in his journal that she had auburn hair around an oval face with a firm chin. They exchanged smiles, and in one brief conversation she told him her name was Odette. He wanted to learn more about her. But the *surveillante*, Madame Lambert, always intervened to take her away.

Remy tried to picture lying with Odette in his hammock or on a mat in the steerage. Even in imagination that was hard to do. Yet the thought was so pleasant he tried to stay awake and speculate about her. Sometimes he recalled his friend Le Coquin with a tinge of regret that they were not able to see the "girls" in that red-lamp house that they had tried to visit.

In their seventh week food supplies ran low. Salted beef and sea biscuits became daily fare. Heavy seas frightened them all and brought on even more *mal de mer*. There was speculation and wagering among passengers and crew as to whether or not they would reach land by the end of the ninth week. One morning on the next to last day of that week a sailor on the forecastle called out, "Land ho!" The blur on the horizon was Cape Race, Newfoundland.

As *l'Esprit de France* approached its destination, wind from the west-northwest forced the crew to tack for five days before switching north as they reached the Grand Banks of Newfoundland. Sailors began to haul in great catches of cod that the hungry passengers devoured. When Captain Merck authorized a ration of wine their spirits lifted.

At this point sea custom required a ceremony called baptism into the New World. For several days there had been rumors spread by sailors about passengers who had refused the ritual and were thrown overboard to perish in the sea. The next day the old Salts blackened their faces and wrapped themselves in sea ropes.

A large wooden tub was set out on the forward deck. At the last minute Madame Lambert demanded that her charges be exempted from this undignified performance. After some discussion they agreed to bring the young women on deck and sprinkle them with a bit of seawater. The sailors wanted the girls to dance or sing in payment and a few did until their directress stopped them. Odette, who had started to dance, met Remy's glance with a twinkle.

Not knowing how much money was expected to escape the ritual, Remy had chosen to be ducked. Two sailors grabbed him. After being led to the tub he started to struggle and another old Salt stepped in to hoist him up over the rim and plunge him into the icy water. Although dripping on the deck he stood tall. Now wasn't he an experienced sailor?

To complete the ceremony passengers had to kneel and take a solemn oath on a book of hydrographic maps that in the future they would never permit fellow passengers to cross this line for the first time without undergoing the same initiation. Remy folded his "Baptismal Certificate," the first document he had ever received, neatly into his journal and kept it tucked away in his baggage.

L'Esprit de France sailed west and north between the Islands of Newfoundland and Cape Breton into an area of smoother water called the Gulf of Saint Lawrence formed by a stream bearing the same name.

The ship was then sailing upriver against an ever-present ocean current. Crowding to the rail everyone watched the changing landscape bordering the river. On both sides pine, spruce, fir and cedars blanketed the sloping hills. While their ship tacked against the current passengers observed a shoreline of stones and pebbles as variegated patterns of nature passed before their eyes.

L'Esprit de France approached the great rock called Kebec that the Captain said was the Indian word for "narrowing of the waters." Nearby came into view a large island with houses and cultivated fields from which the landing place at Quebec Village could be seen. More than a century before, Jacques Cartier, impressed by the lush wild vineyards, had called this the Island of Bacchus. The

Hurons once called it *L'ile de Sainte-Marie* but for the French it had become *L'ile d'Orléans*.

Flowing north by east the wide river began to narrow above the island. Built on the western shore of the Saint Lawrence close to the water's edge, the town occupied a strip of land between the main river on the east side and the Saint Charles River to the north. The mountainside (Rock of Quebec) on which the village was clinging climbed steeply toward the sky. The upper town seemed to sit atop the lower part nestled against the river.

Odette and the other women were unloaded quickly when the ship docked at Quebec. From on shore she sighted Remy and waved. He wondered if he would see her again. After landing he was placed into a camp with those who had worked for their passage. He and Jean Fauvet managed to stay together.

Remy arrived carrying papers from the Paris Diocese stating that Bishop Laval would have first claim on his services. To complete payment for his passage Remy was obliged to work for two years, after which he would receive thirty *sous* and be free to make his own way.

The first day some of the passengers walked up a trail to Cap Diamant, which overlooked the St. Lawrence River. Below them they could see the Bishop's palace and gardens. Remy looked down upon steep gray roofs.

The day after their arrival, Remy and Jean met a gentleman recruiting for the Sieur de La Salle who had established several forts and needed men to help construct a ship for sailing on the great inland seas to the west. Remy said he knew nothing about shipbuilding but could read and write. He was told that he could learn carpentry skills or might be useful for clerical duties.

Then wishing to know more specifics about the jobs, they met a recruiter named Mansion, at the house of a merchant, Camille Marne. After agreeing to accept employment with the Sieur de La Salle they found themselves three days later, with four other men recruited for La Salle by Monsieur Mansion, sailing up the Saint Lawrence River in a crowded, gaff-rigged launch.

After two weeks of travel they reached *Ville Marie*, also known as *Montreal*, where they transferred to canoes. Being light in weight these boats were easy to portage but unsteady in the water. Remy

thought it would take many days of practice to manage these unsteady craft.

Arriving at Lake Ontario they were transferred to a larger boat.
Late August wind-storms forced their brigantine to follow the
north shore to a dock on the river before reaching the great falls
of Niagara. Men with heavier loads were to portage up the narrow inlet past the falls. Jean and Remy accompanied others with
lighter packs on an overland trail by passing the *chutes d'eau* called
Niagara. They could hear the distant thunder along the route.

Excited by roaring water of the falls and the rugged terrain
Remy had written in his journal:

> *August 1680*
> *This wild country may be a grand adventure,*
> *more dangerous than the Latin Quarter of*
> *Paris after midnight.*

Chapter 17

PRELUDE TO PARADISE

Morning sunlight filtered into the bark hut where a wooden cross and beaded doeskin wall hanging appeared before Remy's eyes. Then he heard voices and approaching footsteps.

Moon Cloud's arrival brought a realization that he was in Tika's hut where her mother had hastily prepared a bed of furs after his arrival late the previous day. Carrying a pot of warm fish oil she offered a foot massage. Supple fingers stroking his aching feet brought instant relief. He drifted back into sleep.

An insect attacking his face disturbed his slumber. He slapped at the pesky creature to no avail, finally opening his eyes to recognize Tika as she leaned over his bed tickling his nose with a blade of grass.

"*Maman* tell me," Tika seized his hand, "that yesterday you walk like old man."

Remy had lost his way coming from the shipyard, veering too far west after the River of White Waters. He had spent two days trying desperately to find the trail again. He had consumed his food supply and in his haste he did not wish to spend time hunting. Finally he had reached the village late in the afternoon hungry and exhausted.

Moon Cloud, the first person to spot him making his way up the trail hurried to greet him and soon placed before him food and water. He devoured the smoked trout washed down with cold water. Tika was away in the forest at the moment, enjoying a rest from studies while Father Laurent visited a Jesuit brother.

The first day Tika and her mother carried food to Remy while he lay in his warm furs. Two elders then escorted Remy to a sweat lodge where he soaked up as much heat as he could bear.

When he emerged Tika was waiting with a blanket and a pair of snug-fitting moccasins. As he was walking to the hut his body seemed to be floating. Perhaps he was learning to find pleasure in Wendat ways.

Moon Cloud quietly attended to Remy's needs. The two young people would share an evening meal with her and the chief, often fresh trout. Tika had somehow come into possession of a bag of salt that had taken on moisture and become a solid lump. With a knife he could chip off enough to season his food.

"Anu,magh,ke,he,one," she said.

"What is that?"

"We call it 'the white man's sugar'."

Moon Cloud politely tasted the salt he offered her and said nothing.

Some members of the tribe were in hunting camp so the long-house was less crowded than on his last visit. Remy could never quite become accustomed to the smoke. But they did not object to him pushing aside the hanging mat.

Their space was near the door so each person entering had to pass them. Several began to know him, stopping to tap his shoulder with the words *tu,hugh,car,o,no* which Tika said meant Frenchman.

Or he would hear *ne,at,a,rugh* meaning "friend."

Evening meals were pleasant. He listened carefully and began to understand simple expressions. Even the chief would help by repeating words when Tika prompted him. Proud of his daughter's skill he would nod. To the amusement of the family, Remy sputtered out a little Wendat.

After their first repast Remy and Tika set out for an evening promenade. Moments later Moon Cloud caught up with them. Addressing Tika she thrust a cooking pot into her hands.

Without a word Tika snatched it and marched down to squat by the stream. She scooped in sand and swished it around before rinsing it out.

After returning it to the longhouse in silence they climbed a slope rising from the river. Remy matched Tika's rapid stride and accompanied her into a stand of spruce before he finally spoke.

"What did your *Maman* tell you?"

"She say must put into Circle of Life as much as you take out."

"You were angry."

She nodded. After a pause a smile appeared on her face. "What she tell me is wise."

Moon Cloud's calm authority prevailed over the family's daily life. From the first day, after massaging Remy's feet, she would put her hand on his shoulder as he passed.

It occurred to Remy that he might prefer to just stay on and never go back to the expedition. He was, however, under contract to La Salle. And in truth he could not resist the call of adventure in exploring the unknown world to the south with the two men he most admired.

Tika cancelled her sessions with the children and spent her days in the pleasure of being with Remy. She was conversant enough in French that they could explore their feelings with words, a sharing of each other's world that was new to them.

For more than a year Remy had been sleeping in a blanket of skins on the hard ground of his cave. Now coupling with Tika's warm body on a bed of supple fir boughs was *le paradis*.

One evening the chief invited his guest for a parley where Remy, with Tika's help, did much of the talking. A man of few words, Chief Owassoni simply wanted to know how much his people could depend on the French for protection against the Iroquois. He invited Remy to speak with the elders before departing.

"If we are friends why you do not help?" Tika stopped in the trail leading from her father's hut.

"The Sieur de La Salle wants to make life better for all your people everywhere. He does not yet have enough men and wampum to do that."

"If Iroquois attack, you come?"

"In truth I think we can't. Fort Frontenac is far away. Only a few men are there and most are not trained soldiers."

"Why you say at powwows we your friends?"

"Some of us say that to make you happy. But I believe La Salle and Tonty really want to be friends. You would like them."

"If no help, not friends."

Tika was troubled by the new circumstances that the arrival of the French had brought into her people's lives. How should

Wendats think about these strange newcomers? Can they be trusted? Aware now that there were many of them in her country, Tika knew only three white men. Brassart she liked. He was courteous and wanted to practice Wendat while helping her with French.

Father Laurent obviously wished to help her people in his own way. But he tried to persuade her not to give her heart to a wandering Frenchman.

Some of his countrymen, the priest told her, were doing wicked things like trading firewater and guns for furs and wanted only to gain wealth from the exchange. On the other hand, God and his representatives, the Jesuits, desired to be their friends. Inspired by the love of Jesus they did not request wampum in return. He was prepared to remain there as long as they wanted him.

Tika nodded.

"Give your heart only to Jesus," Father Laurent told her.

She enjoyed learning French and making herself understood. Curious about the process of creating letters, she was tempted to pursue further studies some day in a convent as Father Laurent was urging her to do. But she found Remy fascinating.

"Like drum beats in my heart," she told Moon Cloud.

He had such strange ways. Could he be content to make his life with her friends of the forest? When they were together he seemed devoted. Yet he kept coming and then leaving. Was that the way of white-faced men?

Remembering that Brassart had once told him about living with natives—that he had rarely seen happy mixed marriages—Remy wanted to believe that he could all the same fit into Tika's family and tribal life. One day in a burst of enthusiasm he put his arms around her mother. Surprised, Moon Cloud accepted the embrace and held him for a moment. It occurred later to Remy that she was the only mother he had ever held in his arms.

Remy observed how much Tika had changed this past year. Serious and beautiful, she now appeared self-assured. He noted that she felt comfortable with Father Laurent, whom she admired. Like Remy she faced hard decisions. Being the one surviving child in a loving family she was bound closely to her parents.

Remy had cautiously broached the idea of Tika going away to live with him one day.

"Have you talked with your family about that?"

"With Moon Cloud yes."

"Do you feel," he pursued, "that leaving with me would be abandoning your own people?"

After another pause, "Perhaps."

"Why?"

"Your people take our land."

"But there is enough land for all to share. And there are many tribes with different dances and spirits. You are not like the Iroquois, for example."

"No. They want only to make war. But your French soldiers use guns—not parley and peace pipe. Little Eagle say they try to make us depart so can have our land."

"He is mistaken. We can all be here in peace."

"If you go off to live with Indian woman, what think your friends?"

"We should all be free to make choices. Perhaps we are intruders in your land. But neither you nor I are to blame. No need to kill one another."

When finally Chief Owassoni called on him to meet with the Council of Elders, the chief was disappointed that La Salle's emissary could not speak officially for France. Tika was interpreter and had only recently acquired a new consciousness of the importance of words. She was sorry that Remy could not bring a message of comfort.

On birch-bark scrolls Tika would scrawl out letters of the alphabet. Putting them together with the sounds was a new experience. Her people had communicated by voice or by pictures. Writing for her was a painfully slow process. She let Remy share her supplies to work on his journal. It was amusing for him to read passages aloud to Tika. She admired his ability to record his thoughts.

When he related an incident where La Salle took hostage a Miami warrior and threatened to kill him if stolen goods were not returned she became angry.

"La Salle did bad thing."

"You think a Wendat warrior would have done the same thing?"

"No."

"To an Iroquois, perhaps?"

"An Iroquois, maybe yes."

"And that would not be bad?"

She looked at him.

"Before you come, life not so hard."

"Being with you," he told her, " makes me happy. What do Wendat boys do when courting a girl they like."

"Courting?"

"Trying to please a woman they wanted to be with for many moons."

"Our way, man run the light to girl."

"Run the light?"

"Young man come with burning stick to wigwam where girl is lying. Come near. If she blow out light he gets into furs with her."

"And if she does not want to be with him?"

"She turn away and cover head. Man go away sad."

"Does he always leave? What happens if he tries to embrace the girl?"

"Tribe no like that. No force a girl or a boy together unless they both want that."

"And if a woman has a baby and does not want to be with the father?"

"She take it to live with mother. Maybe try not to have baby."

"How would she do that?"

"Drink medicine."

"What would it be?"

"Made from root, "Tika responded. "Only Onendo know. I ask him how."

"If I tell," he say, "Great Spirit angry. Maybe punish whole Clan."

After a day of rest Remy was ready for long walks. Father Laurent, away visiting a mission near Lake Simcoe, was expected to return in a few days. Remy was eager to learn whether Laurent knew anything about a Jesuit plot to foil La Salle's grand plans for a route to the southern sea. If he were a truly devout priest he might tell the truth.

When Remy told Tika that he thought Laurent might know of intrigues to stop La Salle's journey through the wilderness she replied quickly.

"Father Laurent no do that."

So Remy did not talk with the priest.

"Your people make war like us?" Tika asked.

"Far across the great sea we have many wars."

"Peace not easy. I tell you story:

> "Mokanoa say that long ago a Wendat woman give birth to holy man named Deganawida. In Wendat that means 'peace-maker'. He go to warring tribes. Tell them stop making war. But no one listen. He paddle out across Lake Ontario. Meet Ayonhwathah, Mohawk leader and fierce warrior, full of hatred because daughter killed by enemy tribe.
>
> Deganawidah tell Ayonhwatha make peace with enemies. Tribal wars hurting all their brothers and sisters.
>
> 'Go away,' Mohawk leader say, 'What I do not your concern.'
>
> Their talk become fight. The men wrestle for half day. No one can throw other. As darkness fall Mohawk tell peacemaker leave him alone. Deganawidah refuse. He go to angry man next morning. They fight with sticks until both exhausted. Finally throw down weapons.
>
> 'You are great warrior,' Deganawidah tell his opponent. 'Our brothers will listen to you. Let us be friends.'
>
> Then he and Ayonhwatha go about counseling cooperation instead of war. They travel among tribes. Say they should live in peace. Not all Indians ready to listen."

"Did you recount that to Father Laurent?" Remy asked when she paused.

"Yes. I think Deganawidah like your Jesus who teach about peace. Father Laurent say we take it from your *Sainte Bible*. But Onendo tell me is ancient legend. Just think. The son of Wendat woman."

Tika's interest in peace had perhaps been aroused by Iroquois raids on beaver dams in Wendat territory. There had also been recent traces in the nearby forest of night visitors believed to be Iroquois.

On the eve of Remy's departure they climbed a rocky bluff to share once again Tika's favorite view. In the stillness of the night they heard a rustling in the bushes below them. Remy stopped.

"That sounds like somebody slipping through the woods. Who could that be?"

Tika cupped a hand to her ear. "Maybe Little Eagle and another warrior."

"Why are they out at this time of night?"

"They protect us. Think Iroquois come at night. Find traces in forest. Wendat beaver dams broken."

"Why would the Iroquois do that?"

"Perhaps attack us."

Remy and Tika reached the top of the bluff in silence. As a bright moon glided across the heavens they reclined under the pine-scented glow in a clearing. In the night sky a thousand points of light glistened.

"See four bright ones in middle?" Tika pointed to a cluster of stars.

"Yes?"

"There is Dehndek."

"Who?"

"Mokonoa tell me story of Dehndek. So sad at the death of his daughter, Mahohrah, he also pass into land of spirits. He go up into clouds with team of three deer. Always journey through sky searching for her. Mokonoa say that story teach not try to bring back people from death."

"Why is riding through the sky bad?"

"Mokanoa say is better to help living person after loved one gone. He tell of man who lose wife and two daughters. He work to help everybody find happiness. After time, spirit of younger daughter bring him tobacco plant as gift for all our people."

In the chill of late evening they returned to make a small fire in Tika's hut. She had little to say before they drifted off to sleep on fresh-cut fir boughs.

Moon Cloud wept when she embraced Remy the next morning. Tika walked with him for a time. They sat down on a rock to rest in the sun.

"How long you gone?"

"I once said I would be back soon but now I don't know. Our journey may take many moons. I will come to see you when we return."

"Maybe I be here."

"Where else would you be?"

"Maybe I study in convent. Father Laurent say I can go to visit family sometimes."

"If I offered wampum, would you wait for me?" He smiled. "And how much do you think you are worth?"

She paused in thought. "All the beavers in the forest."

His first night back at the shipyard Remy wrote in his journal:

September 1681
I know now that I love Tika. Why did I not tell her?

Chapter 18

JESUIT LETTER

My Reverend Father Laurent
The peace of Our Lord
September 1681

Your letter, *Cher collègue*, was an occasion of joy bringing me renewed enthusiasm for the work of this mission. I agree that we should give more attention to Holy Days and try to bring our Savages into the observance of them. I like the idea of St. John's fire but you ask me what I thought of dancing and drumming.

I would urge caution in combining church ritual with native customs. We risk creating a bastard religion with the native elements having ascendance in the minds of these simple people.

You mention the ravages of smallpox. Many people pass through the trading centers at the Sault and Michilimackinac carrying sickness along with trade. Epidemics of influenza, *variole, rougeole*, diseases common to Europe but hitherto unknown in this part of the world, have left only a few survivors, some of them disfigured. Less robust than we are, many natives succumb.

Your young Mademoiselle Tikanaka appears to be a most unusual native. You do well to instruct her in French but I would counsel caution for two reasons: because we can have little confidence in the Savages and because she is a woman.

We must teach them that monogamy is the only form of marriage God permits. They need to be persuaded that customs whereby women hold property and wield power within the tribes are immoral. A worldview that considers an Earth Mother to be more significant than God the Father is pagan in the extreme.

You have no doubt observed that promiscuity is rampant among the native boys and girls at a certain age. And I have been informed that women have the freedom to change mates whenever they wish. One Huron warrior confided to me, "If I can have but one wife at the first whim she might leave me. I would have a wretched time because she does the planting and cultivating of land and prepares the food I eat."

Remember that Ecclesiastics entreats us, "Give not thy soul to a woman" and Ephesians, "Wives, submit yourselves to your husbands, as unto the Lord."

You may, however, gain a perception of native ways talking with this exceptional young woman and through the use of Biblical French help us all to develop more skill in changing their way of thinking.

When your young convert is fluent enough in French I would advise teaching native children in our language. Perhaps they are incapable of grasping the true Catholic message delivered in their tribal dialects.

With limited success up to the present I have sought ways to convince them that there is but one God. Their superstitions are infinite. Almost their whole life turns upon this pivot. Dreams, above all, inspire them. They are considered to be an inner voice from the spirit world. The messages of these night visions are accepted as literal truth even if contrary to life's experiences. Familiar demons, or Oki, manifest themselves under assumed shapes—a bear's claw or the skin of a snake. It is their belief that even animals have souls.

There seem to exist various kinds of shamans. Some diagnose diseases; others cast spells, predict future events, or claim to control nature. A fear common to all natives is that in abandoning their old allegiance to spirits they risk terrible dangers should the old gods seek vengeance. Have you observed this?

In evangelizing these natives the one element upon which I hope to build is their rudimentary notions of immortality. Providing gifts and even food for departed spirits demonstrates that they do look forward to some kind of life after death.

If we were endowed with the gifts of miracles like those who first announced the gospel to the world we could convert these barbarians with little difficulty. But God dispenses such favors to those who please Him. It may be that He wishes us to develop patience as we wait for the harvest of souls. Meanwhile by clearing fields with iron tools we can begin teaching natives how to fill their stomachs in all seasons.

When Jesus went to the sea of Galilee and fed the multitudes with loaves and fishes He said to them, "Verily, verily, I say unto you, Ye seek me not because ye saw the miracles, but because ye did eat of the loaves, and were filled."

We can demonstrate to these Savages that the power of prayer will aid them in providing for their daily needs. We should concentrate more on teaching them agriculture and demonstrate the advantages of permanent communities around a church. Although the season here is short they could thereby be assured of a dependable supply of food.

Your letters are a great comfort to me. I look forward to hearing more about your French-speaking convert

You mention that La Salle may be launching his boat shortly. My Hurons have let me know that the Miami Indians to the south of us are fearful of any extension of French trading into their area. Should they join their neighbors, the Fox, they may be able to offer serious opposition to his grandiose plans. He may end up getting himself killed.

IN UNION WITH YOUR HOLY SACRIFICE, I REMAIN
FATHER R. NICHOLAS, S.J.

Chapter 19

JESUIT LETTER

My Reverend Father Nicholas
The Peace of our Lord
October 1681

Your recent letter suggested that we give more attention to growing food so our natives might, in the words of Jesus, eat of loaves and be filled. I have learned enough Huron to discuss with Mademoiselle Tikanaka her translations of our prayers. She informs me that her people delight in the words "give us this day our daily bread," although they are known to endure occasional hunger with a certain stoicism.

I am also attentive to your caution about women. Native customs have indeed endowed them with great influence. Perhaps this explains why they are so gentle in guiding their young ones. Sometimes when children are sick or dying mothers have allowed them to be baptized.

Huron women hold what little property they have. There is more rejoicing at the birth of a girl than a boy. Moreover young women are free to select any mate they desire and change partners whenever they wish. The strict control of marriage customs we have in France does not exist in this culture.

I fear that even Mademoiselle Tikanaka assumes she can include ancient Wendat belief in the spirits of nature with her interpretation of our Christian God. Yet I have great hopes for her since she is intelligent and open to learning. In truth some of the questions she asks challenge my ability to give her a clear understanding.

Recently she inquired, "Who is mother of people after Adam and Eve?"

I replied that Eve was the mother of Cain, Abel, Seth, and other sons and daughters who followed.

"Why Eve not in command?" she asked.

"Adam," I explained, "was made in the image of God as the first human and agent of propagation for all his descendants. Eve was created as his helpmate to cherish and obey him."

She replied that Moon Cloud would not like that since mothers are life givers to warriors who then protect the tribe.

You see my dilemma. She listens, remembering what I say to her, and she is willing to consider new ways of thinking. I am convinced that her conversion is possible.

This young woman gathers children together to tell them our Bible stories in their language. Yesterday she was relating how Jesus in the desert took five loaves and two fishes dividing them to feed the multitude. My knowledge of her dialect did not enable me to check the complete accuracy of her account. But the wide-eyed attention of the children attested to their interest.

Afterward the young girls and boys were eager to compete, pointing out fishes they had etched in the sand. Mademoiselle was pleased. She likes to hear them laugh.

At the moment she is sad because this boy called Remy is departing with the La Salle expedition. She may never see him again, which would be a good thing. The only benefit of their unfortunate time together is that her French has improved remarkably. I am certain that she is now capable of receiving advanced instruction in our faith. Her childish pranks seem to be something of the past.

The first time she understood printed text she laughed and responded in Huron as if in conversation, entranced by talking with the writer. She calls letters of the alphabet "little pictures."

Recently some words she wrote out for the children were very well done. I hastened to praise her efforts having watched her labor to fashion each letter with meticulous care. She now has the basic idea of how to put letters together with sounds.

"They are like magic," she says.

If we should combine the mystery of writing with that of the Resurrection at Easter we might excite the curiosity of these Savages. When I discussed this with Mademoiselle she immediately thought of relating in Wendat the story of Christ arising mysteriously from the dead. Thus we can illustrate a true miracle.

Then she thought it could be even more dramatic if accompanied by drumming and dancing. She was puzzled when I told her that would not be respectful of the Almighty God.

Mademoiselle Tikanaka, as you can see, still struggles with the basic ideas of our faith, reverting easily into the mythology she has known from childhood.

Do you find that your Hurons can enjoy simple prayers? My people show a great interest in rosaries. Both for decoration and remembering prayers I find the rosary beads useful.

Mademoiselle tells me the Wendats often carry amulets—a smooth stone, beads, the beak of a raven—with magic qualities for healing or protection. Their belief in departed spirits offers us an opportunity to introduce the idea of eternal life in Christ. Thus, might we use Church ritual to replace their superstition.

La Salle's ship, the *Griffin*, has been launched and will depart soon for Michilimackinac to be loaded with furs. These will presumably be transported to Quebec for shipment to Europe where they will help to finance this journey. We hear that his band of adventurers will then follow rivers to the south in canoes for the expansion of trading routes. La Salle is reported to be in debt and pursued by creditors. That man seems to have a charmed life in dealing with problems by ignoring them.

This is a critical time. Our efforts will affect not only the mother country but also the Savages in this new world. If our countrymen are encouraged to value commerce above salvation we are inviting constant disputes over wealth and power—whatever be the consequences for all the people.

Now in the absence of her young Frenchman we shall see if Mademoiselle Tikanaka will consent to further study in the convent at Montreal or Quebec. She is as yet undecided. Moon Cloud and Chief Owassoni do not like the prospect of their daughter going far away for training. Nonetheless they are proud of her and have been indulgent parents. I believe they might accept her decision in this matter.

IN UNION WITH YOUR HOLY SACRIFICE, I REMAIN
FATHER M. LAURENT, S.J.

Chapter 20

THE VOYAGE

"*Vite*, Remy, to the halyard." Tonty spied him clinging to the rail as a wave lifted the bow skyward. On his knees Remy inched along the slippery boards toward the mast.

The *Griffin*'s ensign twisted wildly in the wind over a ship listing sharply to starboard. The vessel of sixty tons' burden bounced like a canoe on the waters of Lake Huron. Plumes of foam scudded across the deck.

La Salle and Tonty had sailed in a variety of vessels and Remy had acquired a certain experience crossing the Atlantic. Working the ropes and sails of a small ship like the *Griffin* was a new challenge to the other voyagers as they struggled against the tempest. Water sloshed from La Salle's oilskin as he pushed into the cabin.

"*Mes amis*," his voice rang out, "we must place our enterprise into the hands of God."

He closed his eyes:

> "*Blessed Saint Anthony of Padua*
> *We invoke your benign protection*
> *If you save us and our ship*
> *I pledge to your blessed memory*
> *the first chapel I will build in Louisiana*
> *bringing to ourselves and to the Savages*
> *your holy presence and protection.*"

Tonty grasped the sense of urgency in his leader's voice. He rushed back on deck to get all sails down and the ship to anchor.

The calm presence of Pierre Chandavoine on the ship was reassuring although he was no sailor. Remy found comfort in checking the ropes alongside stocky Pierre. They steadied themselves by the rail near the bow as they plunged and lifted with the waves.

"I hope these lines hold. I have no confidence in that cable." Remy peered over the rail.

"I trust it more than I do Saint Anthony," Pierre shouted into the gale.

After topsails had been lowered and yards fastened at the clew, La Salle's ship remained broadside to the Lake Huron shore. With horror the men had witnessed the fury of the gale threatening to break up their precious ship. Tonty was uneasy with his raw crew. And on this its maiden voyage he was unsure whether the *Griffin* had enough ballast to control its direction.

Before they left the shipyard while La Salle was away in Quebec Village, Luke, their pilot had made a trial run with the *Griffin*. Absolutely unable to make headway against the current, he warned that they could never stem the strong Niagara flow with sails.

Upon his return however, La Salle proved to be the better sailor. At the helm he would advance when the aft wind was strong and at other times put men on shore to tow with ropes. Even so the labor was slow and arduous.

With their ship now buffeted in the gale they all looked to La Salle for leadership. The storm lasted well into the next day. Finally, pushed by a gentle southwest wind the exhausted thirty-four-man crew could enjoy some respite.

In the interim La Salle and Tonty pondered their prospects. They missed the wise and stalwart Brassart, who had been left behind to supervise moving the shipyard to Fort Frontenac. And Father Hennepin had chosen to leave the expedition at this point to explore possible future missions in the Miami territory. He would rejoin La Salle further south on the Illinois River.

Coming from peasant stock, young Remy Moisson was unexpectedly adaptable. He had a spirit of adventure and learned quickly. However, with his superior education, he did not always seem to fit in with the men. Some of them resented his independence. Paul Crevel, a recruit from southern France and hostile toward the natives, seemed anxious to pick a fight with the boy.

This calm stretch of water was the first time Remy had a chance to reflect upon his last ecstatic visit with Tika at the longhouse village. Moon Cloud's parting embrace remained in his memory.

At the last minute before the *Griffin's* departure he had written:

> Chère Tika,
> I love you. I want to be with you always. As soon as we return I will come to you. Please wait until then to decide what you will do.
> Forever yours,
> Remy

He dispatched his message with Weasel Tail, a young Indian who assisted the cook. Remy feared that the crafty boy might take the wampum and never make the journey. But he had no other way to let her know.

Now, four days after the storm the *Griffin*, anchored in six fathoms of water in Michilimackinac Bay, was sheltered from the violent winter weather. At this location La Salle had placed a store of furs accumulated by traders whose pelts he had purchased before the *Griffon* was launched. These were loaded onto the boat with additional bales for which he had just traded.

The Potawatami Indians had welcomed them with a calumet dance. Their chief tried to dissuade La Salle from sending the *Griffon* off until the weather was clear. His men had informed him that an even greater storm was headed their way from the south.

Tonty and Father Membré also tried to reason with La Salle but he would not listen. He insisted that the loaded vessel sail immediately.

"What a stubborn fellow." Father Membré shook his head.

"Once he has made a decision he does not change." Tonty joined them on deck. "But remember that his creditors in Montreal and Quebec are giving him no peace. He wants these pelts to reach their destination in the shortest time possible. He could come back from this expedition to financial ruin."

Little did the men know, Tonty was thinking, how precarious were their prospects. Since French law made it impossible for a priest to ever renounce his oath of poverty La Salle had been denied for all time access to his family's wealth. And he was already thousands of pounds in debt.

The *Griffin's* cargo was destined for the river Niagara, from whence it would be portaged to Lake Ontario and eventually to Quebec. Sailing southeast the ship departed toward yet another ominous storm. Doubts about the competence of Pilot Luke did nothing to ease Tonty's mind.

Jean Fauvet had decided not to come on the expedition because he could be head woodworker at Fort Frontenac. And at Michilimackinac Pierre departed to resume his fur-trading life. Tonty hated to see him leave.

"I am abandoning ship," Pierre told Remy. "I hear my beavers calling."

"You dislike La Salle and Tonty."

"La Salle is not my hero. Tonty is an admirable woodsman. In truth I could learn from him. But I love the freedom of being alone in the wilderness. Nobody giving me orders."

"I hope we can get together when the expedition returns, perhaps meet at Fort Frontenac or Quebec."

"I will try to do that. *A la prochaine* (to the next time)." Pierre lifted an imaginary glass.

One day Tonty told Remy that the Sieur de La Salle desired to speak with him. Somewhat apprehensive Remy found him in his hut examining a map.

"Father Hennepin told me you studied in monastery school and that you know your letters. The Sieur de Tonty has observed that you write well. I want you to help with the journal of our expedition."

"That would please me," Remy responded, "but I thought Fathers Membré and Ribourde were recording our journey."

"There is work enough for three. Father Hennepin will not be with us for a while. Remember, Remy, we are making history for our King and country. Our maps and notes will be a guide for all who follow. Of course I will expect the highest level of accuracy."

"*Merci, Sieur.* That will indeed be my objective."

He was excited by this opportunity to be an official scribe. Above all he did not wish to displease again this *grande homme* of noble birth. He remembered the explorer's silent disapproval when he fired his musket wildly into the night, warning the fleeing Iroquois. Working with the journal could make this adventure even more rewarding.

Remy had returned to the shipyard from his visit with Tika in the Huron village to learn that in Quebec La Salle needed more time to get his affairs in order. From week to week he sent notice of further delays. Remy wished he had stayed longer with Tika.

La Salle's party, when finally it arrived, included Nicolas de La Salle, a former naval officer not related to Robert; Franciscan Fathers Zenobé Membré and Gabriel Ribourde; Jacques Métairie, a notary; and Jean Michel, a surgeon. From the east La Salle had also recruited eighteen Abenaki and Mohegan natives, ten of whom joined on the condition they could bring their wives. The new Frenchmen included a gunsmith named Pierre Prudhomme.

All of the recruits except those chosen to man the *Griffin* set out in canoes for Michilimackinac where they would await the arrival of their leader. Two of La Salle's Indian guides were to show them the way.

The *Griffin* had already been launched on the south border of the stockade into Cayuga Creek where it joined the Niagara River. There the ship was outfitted with sails and equipment. This required another five weeks.

The storm on Lake Huron in early November had given warning of what the coming season might hold in store for travelers. From Michilimackinac the expedition departed in canoes on a December morning in 1681 as winter made a bitterly cold entry. They circled the southern tip of the lake of the Illinois and discovered to their dismay that their chosen route, the little Chicagou River, was frozen solid. They were obliged to fashion sledges to drag along their equipment including canoes. The men strained ahead for almost fifty leagues, feet slipping on the rough ice. From that point they could abandon the sledges and portage southwest toward the river of the Illinois. The journey was such an ordeal that Remy had not the courage to make journal entries for several days.

The expedition then numbered more than fifty people strung out in sections. In addition to the smaller craft, Montreal canoes with several oarsmen in each had been loaded with supplies and equipment.

The great inland sea dwarfed their small craft. Hugging the steep shoreline they were obliged to haul cargo and canoes up to the summit every night so the waves would not smash them against the cliffs. Each morning the shivering men stood in icy water steadying the boats while cargo was reloaded for the day's journey.

Pierre Chandavoine's training had helped the men sharpen their skills for camping and handling canoes. But most were not prepared in spirit for the demands of constant travel, irregular hours, and uncertain food. Paul Crevel and Jacques Hunault, who had been recruited for La Salle in the *Ardèche* region of France two years before, were the first to complain. Crevel nursed an intense dislike for all Indians. He and Hunault were farm laborers who had expected to improve their fortunes more easily than undergoing the rigors of a wilderness journey.

The two of them were loading the tools for joiners and pit sawyers into one of the big canoes as the wind whipped waves against the shore.

"*Dépêchez-vous*. (Hurry)." Crevel, in water above his knees, was holding a small blacksmith's forge. "A few more minutes and I will freeze my *testicules*."

Hunault waded closer, wedging the bobbing craft between them. "Unless you want to bugger a she-bear you won't need them in this God-forsaken country."

Crevel lowered his burden into the boat. "If we had the brains God gave a goose we would have stayed back in France."

Three days later they came upon a settlement of Illinois Indians along the west bank. Hundreds of lodges covered with woven matting spread out before their eyes. A Shawnee visitor who had left the Indian settlement shortly before the Frenchmen's arrival went running back to the village with alarming news. He had seen a host of Iroquois warriors in the forest on their way to attack the Illinois. Many, he reported, were armed with guns.

When the explorers arrived prepared to greet the natives in friendship, the angry Illinois believed them to be scouts for the Iroquois. Illinois warriors encircled the Frenchmen and threw some of their supplies into the river. Meanwhile La Salle was still with the rear guard of the expedition far upriver.

The Frenchmen enjoyed little sleep that night. In early morning to make things worse some Illinois scouts reported that they had spotted the Iroquois and that the Sieur de La Salle was among them. Then they truly believed that the Frenchmen were in league with their enemies. In fact, the Illinois later learned that they had seen one of the Iroquois chiefs, who was wearing a black hat and French clothing purchased perhaps at Michilimackinac.

Now a furious crowd of Illinois gathered around Tonty. He was completely isolated. Remy struggled to stay by his side, but the Indians dragged him away.

The Iroquois had beached their canoes upstream and were approaching by land. As they came into sight Tonty laid down his gun. Snatching up a wampum belt he broke out of confinement and strode toward the attackers as the astonished Illinois looked on. Remy slipped away from the warriors surrounding him and followed.

Three gunshots were fired, upon which Tonty turned to order Remy back. Then, waving his wampum belt, he was among the Iroquois.

More shots were fired—none directly at Tonty. Knives flashed in the morning sun. An Iroquois warrior lunged at Tonty stabbing him, the knife missing his heart but cutting a gash in his side. Another warrior seized Tonty's hair from behind as if to scalp him.

Tonty warned the Iroquois chief that the Sieur de La Salle was nearby, coming with twelve hundred Frenchmen to help defend the Illinois. He was a forceful figure standing there with blood running from his breast. Fortunately his warning had an immediate effect. The attackers believed he would not be so bold if help were not forthcoming. One of the Iroquois warriors, an Onondaga chief who knew La Salle, convinced the Iroquois that they would be wise to set Tonty free.

They sent him back with his wampum belt held over his head while elders and chiefs on both sides tried to separate some young warriors who were still struggling. Staggering back to his men Tonty was near fainting. Fathers Membré and Ribourde rushed up to help. Their surgeon Jean Michel started to bind Tonty's wound.

"I thought it was all over," he half whispered. "I was hoping that they would only knock me in the head instead of throwing me live into the fire as I have seen them do."

Just then La Salle, with his Abenakis and some French soldiers, came into view. He beached his canoe in haste and ran over to rebuke the Iroquois chiefs, reminding them of their treaty with the governor in Quebec. Such was La Salle's standing in the eyes of the natives that even though he had far fewer men than Tonty had claimed, the Iroquois hesitated long enough for their Illinois victims to withdraw. They had already loaded their women and children into canoes as they started setting fire to the village and fled down the river. They knew that in any event the Iroquois would have incinerated it. The French hastened to leave this desolate scene.

Remy noted in his personal journal:

> *January 1682*
> *Will the rest of our journey be like this?*
> *Natives to the south have never seen white*
> *faces like ours. How will they receive us?*

Chapter 21

THE PROMISED LAND

Cloistered in moonless obscurity where the Illinois River empties into the Mississippi, the expedition would start south at daybreak. In the firelight, shadows of La Salle's waving arms accompanied his words:

> "And the Lord said unto Abraham
> Lift thine eyes and look from the place where thou art
> northward and southward and eastward and westward:
> For all the land which thou seest, to thee will
> I give it, and to thy seed forever.

Mes amis, in a land of promise we are planting the seeds of a French civilization. His Majesty King Louis XIV will rejoice in our success."

Tonty, recovering from his stab wound, resumed command of daily work schedules. La Salle appeared unmoved by weather or river conditions. Always the first man up each day he urged them on. Mornings, hitherto cold and threatening, now welcomed the travelers, arising under skies ribbed with striated clouds.

Spirits lifted. With the adventures they had survived the men were losing some of their fears of this unknown land. But they were nevertheless anxious to see how each tribe would greet them. They were warned that most natives down river had never before seen white Europeans. Savages in clumsy dugout logs called *pirogues* began to appear on the river that some natives called *Mitchi Sipi*.

The Mississippi, as the French named it, was a broad stream with a constant but mild current. Requiring little effort the canoes of the expedition glided southward with the current through forests and plains past the mouth of a river La Salle called the Hohio, whose northern headwaters he had already explored.

They passed cliffs that a riverside native called Chickasaw and made camp to send out hunters. Pierre Prudhomme, the gunsmith, went with them but did not return that night. The next day search parties found no trace of him. La Salle feared that he had been killed, but since they were comfortably camped he decided to build a rude log fort in the hope that Pierre would reappear.

One week later they found Prudhomme floating on a log far downriver, half dead from hunger and exposure. They named the place Fort Prudhomme, leaving him behind to recuperate in charge of a few *compagnons*.

Spring breezes, hazy sunlight, and blossoming flowers mantled a land of enchantment. Stags, bears, wild turkeys, woodcock, and ringdoves came into view. Green beans grew wild. Bean stalks as thick as a man's arm climbed to the top of trees. All this was noted in the expedition's journals. Some day Remy hoped to tell Tika about this beautiful land.

One evening after a day of pleasant weather La Salle gathered the men around the fire to share with them his hopes for the voyage, tracing in the sand by firelight a map of the route they had already traveled.

With his stick he pointed out their location. "Some day we will dig a canal to join the inland sea of the Illinois with rivers flowing south, completing a route all the way from France via the river Saint Lawrence to the Mexican Sea. Furs, minerals, and lumber could be shipped along the length of New France."

Their eyes followed the stick.

"Our country will enjoy a better life than any people in history. The Savages know many things about this land that we have yet to learn. Sharing with them our civilization may take time and patience, but we can all benefit. It will be a partnership."

"He's just bragging," Remy overheard Hunault say that evening. "Look at what we've already endured. We'll all finish with arrows in our backs."

Crevel, strong of voice and muscle, replied that La Salle's only interest was building a grand empire for himself.

"Imagine making these Savages *partenaires* or *associés*." He rolled his eyes.

The other men laughed.

"We can learn from the Indians," Remy countered. "They know how to survive in this wilderness."

"We should find a way to rid ourselves of these people so we can settle the land without worry."

"La Salle is right," Remy persisted. "We have nothing to lose in gaining their friendship."

"Nothing to lose but our lives, *imbécile*." Crevel grabbed Remy's arm. "Those wild men you like so much are the ones who murdered our friend Henri. Have you forgotten?"

Remy pulled back but his adversary held firm. Then breaking the man's grasp Remy struck him squarely in the stomach and knocked him to the ground.

Crevel scrambled to his feet and came roaring at his antagonist. Remy stood up to him, ducking and warding off his blows then hitting him again. Big Jean Paul stepped in and pulled them apart.

Hunault had fetched Father Membré who took Crevel aside. The other men stood silently around the dwindling fire before saying goodnight.

"Morale is already low. Brawling among the men only makes it worse," Father Membré told Remy next morning.

"He attacked me, Father."

"Crevel thinks you should excuse yourself for punching him."

"I have to defend myself. But I will try to talk with him about it."

Remy greeted Crevel with a *bonjour* several times in the next few days but got no response.

One week below the Arkansas River, just north of Natchez country, they found the most marvelous native settlement imaginable. Guides had told them about the great village of the Taensa, some distance in from the river. An advance party with Tonty, Father Membré, an interpreter, and Remy started out in two canoes. Crossing a swampy area, they entered a long canal leading into a great inland lake. After three hours of paddling they discovered the biggest habitation any of them had seen in the New World.

They rounded a turn of the lake to see more and more dwellings. Children playing by the beach ran to tell the village of their arrival. The travelers were such a surprise that a crowd of women and children surrounded them before warriors appeared armed with bows. Absolutely without fear the Indians greeted their visitors.

The explorers looked around in amazement. Large square buildings of baked mud and straw arched over with dome-shaped roofs of sugarcane stalks had been laid out with open spaces between. The two most important structures were a great temple and the residence of the chief. He received them at the entrance with his three wives. He had quickly assembled a council of about fifty elders in white cloaks.

After accepting gifts from the travelers, the Taensas showed their visitors through the temple. A thick mud wall surrounded it marked at intervals with stakes upon which were suspended skulls of enemies the Taensas said had been sacrificed to the sun. Remy was to note this detail in his journal.

Through an interpreter and Tonty's language skills the Indians were asked if they would like to meet the Sieur de La Salle, the representative of the Great White Father. The Taensa chief surprised the explorers by offering to visit their camp along the river.

Remy wondered how Tika would like living in such a settlement. She was often in his thoughts. Had she received his letter? Could she already be in a convent?

Accompanied by elders in white robes the Taensa chief appeared the next day bearing gifts of woven baskets and blankets. The Sieur de La Salle had donned his scarlet robe for the occasion and received the visitors graciously. He thanked them for their visit and presented the chief with a bundle of the tobacco from the Petun tribe he carried with him for trading.

One day Remy queried in the journal: "Should we put into our treaties with the natives a promise not to take possession of their land? Should we be giving them money or useful items like sawpit tools to make lumber in exchange for some land for our towns and farms?"

The next evening La Salle read back to him these sentences.

"Your task, young man," he said, "is not to question the policies or practices of the French crown. You write well in recording our events up to the present. One more outrageous presumption and you will have no part in the journal."

"But, Sieur, some Wendats fear that we are taking away their land. That is not fair."

"I am in contact with native leaders and am authorized to take measures that provide justice for them. Is that clear?"

"Oui, Monsieur de La Salle."

"You are to write in the journal only descriptions of the country and the work of the expedition." Then he turned away.

"Keep an eye on the lad," La Salle said to Tonty. "He must learn to know his place."

Tonty's sole admonishment to Remy was, "Watch what you write."

Warm weather, once so welcome, turned hot and humid. The river was bordered on both sides with tall stalks of cane growing in vast canebrake thickets too dense to penetrate. Some of the plants—twice the height of a man—resembled a tall fence along the water's edge. The ground was swampy and there were swarms of *moustiques*. It was impossible to hunt and food supplies threatened to run out.

Late one evening they arrived at a point where the river had grown much wider and seemed to separate into three channels. La Salle wanted to press on, but darkness descended upon them. Finding a dry camping spot would be difficult.

"I think we are near the mouth," Tonty announced.

With three canoes six of the explorers set out next day at dawn. In a warm morning mist they drifted downstream. As the first rays of light mirrored the river Tonty leaned over the bow, dipped his hand into the water and brought it up to his face.

"Taste this water."

Remy trailed his fingers in the stream and rubbed them against his lips.

"It 's salty.

"Remy, *mon ami*, we are at the mouth of the great river. Out there is the sea."

In the darkness of the previous night La Salle had stalked through swamp and cane thickets discovering that they had reached a delta dividing the river into three branches. That morning with Nicholas he chose to follow the westernmost course while

Tonty and Remy took the center. Father Membré with La Métairie would explore toward the east.

It was not long before the men in the middle channel came in sight of rolling waves and felt the tide tugging at them. Tonty pulled sharply to the right and called out, "*Vite,* we must beach before we get swept out to sea."

They pulled their craft ashore onto a small island to watch the sun burning through the mist over an endless expanse of water.

"We can stay here a while." Tonty leaned against the canoe. "If the others reached open sea they may have trouble getting back."

The little elevation gave them a spectacular view. They sat there watching the whole coastline emerge as the sun climbed above the horizon. From their islet in the delta the vast expanse of blue-green sea sparkling in sunlight seemed to pull them toward the skyline.

Morning sun had not yet dissipated all the mist. The two of them stretched out for a time and listened to calls of gulls. Remy closed his eyes. The scent of the sea was salty and sharp, the swamps mildly unpleasant. Finally Tonty stood up.

"We should get back and report."

Scanning the horizon as they were leaving they recognized La Salle and Nicholas coming into view along the shoreline paddling furiously against the tide.

Turning upstream from the sea their canoe was instantly caught in the tidal surge. The two men took several minutes to maneuver over to where Tonty and Remy were waiting. Stepping ashore La Salle dragged the canoe out of the water. He rushed over to Tonty and threw his arms around him.

"*Salut, mon ami. Nous sommes arrivés!*"

He turned to Remy and called, "*Camarade de voyage* what think you? *Valait-il la peine?* (Was it worth the trouble?)"

"A momentous discovery, Sieur de La Salle," he responded, flattered to be a part of this historic moment.

He stood in amazement as two great men—neither of whom usually demonstrated much emotion—shouted and embraced. Nicholas de La Salle watched in open-mouthed wonder.

The Sieur de La Salle put his hand on Remy's shoulder. "It is a day of glory for *la France.* Note that in the journal."

"And I will give you an exact reading on our location," the practical Tonty added.

"We must commemorate this place and take possession of the territory in an appropriate manner," La Salle announced. "It is still morning with good weather. We should organize proper ceremonies this very day."

Back at camp men set to work preparing a grand column and a lead plaque with material their blacksmith had carried from Canada. Le Métairie and Father Membré in the third canoe returned in time to help. La Salle was directing the surgeon Michel and the smithy exactly how to inscribe the message he wanted to leave.

They moved upriver to a place beyond the reach of inundations. There, on a rise of ground in the presence of the entire company they planted the column and attached thereto the arms of France. At this spot the elevation of the North Pole, Tonty announced, was 27 degrees.

They stood in formation around the noble column. Orders were given for volleys of musket fire among shouts of *Vive le Roi*. Before the amazed eyes of the Indians they chanted the *Te Deum*, the *Exaudiat* and the *Domine salvum fac Regem*. Again they shouted *Vive le Roi* as René-Robert Cavelier de La Salle, arrayed in his flowing scarlet robe, with Henri de Tonty at his side, placed in the ground the post bearing a plaque with this inscription:

LOUIS LE GRAND
ROY DE FRANCE ET DE NAVARRE
REGNE: LE NEUVIEME AVRIL, 1682

La Salle waved aloft the royal document authorizing this expedition as he intoned, "In the name of the most high, mighty, invincible, and victorious Prince, the Great Louis, by the grace of God King of France and of Navarre, Fourteenth of that name, I, this ninth day of April, one thousand six hundred and eighty-two, in virtue of this commission of his Majesty do now take, in the name of his Majesty and of his successors to the crown, possession of this country of Louisiana."

He then declared that he was acting with the consent of the nations dwelling in the country, naming several tribes including the Illinois, Chickasaws, Arkansas, and Natchez. Had Tika been there,

Remy was certain that she would have asked who gave the approval. Was she still with Father Laurent or in a convent?

A cross was planted beside the column, its lead plate bearing the arms of France with a simple inscription, *Ludovicus Magnus Regnat*. Then they all sang *Vexilla Regis*: "The banners of Heaven's King advance...The mystery of the cross shines forth..."

In the evening Remy would write that indeed discovering the mouth of the Mississippi was worth the toil and sacrifice of these past months.

Camping apart that night, the Indians retired early. Exultation was the mood in camp for the French, pride at having accomplished what they had set out to do. Father Membré pronounced a special mass around a blazing bonfire. Each explorer toasted their success by raising a cup to drink *un coup de cognac*. Reluctant to interrupt this happy time they remained awake far into the night with little thought for the morrow.

Returning north against the current would be hard work. And hostile natives, alerted to the French presence in their country, could be lurking along the way to ambush them.

In his personal journal Remy wrote:

> April 1682
> How can I tell Tika about this historic moment? What does this mean for her people? I fear that she may believe Father Laurent. Will she already be in a convent?

Chapter 22

JESUIT LETTER

Could Father Maurice Laurent be a captive of the Iroquois? Is he alive?

Quelle inquiétude! Quelle grande tristesse!

His mission north of the Niagara was attacked and, we hear, destroyed by the Iroquois. I have had no word from him since early this year. We have tried in vain to learn more about that raid and its consequences. We are uncertain of the date. The Iroquois have been on the warpath for some time. Early this year they demolished by fire a settlement of the Illinois Indians, who fled down the river that bears their name.

I recall that you and Father Drapeaux have known Father Laurent. He has become one of my dearest friends since I made his acquaintance in *Trois Rivières* shortly after you departed. We have corresponded frequently the past two years. He is a man of extraordinary strength and devotion.

Are any members of the Iroquois Confederation in your region engaged in raids on isolated settlements? Here a growing fear of attack is shared among our countrymen and the Hurons. Is there any danger to your mission near Quebec?

Father Laurent often mentioned a young Indian woman named Tikanaka. He thought she had the qualities to become a native nun.

We must consider her as one of our own family. If you find news of her we would be most grateful to know of her fate.

This young woman had some success telling Bible stories to native boys and girls. Here at the Sault we try to baptize infant natives whose parents have accepted the Christian faith. We must remember that the Lord said, "Suffer little children to come unto me, and forbid them not; for of such is the kingdom of God."

The natives are as our children and under our care whether or not they accept Christ's message. We are responsible for leading them to salvation.

Around our mission we have second-generation native Christians and a few of their children. Their numbers are small but offer us encouragement. They have a difficult time not so much for religious as for cultural reasons. Our natives are surprisingly tolerant of each other's ways but they have deep suspicion of white Europeans. They call us *ondaki* (demons) meaning that we can do marvelous things but that we are to be feared.

As you know, our Hurons have suffered unspeakable wrongs at the hands of the Iroquois. About a quarter century ago they slaughtered more than half of the entire Huron population. Among them at that time we had the most active Christian mission of the New World around Toanché and Sainte Marie on Georgian Bay, thanks to the heroic work and martyrdom of Father Jean de Brébeuf.

Working near Iroquois territory what are your prospects for turning them toward Christianity? They seem to be without mercy. Their domination of enemies through fear is one of the greatest obstacles in our efforts to bring God to this continent. I continue to pray for our success.

We have received word that La Salle's expedition has penetrated far to the south and that he has constructed some forts along the way. An extension of the fur trade into such a vast new area without an accompanying presence of the word of God distresses me indeed.

I think of the martyrdom of our brothers. These killings by torture of Fathers Garnier, Brébeuf, and Lalemant haunt my dreams. So much blood we have shed to further the noble work of salvation amidst the corruption of those who would sacrifice precious souls to the profits of trade.

Father Laurent was enjoying some success in speaking the language of the Hurons and in pleasing the children who came to lessons with Mademoiselle Tikanaka. If one native woman can learn our language for Bible study as she was doing, there is hope for the world.

We can only pray that Father Laurent and the Wendat maiden escaped the attack.

I await any news that you may have.

IN UNION WITH YOUR HOLY SACRIFICE, I REMAIN
FATHER R. NICHOLAS, S.J.

Chapter 23

THE LONG WAY HOME

What could have happened to their leader? Apprehensive, La Salle's men were waiting on the shore of the Mississippi. Standing by the riverbank Tonty shaded his eyes with his good hand and peered downstream from Fort Prudhomme.

"The Sieur de La Salle probably spotted a site to investigate. He is always doing that." Tonty was visibly irritated.

"Maybe he encountered hostile Indians." Remy regretted his quick reply. They were all worried enough now since the explorer was already three days late.

La Salle, with his Indian contingent and the surgeon Michel, had planned to spend an extra day to study an area near *la Pointe d'Osiers* north of where the Arkansas River emptied into the Mississippi.

Tonty had already anticipated the challenge of their return. But only now were the men beginning to realize how grueling the journey back would be. Making their way upriver from the mouth had been increasingly difficult these past weeks. Nightly meals of Mississippi alligator were an ordeal. These monsters swam with surprising speed, making snorting noises and rippling the water. The scaled reptiles floating just below the surface of the water or sunning on the riverbank like New World dragons hardly appealed to the imagination as dinner fare. Found mostly in the tail, their meat resembled pork but smelled different and was certainly less tasty for the Frenchmen's palates.

The glow of excitement after reaching the sea and the glorious *prise de possession* had faded. Somebody suggested that La Salle had put all of his wealth into this trip and would be in trouble with his creditors when he returned.

"Then there will be no money to pay us," Crevel concluded.

"Some of the Indians who watched us coming down the river may be prepared to attack as we go back," the guard Cassier added.

"We are getting out of alligator territory, thank God, but where will we find Indian wheat?" Hunault placed a hand on his stomach. "I'm starving."

Three weeks before, with depleted provisions and morale low they had come upon a Quinipisan village on the east bank of the river. The Frenchmen had encountered several of their warriors a few days earlier and inquired about trading for wheat. The Indians appeared frightened and not at all friendly. La Salle sent messengers to their village to bargain for grain. They returned saying that the Quinipisans would not trade.

To lift his spirits Remy had left the camp behind and pushed his way through the brush. In a clearing he sat down and made entries in his journal. Returning to camp he was surprised to see three native women sitting on the ground, surrounded by axes, knives, and beads, presumably useful for a future trade. One of the women was in full afternoon sun.

"What are they doing here?" Remy demanded of the guard Cassier who was standing by with a musket.

"They are hostages," he replied. "We found them gathering herbs near the river. The Sieur de La Salle decided to hold them until the Quinipisans agree to trade us some wheat."

The captive woman in the sun was bending forward to shade her head. Vaguely she reminded Remy of Moon Cloud. He carried a jug of water over to place before her.

From the front, however, she had little resemblance to Tika's mother, being older and having lost some of her teeth. When Remy offered her the drink she drew back in fright, not meeting his eyes. He left the gourd on the ground.

"Where are La Salle and Tonty?" he asked Cassier.

"The Sieur de La Salle has gone with some men to the Indian village to demand a trade for wheat. The Sieur de Tonty had set out along the south shore with a small armed force to protect our position in case the natives attack."

At the edge of camp Remy encountered Father Membré and took him by the shoulder. "We can't hold those women against their will, Father. We must let them go."

Remy drew back embarrassed when Father Membré did not shake loose from his grasp.

"You are right, my son. That is what I told the Sieur de La Salle. He just shook his head and turned his back."

Drawing near the sitting women Remy saw that the jug was empty, but did not approach any further, not wishing to frighten them again. Then without reflection he set out in the direction Tonty had taken. Before long he saw some figures approaching in the distance. It was La Salle's party, with five Quinipisans bearing baskets of wheat.

After the evening meal Remy spoke with Tonty about the hostage taking.

"We had to do something," Tonty told him. "We were all hungry and the men are in an angry mood."

"So we abduct and terrify their women. That is not right. How can we say we respect the natives when we treat them like that?"

"We have to take care of our men, Remy."

"You know, Sieur de Tonty, we are as deceptive as the Jesuits and as cruel as the Iroquois. I would like to tell the Sieur de La Salle."

"Remy," Tonty responded, "I admire your loyalty to our native friends. You are right that taking women hostages was not a kind thing to do. But no harm to them was ever intended. They are almost back in their village now and we are no longer starving. We must stay alive in body and spirit to complete this mission. Speak to La Salle if you wish but I would not recommend it. He has enough to worry about."

Remy sat in silence.

"When you take command of men for an enterprise like ours, you may be obliged to do things that are not just. You, Remy, may one day be a leader. Men who go to war or risk their lives for a great cause have many loyalties—families, King, and comrades in arms. Often they must decide which obligation to honor."

"I don't see how mistreating people can be justified."

"Think about this, Remy. What would you do if you were in charge of this expedition? Father Membré agrees with you about the women but he also sees a need to care for men under his spiritual guidance."

"I did talk with him, but to be honest I didn't really hear much about what he thought."

"It would be wise of you to give him that opportunity."

Remy did think about what he would do if he were the leader. Remembering Moon Cloud and Tika and the frightened eyes of the old woman he went in search of La Salle.

The explorer was sitting on skins near a small fire in front of his shelter. He looked up from studying sketches he had made of the river's course.

"Sieur, those women hostages we took were terror stricken. I don't think we should have done that."

"Then it is fortunate for our hungry men that you are not their leader."

"Sieur, I looked into the face of one of those women. She looked like a frightened animal. How can we do that to Indians who have done no wrong?"

Sitting up straight, La Salle looked at Remy.

"I need no instruction from you, young man, on how to bargain with my native friends."

"Some Indians think we are taking their land. Forcing them to trade with us makes them believe that we are enemies."

"Remy, your task is to record our activities and help our crew keep moving. You were not engaged to direct our decisions."

He resumed studying his sketches. Remy started to walk away then turned back.

"I think we are making a mistake," he said.

"Moisson." La Salle rose to his feet. "Tell the Sieur de Tonty and Father Membré that you are no longer assigned to the journal. Do you understand me?"

"Oui, Sieur de La Salle." Remy stalked away.

"I agree with you about the women hostages," Father Membré said, "but remember, my son, that bringing Christianity to the natives may require actions we do not like."

"Did Tonty say anything to you about that?" Remy asked.

"No, but he told me for the journal that the distance between the delta and the junction with the Illinois River is almost four hundred leagues."

"How far do we have yet to go?"

"Tonty thinks we are more than twice that far from Fort Frontenac. We are a long way from home."

"Remember that you had fair warning some time ago," Tonty told Remy. "You can start working with Big Jean Paul tomorrow on loading boats and making camp."

Now, more than two weeks of travel after trading with the Quinipisans, Tonty and the French explorers had stopped to let La Salle and their Indian companions rejoin them. While the advanced party waited, the explorer's abrupt dismissal of Remy from the journal still rankled in his mind. But anger became tinged with worry after his leader failed to appear on the third day. When La Salle's canoe did not arrive during the following twenty-four hours they all became alarmed.

La Salle had ordered the men to help Pierre Prudhomme and the half dozen men who had remained with him to reinforce the fort for possible future use. The discontented crew now took advantage of his absence to slow down in their work.

Meanwhile they had distressing news. There appeared from the north Chapelle and Leblanc, two men whom La Salle had dispatched during the trip downriver to get news of the *Griffin*. The explorers learned to their horror that the precious ship with its crew and cargo, laden with goods of 10,000 crowns in value, had disappeared in a storm on Lake Huron. Luke, the pilot had departed from a sheltered bay despite the advice of some Indians who warned him of a great storm moving in from the southwest. The natives lost sight of the *Griffin*, believing she had been driven onto a sand bar or had foundered.

The messengers also bore the news that Father Hennepin had been captured by the Sioux on his trip south from Michilimackinac. Unrest in camp increased. What could have happened to the Sieur de La Salle? Could he have been captured by the Indians?

That night Remy wrote:

> March 1682
> Did some Quinipisan warriors ambush La Salle? I pray that La Salle has not been harmed. I am more and more anxious to see Tika.

Chapter 24

A SPECIAL DELIVERY

For an entire week the expedition waited for the Sieur de La Salle to rejoin them at Fort Prudhomme. Midmorning of the following day Big Jean Paul shouted that a canoe was coming up river. They rushed out and saw the surgeon Michel with one of their Indian hunters.

"The Sieur de La Salle is gravely ill," Michel told Tonty. "We must quickly prepare a comfortable resting place."

"What is it?"

"A fever came upon him abruptly. He is too weak to sit up in the canoe and now has a raging temperature. They should be here at any moment."

When they arrived La Salle appeared dazed. He did not respond to greetings from those who gathered around as he was carried up into the Fort. All that night and the next day he lay in feverish sleep. The surgeon Michel stayed at his side administering medicines and applying wet cloths to his body.

The Indian contingent of the expedition, who had been with La Salle when he fell ill, had caught up with the others and camped apart.

La Salle had planned that on their return trip Tonty would reach the fort at Michilimackinac in advance with the precious journals and maps of their voyage in addition to messages for Quebec. He was anxious to spread the word immediately of their grand achievement in carving out vast dominions in the New World for France.

Reluctant to leave his leader in such a frightful condition, Tonty conferred constantly with the surgeon. The fever broke two days later. La Salle, still stricken but quite able to command, ordered Tonty to depart on the morrow. Remy, who had remained close by, marveled at the calm manner in which La Salle received the news that the *Griffin* and its cargo had been lost in Lake Huron.

To prepare for his trip Tonty asked Remy to help him check over official papers as they were rolling them up into doeskin bundles.

Remy turned abruptly to Tonty. "Monsieur, may I accompany you?"

Tonty looked surprised. "Well, under present circumstances I think that the Sieur de La Salle would have no objection, especially as that would speed up my journey."

Remy felt a surge of gratitude and he hurried off to prepare his pack while reflecting upon his good fortune. They set out that afternoon.

Tonty managed well at both port and starboard but his stroke was definitely stronger on the side of his good left hand. Fortunately he had a remarkable memory of the river's course, often anticipating the shoreline around the next bend.

Even in their haste, however, they took time to prepare a comfortable camp at nightfall. An ample supply of fish and game provided adequate meals. Remy began to feel a pleasant glow of anticipation at the prospect of seeing Tika.

Had Weasel Tail delivered his message? Did Tika confide in Father Laurent? Could she possibly be studying in some convent?

He kept their journals and maps along with the private papers of the Sieur de La Salle bundled in the center of the boat. Every night Tonty watched him take them out after entering a few notes in his personal journal. He would then find a dry, safe place to stow them.

"*Bien fait,*" Tonty remarked the first night. "Have you heard the story of Father Marquette? It happened about ten years ago. After descending the Mississippi past the Arkansas River, Father Marquette and his friend Louis Jolliet suffered a tragic accident. Their canoe hit a submerged rock and overturned into the current. Two of their men and an Indian boy were drowned and they watched all of their precious papers swallowed by the rapids."

Remy could scarcely believe such misfortune befalling those two God-fearing men. He was still pondering the matter as he and Tonty made a relatively easy portage to reach the little Chicagou River. The most hazardous part of the journey turned out to be along the west shore of the great Lake of the Illinois in some rough water and buffeted by changing winds. They were happy to glide finally into the bay and enjoy the comforts of Fort Michilimackinac.

A man approached them as they walked toward the trading post.

"You are the Sieur de Tonty?"

"*Oui monsieur.* Why do you ask?"

"A representative of the Sieur de La Salle desires to meet with you as soon as possible, also there are messages awaiting you from Quebec."

The remainder of the day Tonty conferred with several gentlemen while Remy remained with his precious cargo in a designated hut. He was especially protective of the journals. They would influence further the plans of La Salle and Tonty, and assuredly become important historical records. A military courier boat would transport the documents to Quebec.

Remy and Tonty shared a hearty *pot-au-feu* and a bottle of red wine at dinner that evening. Yet both of them were thinking of the future. Tonty of course would head downriver to rejoin La Salle.

"I will miss you, Remy. What are you planning to do? How will you begin your new life? Your years of service are completed."

"Sieur de Tonty, have you ever loved a woman? I mean someone you wanted to be with always."

Surprised at the question, Tonty waited for a moment to answer.

"Yes, of course. I was about your age." He shook his head. "She would not have had an easy life following me around. Anyway that was well before I served in the navy and lost my hand. I have no idea where she could be now."

"I've learned a lot working for the Sieur de La Salle to pay my passage. Now I am certain that I want to be with Tika as soon as possible. Perhaps she will agree to marry me. We can make plans together. What will you do next?"

"I'm not certain what my plans will be after returning with the Sieur de La Salle." Tonty sat in silence for a time. "The two of us have spoken of building a series of trading posts reaching far to the south. You are an experienced woodsman now, Remy. There may be the possibility of a generous parcel of land for you."

Remy laughed. "The Sieur de La Salle once mentioned that to me. I would hazard a guess that he now wants to see no more of me."

"I doubt that. He is always quick to anger. I believe that he has forgotten all about the dispute over the hostages. I think that basically he appreciates you. Your monastery education and experience on the expedition make you a valuable man. But, *mon ami*, you must develop self discipline. Even I have learned to accept the authority of a wise leader. And also you have to decide which way to direct your life."

"Well, right now I want to see Tika so we can plan our future together."

"You may have to make some hard choices—decide between a French future or an Indian past."

"The Sieur de La Salle claims he wants to help the native tribes to profit from his enterprises. If that is true, perhaps I would wish to be a part of it. In any event I want Tika to be with me. She might keep us honest."

Remy received half a bale of furs and thirty sols in payment for his services. Now he had to find a way back to the Niagara River. Preferring not to travel alone in a canoe, he roamed the marketplace to find somebody he could join heading east through Lake Erie. For two days he had no luck. Then one evening a young Frenchman walked up to their hut as he and Tonty sat by the fire.

"*Bon soir messieurs,* I am looking for the gentleman who was seeking transportation east.

"*C'est bien moi, monsieur.*" Remy stood and they shook hands.

The man identified himself as François Siloret and said that he was working for the new trading *Compagnie du Nord* in Quebec. The Indian he had engaged to take him back in his canoe had departed with somebody else.

"I've had little experience with a paddle and don't want to attempt this voyage by myself. If you're interested I can provide the boat and our food. *La compagnie* would compensate you when we arrive in Quebec."

"I'm only going to an area above the great falls on the Niagara river." Remy described the location of their old shipyard.

"That will be fine with me." François nodded. "I wouldn't hesitate to continue by myself from that point. A person from our Quebec office will be coming out to meet me between Lake Erie and Fort Frontenac."

The next day Remy and Tonty parted with a firm embrace, promising to keep in contact with one another. However, Remy wrote in his journal:

> *June 1682*
> *I wonder if I will ever see Tonty again. I shall never forget his lone act of courage with the Iroquois. He has been like a father to me. Will Tika be at her camp?*

Chapter 25

ASHES OF A DREAM

Not a man to boast, François Siloret was quite able to manage a canoe paddle. He simply lacked experience. Growing up in Paris, he too had studied in a Jesuit school and liked the discipline. Remy had no desire to reveal his own resentment of monastery life.

Supplied with smoked venison and dried corn supplemented by fresh-caught lake trout, they reached the *détroit* (strait) entering Lake Erie in ten days. In one cove along its shores they encountered flocks of huge birds that scattered with surprising speed.

"Whatever are they?" François stopped paddling.

"*Les dindes sauvages,* (wild turkeys). I wish we could match their pace."

Borne along by a steady west wind the two men finally entered the Niagara River. Remy offered to camp briefly with his companion at the old shipyard and help get him on his way.

"I'm not afraid to go on from here," he said. "I had word at Michilimackinac that *mon directeur* would be coming along to meet me between Fort Frontenac and Lake Erie."

"We're more than half way to the great falls now." Remy looked around. "I can recognize the shoreline here."

A wooded stretch of the stream reminded Remy of the *Griffin's* maiden voyage as they entered the Niagara. He tried to picture the ship lying on her side at the bottom of the inland sea with fish gliding past her hulk. When they reached the stockade he felt nostalgia for the *Griffin* taking shape amidst the clamor of pit saws, axes, and hammers. Now there was only silence. He was a bit comforted to find some of the walls still standing.

A man sitting on a log far back in the clearing arose and walked toward them. For one wild moment Remy thought he was seeing a specter. Then he recognized the real Brassart, tall and courtly in bearing. They embraced for a long moment.

"*Quelle bonne surprise, mon ami*! I had expected to meet Monsieur Siloret near Lake Erie. But passing the shipyard brought back rather special memories so I decided to spend the night. Tell me how you happen to be here. And is it true that La Salle is planning a trip to France to get an audience with the King?"

"That may be true. He suffered a raging fever. Tonty and I left his party down-river to deliver precious documents at Michilimackinac."

Brassart, of course, wanted to know all about the great adventure. Remy kept remembering different events as they unloaded the canoe. Since Brassart would be accompanying François back to Quebec he offered to take the half bale of fur and store it for him.

"As you see, I'm now working for *la Compagnie du Nord* in Quebec. But we can talk more about that later. You actually reached the mouth of the Mississippi?"

"*Mais oui*. It could have been on the stage of a Paris theater. We had a magnificent ceremony out there in the wilderness. La Salle was wearing his red robe. We set up a column with a plaque proclaiming that all the territory would belong to our Louis, *le Grand Roi de France*."

"Now what would the Spanish think of that?"

"Fortunately we encountered only native tribes. All the same, it was a strenuous journey. We came upon strange new creatures: huge alligators like monstrous New World dragons sunning themselves on rocks along the river. Then many in our crew were unhappy working in humid heat, hungry most of the time and fearing hostile Savages. Some men deserted. They probably tried to find their way back."

"Remy, there are vast political changes in Quebec," Brassart informed him. "The Sieur de la Salle's friend Count Frontenac has been called back to France. The new Governor de la Barre will likely not receive cordially Robert Cavalier de La Salle. La Barre will not appreciate his grand ambitions."

"The Sieur de La Salle and Tonty plan to expand their trading south all along the great river, "Remy replied.

"Will you be waiting to meet La Salle at Fort Frontenac?

"No. My two years of service are finished. Anyway, La Salle dismissed me from the journal. He was angry with me. I have different plans for my future."

As they prepared the meal Remy began to have the impression that something was amiss with Brassart. Several times he started to speak and stopped. He appeared nervous as he tended morsels of meat over coals.

Food and drink in the warmth of the fire was restful. Brassart shared a bottle of excellent red wine.

"*C'est merveilleux*. Let us drink to my reunion with Tika."

Then Brassart, who had eaten little, turned to Remy, "*Mon cher ami*, I have bad news for you. I don't know how to relate this."

"Did something happen at Fort Frontenac?"

Remy waited for a few moments as Brassart swallowed a bite of venison and cleared his throat.

Finally he said, "The Iroquois went on the warpath and attacked chief Owassoni and his settlement in—"

"When did that happen?"

"About three months ago."

Remy tried to get his head to stop whirling long enough to ask, "Could the Wendats hold them off? What about Tika?"

"The Wendats were completely overrun. There are rumors that a handful of people escaped. First we heard that the survivors went west toward the Huron mission at the Sault. Then we were told they headed for Quebec. A business trip to Montreal took me away at the time the news came. I have been unable to learn anything about Tika. Please believe me I have tried."

"Where did it happen?"

"In their winter camp."

Jumping up from the fire Remy grabbed his pack and musket and started running.

Brassart followed him calling, "Come back. Wait. I will go with you."

Remy rushed on. Short of breath in the night air he slowed to a walk, losing any sense of time. Once he stumbled over roots and scraped his face.

His mind replayed scenes of the Iroquois attack when they had murdered Henri. On the trip down river he had had a frightening dream about Tika. Now it was coming true. He remembered how he had once been tempted to stay with her instead of leaving with La Salle.

Exhaustion eventually forced him to drop to the ground and sleep against his pack without skin or blanket. He snatched bites of dried corn along the way and completed the trip in two nights and one day. The hunting grounds came into view on the second morning.

For more than two hundred paces the underbrush had been trampled down, the forest mangled. Even the birds and wild animals were gone. The still air held no shouts of children, no barking of dogs.

A smell of scorched earth filled his nostrils as he crested the hill. Before him lay an immense circle of burned grass and shrubs. Black skeletons of trees stood against the sky. Mounds of ashes lay scattered about: tops of tents, the skin almost intact above a pile of charcoal and carbonized shapes, a blanket almost whole.

In trying to find where Tika's hut had been memory failed him. Remy made his way around the circle of destruction, stirring up clouds of ashes. Without plan or purpose he wandered among human remains.

Came a horrific thought. There had been nobody left to care for the dead. His mind refused to accept what his eyes were revealing.

He picked up a long stick and started poking around in the mounds of ashes, uncovering fragments of melted cooking pots, children's toys, the skeleton of a dog. From pile to pile he went digging furiously. In one heap of blackened remains he uncovered almost at eye level something that caused him to stop short.

Remy was looking into the remnants of a woman's face surrounded by wisps of singed black hair. He stared into those eye sockets and tried to reach out but his arms would not obey.

He dropped his stick. Through waves of nausea he made his way toward a tree at the edge of the circle. Wrapping himself in a deerskin cover beneath its shelter, he pulled the skins up over his head and waited for sleep to come.

Chapter 26
THE TRADING POST

"*Salut.* Awake?"

Remy raised his head and looked around from his place under the tree.

Nearby a man was bringing tiny flames to life in wood he had gathered. He smiled as Remy stared.

"*Eh bien Mon ami*, you have given me a great fright."

It was Brassart.

"How did you get here?"

"I followed a friend who went like a madman."

"Do you think any of the Wendats could have escaped north to the longhouses?"

"Impossible. The longhouses were burned to the ground. I talked with a trader who visited the site."

"Brassart, I must apologize. I haven't even said *Merci, Mon ami* for remaining such a faithful companion. I feel devastated not knowing what to think or do."

"For once my young friend, I will tell you what to do. First, you must rest here for one day to regain a little energy and spirit. We shall then go back to the shipyard where some canoes are cached. There you can start planning your future. Remember that François Siloret is waiting for us at the Niagara site."

The day of rest gave Remy an opportunity to get Brassart's news of his old friends after they left the shipyard. When they had finished breakfast the next morning Brassart assembled their packs.

"Are we ready to get back to the trail?"

Remy nodded. He had slept well and he was anxious to leave the horror of the massacre. With a capable companion preparing the meals and finding their way along the trail his sleep was deep and refreshing.

At the former work site two canoes had been cached. Brassart insisted on sharing his venison. Equipped to start out, Remy had first to decide on a direction.

"If you come to Quebec," Brassart had said on the trail, "I can help hunt for Tika. But to be honest, the first rumors we heard were about a few survivors who started west toward Sault Sainte Marie where there is a Wendat settlement."

"I'll go to the Sault."

They grilled fresh trout and discussed the best ways of conducting a search for Tika. There were now regular contacts between Quebec, Montreal, and Sault Sainte Marie. They could exchange any news of Huron refugees at the trading posts. For a long moment Remy held Brassart in a parting embrace.

Now, in full summer he was heading back toward Sault Sainte Marie. His Algonquin canoe was a fine one with a low bow, less likely to be buffeted about by wind on Lakes Erie and Huron. With a small load it set too lightly on the water's surface so he stowed forward a few flat rocks until it handled well.

Strange questions passed through his mind as he was traveling alone in his boat. His nights became even more disturbing. Images of Tika fleeing from attack filtered into his sleep. Weeks ago Remy had dreamed that she was running through a flaming forest. She seemed to be almost flying along the ground. He knew Indians believe that night visions have spiritual meaning. Could Tika have been trying to tell him something?

Rough water on Lake Huron can be treacherous for a canoe. Paddling close to the shoreline, however, he enjoyed fair weather with a gentle breeze. His main food supply through Lake Erie was Brassart's dried corn and the venison placed in Remy's pack. Canoeing alone of course took more time than stroking with a companion. And he missed the company of his wise and courageous friend. Sometimes with Tonty they had felt as if they were skimming the river's surface like waterfowl. It seemed an eternity before he glided into the channel leading to the Sault on a late summer afternoon. He could have beached easily enough after the first rumble of thunder. But thinking he was protected where the bay narrowed he pressed on.

A sudden gust of wind hoisted the prow of his light craft into the oncoming waves at the same time that lightning struck the surface nearby. He struggled to control the bow of the boat as waves came rolling his way. Then Remy lost all sense of direction. When he wriggled forward to get better balance his weight shifted and he was overboard.

The chill of the billows penetrated his skin. He swallowed water as waves beat at him. Never a strong swimmer and fully dressed he began to sense that something was pulling him under.

Then he realized that his feet were scraping along the bottom. His hands encountered solid ground when he reached down into the water. He lurched forward and crawled onto the rocky beach.

Exhausted and confused he lay there for some moments. When he heard voices he thought it was his imagination. Then somebody turned him over. Remy peered up into the rain. He could make out the form of a man leaning over him.

"Nasty storm. Are you all right?"

Strong hands under his armpits helped Remy to sit and then stand. Back on his feet Remy managed a weak *"Merci, monsieur."*

He swayed against the man who signaled to two soldiers at the water's edge. They were using ropes to drag the prow of their boat in toward shore against the backwash. One of them came forward to help and the two men yanked the befuddled canoeist into their boat.

The first rescuer shouted into Remy's ear, "We were out to get some fish and then tried to beat the storm back to port." The man held firmly to Remy's arm introducing himself as *le Capitaine* Baptiste Charron, military surgeon at Fort Michilimackinac.

"We saw you spill out," the doctor told Remy, "then we lost sight of you in the waves. You're lucky the channel is shallow here."

Huddled in the center of a small *chaloupe* with long oars and no sail Remy began to feel more secure. The sky continued a steady downpour but the wind had subsided. Even with strong oarsmen it seemed to take a long time to reach the wharf. An oilskin the doctor had thrown over Remy protected him from the rain but offered little warmth. It was early evening when they touched land.

Remy had to lean heavily on Dr. Charron on their way into the town. As they approached the trading post a lone man came forward in the dim light to meet them at the entrance.

"What have we here?" His French was heavily accented.

"We were out fishing when the storm came up," the doctor answered, "and this is the biggest one we caught. *Adieu,* I'm overdue at the fort. I think he will be fine, but I'll come back in the morning to take a look." He was gone.

"What's your name, Laddie?"

"I'm called Remy."

"I'm a Dutchman and proprietor of the best trading company in the west. I'm known as Angus. Now you best get out of those clothes."

Angus found a wool blanket that Remy wrapped twice around himself. From a storehouse behind the shop the trader brought another cover to put on a layer of hides.

"This will do for a sleeping place tonight. Would you be wanting something to eat?"

"*Non, merci monsieur.* I just need to rest."

Enveloped in warm covers Remy fell asleep.

"Look for a fine plush of under-hair. Brush gently back and forth with your fingertips in a cross light. If it has a sheen you know that is a prime fur." Angus's long fingers caressed the pelt.

He was piling beaver hides into bales with the help of Remy who, having lost all his belongings in the channel, was happy to be of service.

Lying in the storehouse that morning Remy became conscious of an emptiness, of what—besides Tika—was missing. His records were his most precious possessions. He had carried with him in the wilderness the small volume of *Ars Poetica* that Father Bernard had given him back in Paris, his certificate of baptism into the New World and most of all, his own personal journal. Thus the precious cargo of his former life had, like the *Griffin,* foundered in the waters of Lake Huron. He remembered Tonty's story about Father Marquette and his friend Joliet.

As he sat up in his bed something became entangled with his blankets. It was the cord holding the medallion presented him by Le Coquin, a badge of friendship past still clinging to his neck. He smiled as he pictured the little urchin handing over his most precious possession. It might have been stolen.

Remy took an instant liking to Angus but had trouble understanding his speech. The man always sounded as if he were laughing. Unaware at first of the trader's joviality and having never before met a "Dutchman", Remy believed what he had said in introducing himself. The men around the trading post found that most humorous.

"Angus's accent," Doctor Charron said, "echoes the Celtic music I heard as a child growing up in Brittany. In time I must admit I grew rather fond of that lilt."

Remy had recovered rapidly after his rescue except for a cough and scraped shins. It was good to be working. The trading center was a combined store and warehouse, the biggest non-military building in the area. It handled mostly furs but offered a variety of other goods.

Remy could provide help for Angus, who had a primitive manner of recording all of his accounts in one book. With his excellent memory for numbers he could recall certain specifics of business from months back, but he had never found it necessary to record his affairs in a more efficient way.

"I do not care for bookkeeping," he explained.

He agreed that it might be worthwhile to make an inventory. Remy enjoyed setting up a working arrangement with one register book for furs and another for all other goods. In addition to a barrel of iron axe heads, knives, beads and birch bark for canoe patching, Remy was surprised to find items like vermilion pigment and Irish linen. Angus was surprised and rather pleased to know what he was holding.

Remy observed the trader's skills to learn more about buying and selling. Getting an account of all goods Remy also planned the use of space.

Angus was living with an Indian woman and spoke several dialects. When he said he was most fluent in Mohawk Remy remarked, "That's strange because it is not the language around the Sault."

"Willow Wand, my companion, didn't come from here. She helped us with housekeeping. Then when my wife died she came along with me. We moved from New Amsterdam where I worked mostly for the Dutch trading company along the river they call Hudson."

"It's fortunate that your Indian woman could accompany you," Remy said.

"She's my friend. I also sleep with her if that's what you mean."

"I wasn't asking about that."

"I know. If I thought you were too curious I wouldn't have told you."

Remy was tempted to tell Angus about Tika but decided not to just then. His first full day at the Sault Remy started making inquiries in the village. The Wendat community at the Sault had been informed of the massacre but had heard nothing of survivors. Father Nicholas at the nearby Jesuit mission knew who Tika was. This, the priest thought, must be the young man that Father Laurent had mentioned in his letters. Father Nicholas said he was still seeking information about her and Father Laurent. He had no news of either.

Remy asked traders coming into the trading post from the east if they knew of the massacre on the Niagara. He did not explain his interest in that event to Angus.

One day, when preparing to set up a bookkeeping system, Remy asked Angus his last name.

"Do you need to know?"

"Sorry, I wasn't prying into your affairs but it's customary to have full names on official records."

"You know, our Scottish people are strong on history. Clan wars, clan tartans and names and all that is part of the baggage we carry around. Who needs last names out here?"

Remy didn't answer and kept working on the books.

After a while Angus leaned over and patted his clerk on the shoulder.

"No offense, Laddie. The name is Macpherson," and he spelled it out.

And so it was with Angus and Remy.

Once the storeroom was organized it provided a comfortable place to sleep with one corner reserved for a bed. But Angus soon found a hut for his clerk and spoke of building a small log cabin.

"I don't want a worker of mine sleeping in the storage house. People might think I am stingy. You know how generous the Scottish people are."

Never knowing for sure when Angus was joking Remy stopped trying to figure it out. He was surprised when after three weeks the Scotsman proposed a promotion to manager.

"We have skills that go well together. You can maintain the inventory and keep the books. I know a little bit about hides and furs. We can work out better pay."

"Angus, my plans for the future are uncertain. You have been kind and I don't want to make promises I can't keep."

"Consider it. I need the help and I just like having you around."

"I'm honored. But there's something I have to do that is more important than anything in the world. I wanted to tell you when you talked about Willow Wand."

When Remy finished his story Angus responded, "You do what you must. My offer is open, Laddie. I hope you find your woman."

From that day on he started asking everybody who came into the place if they had heard about Wendat survivors of the Iroquois massacre in their Niagara village. Remy was more and more impatient to resume his search. He sought out *voyageurs* and *coureurs de bois* who came from the east.

One day while counting fur bales he heard Angus bantering as usual in a trade with somebody. Stacking pelts Remy couldn't follow their conversation. Then he realized that they were talking about him.

"That fellow doesn't look honest to me. What is he doing with your bales? He looks at those hides in a strange way. Maybe he doesn't really know what he's doing."

Before Angus could reply Remy whipped around to confront the visage of Pierre Chandavoine. They laughed and embraced warmly.

"Remy," he held his friend out at arms length, "You have been gone so long I thought your hero La Salle had perhaps sold your services to natives in the south in return for trading privileges. I heard you made it all the way to the mouth. Did you find any teeth there?"

"Big ones," Remy retorted. "They are in alligators and would frighten even a man like you."

"I must hear more. A *pension* here serves an excellent *pot au feu*. If this stingy old Scotsman pays me a decent price for my furs I'll take you to dinner and buy a bottle of fine wine. For you too, Angus."

Angus shook his head with thanks and invited Pierre to bed down at the Trading Post. Pierre traded his pelts with Angus at prices calculated by the pound sterling (20 sous). Prime pelts brought five pounds but it was primarily a bartering of pelts for goods. Pierre took some payment in copper sous.

"Gold and silver coins," Angus said, "are extremely rare in Canada."

Remy observed their bargaining with interest. The only gold coin he had ever owned was given to him by his Paris friend Le Coquin who had filched it from a lady's purse.

By the time Pierre had traded his furs the sun was setting. At the *pension* that evening Pierre listened to Remy's account of the expedition to the *Golfe du Mexique* and then, visibly shaken, of his visit to the site of the Wendat massacre. The two men savored the food and conversation over a bottle of wine until the landlady started to close up for the night. Remy led his friend back to the trading post where they lighted an oil lamp and talked until after midnight.

Remy asked about Pierre's partner Camille.

"He is down south now trading with the Dutch along the Hudson River, where he can get better prices for furs."

"You two had some different ideas about the Savages."

"Camille can be a generous person and we enjoyed singing together. But he just could never feel comfortable with the Indians. Then too he is ambitious and he wants to earn enough to start his own business. I'm working alone now."

"*Alors*, I probably won't work for La Salle again," Remy said. "Now I have to find a new life."

"You could start out by joining me in the fur-trading business."

"I will have to think about that."

"Look Remy," Pierre said, " I know the region north of here as well as any man. You told me the first time we met that I might miss a great adventure if I did not sign up to work for La Salle. I don't have a patent of nobility, but you might be making an even greater mistake if you don't join me."

"Pierre, I want to be honest. Working with you would be exciting. I would learn some Indian languages as well as trapping skills."

Remy added, *"Aussi J'adore les chansons des voyageurs.* I shall have to consider this carefully. I like Angus. He has been kind and generous with me. This is a pleasant place to be. I can learn much about the fur trade here. Why should I join you?"

Pierre's answer left his friend gasping in amazement.

"Remy, I'm not talking about the fur trade although we'll have to do that to earn our bread. Do you like games of chance? This is a rare opportunity. I'm proposing a partnership in looking for Tika everywhere she's most likely to be. I wager we can find her if she's alive."

Chapter 27

IN PURSUIT OF DESTINY

Robert Cavelier de La Salle was sitting on a pile of ropes at the wharf with Sieur Henri Joutel, a friend from early school days. They were watching a barge drift into dock at the port of La Rochelle, a familiar sight for the two men who had grown up in the seaport of Rouen.

"Do you know, Henri, I suspect that Captain Beaujeu is plotting against me."

"Why do you say that?"

"He keeps insisting upon loading far fewer supplies than we will need to establish our colony."

"Obviously his heart is not into such a grand project. Perhaps he just doesn't like the idea of the voyage across the Atlantic. And he did have little part in its planning."

"That's clear. I was also told that his wife greatly admires the Jesuits. She has already chosen one to be her confessor, not good news for me."

King Louis XIV had bestowed grand honors upon the Sieur de La Salle after he returned home in triumph to report his discovery. La Salle described in dramatic fashion how he had explored the great river to its mouth and planted plaques that claimed the entire Mississippi Valley in the name of the King of France and Navarre.

More than a century before, the Spanish conquistador Hernando De Soto, in a search for gold and silver, had explored this river basin and indeed was buried beneath the waters of the Mississippi. La Salle's account convinced the Court at Versailles that a colony in

Louisiana could take that vast territory back from Spain and bring further glory to France.

He had requested two ships from Versailles. In fact, *Le Ministre de la Marine* ordered that La Salle be given four vessels: a man-of-war, *le Joly,* with forty guns, and belonging to the royal navy under the command of Captain Beaujeu; a Frigate, *le St. François,* with six guns; a flyboat, *l'Aimable,* of about three hundred tons burden; and, in addition, a barque, *La Belle,* for carrying ammunition and supplies to Santo Domingo, a Spanish island colony in the Caribbean Sea where some French planters had already settled.

Le Ministre issued a decree granting La Salle authority over the soldiers and civilians during the voyage. Once ashore in Louisiana he would be in complete command of the expedition. The Sieur de Beaujeu, a royal navy captain of *le Joly,* was to be in charge of the sailors and the ships during the voyage.

Beaujeu had sailed the seas as captain for thirteen years. Now, unhappy to be sharing power with a common landsman, he complained that he was to be put under the authority of a civilian like La Salle "who had never commanded anything but school boys."

A search for volunteer colonists had already started. In haste men were recruited from ports along the Atlantic coast as far south as Bordeaux. Little did La Salle realize how ill fitted to this expedition some of those future colonists would prove to be. Indeed, several were hapless citizens wandering the streets without skills or employment.

On the twenty-fourth of July 1685 they set sail from the shores of France. The two hundred eighty persons crowded aboard the four ships included one hundred soldiers with their officers, thirty volunteers, and several women who, like *Les Filles du Roi,* were destined to be future brides helping to populate a French colony. La Salle was convinced that these pioneers would strengthen France's claim to the Louisiana Territory.

A command divided between two proud and respected leaders promised trouble. Tension surfaced immediately when Beaujeu wanted to land at Madeira to replenish the water casks. La Salle objected.

"We cannot risk our sailors mixing with others in the port," La Salle told Beaujeu. "The secret of our plans might reach Spanish ears in Louisiana."

Given long-standing Spanish claims to the region, that may have been a perfectly good reason. But Beaujeu was hardly in a mood to listen. During the voyage this clash of wills between the two commanders continued. When they reached Santo Domingo, and while members of the expedition slept, Beaujeu sailed past the *Port de Paix* where La Salle had chosen to land and anchored instead at *Petit Gonâve* on the far side of the island. Unfortunately *Le St. François*, their ship laden with provisions, livestock and tools for the colony, was captured there by Spanish buccaneers. La Salle, on *le Joly*, believed that the loss of this ship resulted from Beaujeu's action.

Beaujeu replied that determining sea conditions for the best landing was clearly the responsibility of the ship's captain. Spanish officials on the island had no interest in restraining their own buccaneers.

In the port Captain Beaujeu kept his sailors under tight restrictions. When soldiers and colonists wanted to debark he referred them to La Salle, reminding him that, "These people are under your command."

Then La Salle became ill with such a severe fever that they were obliged to lie in wait at Santo Domingo for almost a month. With nobody clearly in charge some colonists and soldiers ran off on drunken sprees with native women. When they prepared to sail once again a dozen men were not to be found.

Impatient at the delay, Captain Beaujeu had pressed on ahead, accompanied by *La Belle*, before La Salle was fully recovered. Thus the leader of the expedition was forced to sail aboard the flyboat, *l'Aimable*, with whose captain, Monsieur Aigron, he was already on bad terms.

Weeks of tropical heat augmented by fever, as he lay in an island hut on a mattress soaked with perspiration, had not left the Sieur de La Salle in a conciliatory mood.

His state of mind was not improved when Captain Aigron declared one day, "My ship and I are not under your command. I am obeying orders to accompany *le Joly* under Captain Beaujeu."

Chapter 28

COUREURS DE BOIS

"*Attention*! Rock on the left."

Remy squinted through spray, straining to hear. He had wanted to portage but Pierre could not resist the challenge of rapids.

Down they plunged as the current veered the canoe left toward a jagged boulder. A twist of Pierre's blade rotated them to the right. Remy jabbed out with his paddle. They swept past so close that his elbow brushed the rock. On deep strokes their paddles scraped bottom. They managed to stay mid-current until the stream leveled. Then Pierre pulled them over for a pipe break.

"Well done, *mon ami*." He reached into his sack for a leather pouch.

He measured distances by pipe breaks that occurred every three hours or so, a habit borrowed from the *voyageurs*. At first Remy's tongue had found the tobacco in peace pipe ceremonies somewhat bitter. Now he was beginning to savor the taste as he sat with his back against the tree.

"A three-pipe day on this stream will get us into Nipissing territory." Pierre stretched out against a fallen limb. They had spread on their hands and faces a pomade of turtle fat the Algonquins called *namakwan* for protection from mosquitoes eager to feast on red-blooded river travelers.

On a stream flowing into *le Lac Supérieur* they continued their quest as Remy worked his way into the life of a *coureur de bois*. With regret he had bid Angus and the trading post *adieu*. But he was also eager to resume his search for Tika.

"Find your woman and bring her back," Angus called out to Remy as they departed. "She can meet friends from her tribe right here."

Remy tamped down on his stone pipe.

"*Tabac extraordinaire.*" Pierre puffed out a trail of smoke. "This batch is no doubt mixed with leaves of sumac."

"Why is smoking so important to the Indians?" Remy was having difficulty getting his pipe to draw.

"It is a spiritual act," Pierre answered. "Many ceremonies call for tobacco. It clears the mind and calms the soul." He blew a ring of smoke skyward. "Here you are, Great Spirit."

"And they drink brandy as a spiritual experience?"

"Ah, that's different. For them it's bad medicine."

"I thought *coureurs de bois* traded brandy. You don't."

"Never. One time I went back to see my Algonquin family and offered some brandy to celebrate with them. Kikawana who had been like a brother to me drank a little and started chasing me with a knife. I had to jump into the river. They don't drink for pleasure. They drink to be with the spirits and lose all reason."

"So the Jesuits think alcohol is evil?"

"That's what they claim," Pierre answered, "but I suspect some of them also trade for furs."

"They trade for furs? With brandy?"

"Some Jesuits certainly do deal in furs. I'm convinced some of them offer brandy and firearms."

"Are you sure?"

"I've spotted muskets and fur bales at one of their missions."

"Perhaps they persuaded the Indians to give up their weapons."

"I doubt that. Anyway natives have told me that the Black Robes do trade. I've seen Indians with bottles of wine they say came from priests."

"Do you believe that most Jesuits are in the fur trade?"

"Probably not. But there are those who put the financial interests of the Society of Jesus above all else. This gives them political power. With the support of Bishop Laval they want increasing control over life in Canada."

"I can't imagine Father Laurent dealing in alcohol."

"I don't know him. No doubt he would not, but the Jesuits aren't all of the same cloth. They are a world organization starved for money. I wager that the Jesuit Vicar General in Rome is as interested in the political power of his Society as he is in saving souls."

Remy thought that was an exaggeration because Pierre disliked the church so intensely. However, he was a master of wilderness travel. For several days they were plagued by a leak in the canoe. One morning they pulled out the boat and turned it upside down. From a fire of twigs they lighted their pipes. Pierre pressed his fingers around the suspected location of the leak and bent down to put his mouth on the spot.

Remy stared. "Is that a kiss?"

Pierre lifted his head. "Where there is a hole, you can suck air through it. *Le voilà!*"

On the fire they set down a small metal pot of spruce gum that they carried with them. When it had softened Pierre spread it over the hole with his fingertips and tapered out the edges with his thumbs.

"This gum is tempered with moose fat." He smoothed the patch with a wet hand. "It won't run in heat from the sun. You can soften a lump of gum with spit by chewing it. However that leaves a bitter taste on your tongue."

Pierre was skillful in dealing with Indians. He had asked Angus to pay him for his furs partly in cash and the remainder in trading goods: knives, metal rings, fish- hooks, and beads. Made of polished white and purple quahog clamshells from the eastern coast their wampum beads were highly valued by the natives.

Pierre taught Remy *chansons* of the *voyageurs* that celebrated pretty women, sparkling waters and the sweet calls of birds. Dipping and pulling the paddle to a measured stroke lightened the effort.

Pierre loved to make up his own versions, inventing silly verses that made them both laugh. Remy enjoyed these moments of adventure. But Tika was always in his thoughts.

Early in their search, thinking that Montreal would be the nearest convent, Remy inquired there about Tika. He was disappointed to find that the Ursulines had heard about the massacre at the Wendat village but they knew nothing of survivors.

"Doesn't it seem strange," he asked Pierre later that those Ojibways we talked with yesterday had never heard of the Iroquois attack on the Niagara village?"

"Not at all," Pierre replied. "These natives seldom travel great distances nor do they have the need. That is why they don't make maps. Unless a stranger comes along most of them have little idea of other people on this continent."

For entire days Remy could get into the spirit of their journey. But his nights belonged to Tika. No matter how much he tried to think of other things his mind returned to that awful scene, the burn circle and the woman's face at the hunting camp. He tried to visualize Tika and put her into his dreams, to ask her where she was, how he could find her. But she did not appear. Instead the burned woman's face and the young Iroquois warrior that he had killed peopled his nights. To divert himself he tried walking into the blackness of the woods or even swimming in the frigid waters of the river. Nothing helped.

In memory he relived their last starlit night together. Whenever he saw those same bright stars they became the deer and Dehndek in Tika's story about the grief-stricken father of myth.

"Look, Remy, I mean no disrespect to Tika, but you have to think about something else. Why don't you take a pretty girl from one of the villages for a night. *Qui ne risque rien n'a rien.*"

Perhaps Pierre was right. "Who risks nothing has nothing." In a Seneca village they chose two maidens and brought them to their camp. The setting was a cloudless night with the campfire reflecting in the river. Remy's companion was shy and a bit frightened, not resisting but sitting straight and stiff. After a few embraces he walked her back to the village and left her with a gift of wampum.

Back in his blanket he could hear Pierre and his woman in the woods nearby. Why could he not have coupled with his young maiden? He lay there unable to sleep, feeling as if he had an iron rod between his legs. When he fell asleep he dreamed of being with Tika, playing with her breasts flesh to flesh in a frenzy of ecstasy.

Next morning he awoke, stomach pressed hard upon the earth, his breechcloth and blanket soaked. When he got up Pierre sensed the cause of his discomfort.

"There is an Algonquin word for your plight last night, *ningasimonike.*"

"And what does that mean?"

"Literally it means one is erecting his tent, but also an erection in his clothing. Your body is disappointed," he added. "Sometimes it is wiser than your head."

But he didn't again try to get Remy involved with women.

Evenings around the campfire were a time of reflection. Mosquitoes were a constant annoyance along the streams they traveled. Sometimes their pomade was insufficient protection. Fortunately Pierre was skillful at keeping the pests away with smoke from the fire.

One night he told of his childhood in the village of Surgères, near La Rochelle. His father had a small parcel of land. He worked for and became friends with a wealthy neighbor named Gourguechon. This man was a Huguenot, Protestant followers of a teacher named Jean Calvin.

"The French government saw them as enemies," Pierre explained. "Jealous people in the village rumored that the Huguenots were plotting against the King. Papa was accused of helping him. Soon after Monsieur Gorguechon was arrested the King's Archers came and took Papa away."

"When did that happen?"

"About six years ago when I was fifteen. We didn't even know where Papa was. Three months later he was dead. The soldiers said he was killed trying to escape, which we didn't believe. He could not have a church funeral. Father Duval refused to say a private mass for him. *Maman* thought Papa was going to hell. She went to bed with a fever and lived only about six weeks after that."

Pierre poked at the fire and sat silent for a time.

"You asked me once about God. Those saintly villains who direct God's church talk about love. Yet they feared the Huguenots or anybody who threatened their power. I made a vow that I would have nothing to do with God, His priests, nor His church."

Thinking of Pierre's story Remy lay in his blanket that night. He felt a great surge of sympathy for his friend who was putting his whole heart into their search for Tika.

She was in his thoughts during that first summer and even moreso the following long winter when ice in the river threatened to bring their travel season to an end. Pierre had built a cabin on the river St. François near a northeastern bay of Lake Huron. They were wearing fur mittens and moose-hide boots lined with beaver as they settled into their winter retreat.

Winter was descending and they could see no signs of human life on the frozen landscape. Remy had a suggestion. "This place is cold and lonely. Let's see if we can stay with Angus at the Sault."

Pierre was agreeable and they headed west. In an icy week of canoeing they reached the trading post just in time. The first big storm of the season had arrived in all its fury making further travel impossible.

Angus was delighted to have his accountant once again. The two men were warmly welcomed by Willow Wand. Remy liked working with Angus and felt himself useful as indeed he was. Pierre could indulge his passion for dog sledding, the most rapid transportation during the season. He handled the racing sleds with ease and joy.

As Pierre worked with Angus they argued endlessly but with humor about the quality of certain pelts. At winter's end Angus and Willow Wand treated the two traders to a sumptuous dinner and sent them off with a gift of venison.

Paddling each day up the rivers above Lake Superior after the spring thaw was exhilarating. Remy conceived the idea of seeking information about Wendat survivors from *voyageurs*. They came from all parts of Canada and many were of mixed blood.

At a trading post on *la rivière des Afsinipoils* a red-sashed *voyageur* named Bénédict told Remy that his Algonquin mother knew of a massacre in the Niagara region. A survivor had related the ghastly tale.

"Please tell me everything you know." Remy held his breath.

"There was something about a young girl escaping helped by hunters. But my mother died recently and I have only vague memories of that story."

Remy was encouraged by his words. Starting their third year of search in the unpredictable weather of early spring they inquired about Chief Owassoni and Tika's tribe everywhere they went. But getting into Iroquois country they had to be careful about delving into the story.

Then, near Lake Simcoe, a Petun warrior called Fleet Arrow replied that he had heard of a Wendat woman who survived an Iroquois raid near the Niagara.

"I'm listening."

"The man who told me was Manetera, an Algonquin warrior, passing through my village about two years ago. He related a story of Algonquin hunters helping the woman escape. She was dressed in black. Manetera came from north of Georgian Bay." Fleet Arrow thought for a moment. "That is all I know."

Now Remy alternated between wanting information and fearing bad news. On a stream flowing into Lake Ontario he and Pierre decided to take their furs to Quebec. "Brassart is keeping a half bale of furs for me," Remy told his friend. "And when I saw him at the old shipyard site he told me that my friend Jean Fauvet went to Quebec with him."

They stopped for one night in Montreal, a larger town than Quebec as Remy remembered it. He immediately located the convent to ask once again about Tika. The Ursuline Sisters regretted their inability to help reminding Remy that he had made the same inquiry earlier.

Continuing downstream they came to the town of Trois Rivières. By now the massacre was well known, but again no one had knowledge of survivors.

The next day the sun was well up when they awoke and set out downstream. River traffic was lively. Encountering traders in canoes coming or going on the river, the travelers exchanged information. Among other smaller craft they passed a *chaloupe* working its way upstream and a couple of *barques* going down river.

"How is trading in Quebec?" Pierre would ask them.

They answered that the town was growing each time the ships came in from France.

A week later, as they were gliding along, Remy realized that an ocean tide was pushing against them even though they were going with the current. That meant Quebec was not far. Both men were impressed by the growing number of houses on each side of the river.

Pierre turned toward Remy. "What a difference from three years ago. It is becoming *une grande ville*. I prefer it small and *intime*."

Here, along the river, effects of the sea are indicated with a high and low tide marker on each side of the shoreline. They began to see wire cages along the low-level mark.

"What are those?" Remy pointed his paddle.

"They are traps put out to catch *les anguilles,* sea eels. They try to wriggle back into deeper water and are ensnared when the tide goes out. The harvest is especially good from now into autumn. They are a delicacy."

The two travelers stopped to watch and one of the fishermen handed them a fat eel that they shared for dinner. What a pleasant welcome. The following day they arrived in the village.

The Lower Town of Quebec was the most populated part. Along the riverfront the two traders passed by the new trading company, *la Compagnie du Nord,* storage sheds and hostels with brightly painted signs. Much of the Lower Town had burned down two years before and was still being rebuilt.

Remy and Pierre paddled along the waterfront and passed a series of wooden docks. Pierre guided them to the place where the furs were piled. After they traded their furs Remy had no trouble finding Jean Fauvet.

"Pierre, this is my dear friend from the shipyard. Jean left for Fort Frontenac before you joined us on the *Griffin.*"

The two men shook hands.

"Happy to meet you, Pierre. I often wondered what I missed by not going on that voyage."

"I only went to Michilimackinac. But all you would have missed on that trip was a huge storm and a prayer to Saint Anthony."

Remy was not amused. He looked into the eyes of Jean Fauvet.

"At the mouth of the Mississippi, *mon ami,* you would have witnessed the greatest moment in French history."

Chapter 29

A NEW START

"Henri taught me to always go with the grain. How would you divide this board lengthwise?" Remy turned to Jean.

"The grain runs unevenly." Jean brushed his fingers along the wood. "Mark exactly where you want to cut, and tap a straight line with your chisel, not too deep the first time. Then saw along that line."

Just as he had first settled into life as a *coureur de bois*, Remy was now finding difficulty entering into a different occupation.

Jean and Remy occupied an *atelier* with a high ceiling located on the *rue du Porche*. This short street lead straight up from the river to *la Place Royale* with its open market in front of *l'Eglise de l'Enfant Jésus*. Jean had purchased the property for a workshop and a storehouse for furs.

The Lower Town of Quebec nestled on a narrow shelf of land beside the river while the Upper Town (*La Haute Ville*), some hundred paces higher, sat atop the Rock of Quebec. The two were connected by a series of steps and one precipitous street named *Rue de la Montagne*, along which were located houses and shops that perched upon the slope.

Jean and Remy had moved their equipment to the Lower Town from the house where Jean lived with his wife Colette. One of *Les Filles du Roi*, she had arrived from France the previous summer. Jean also wanted to trade in furs, although he knew little about it. So Remy, using his experience with Angus, became Jean's partner, advising him in buying pelts and setting up a bookkeeping system.

Parting from Pierre and life as a *coureur de bois* had been an agonizing choice for Remy. Pierre had given more than two years of
his life in the search for Tika, even foregoing the annual Beaver
Festival in Montreal. How would Pierre feel about his leaving?
After deciding to accept Jean's offer, Remy dreaded telling his loyal
companion.

To his surprise, Pierre agreed readily with his friend's decision.

"Quebec Village is probably the best place to keep looking for
Tika. Enjoy the good times, *Mon ami, et ne regrette rien.* I will come
to trade more often now that you are here. The river and I will
miss you."

Remy's decision was complicated by learning from Brassart that
he was in danger from the law.

"I must warn you not to draw attention to your arrival. You may
be an outlaw."

"How can that be?"

"The Superior Council has authorized the *Intendant* to issue arrest orders for you, Pierre, Camille Macé and several others charged
with illegal fur-trading. You were aware that only the government
trading company was legal. I recall you saying that Pierre told you
that at your first meeting."

"I guess he did but everybody ignores that. I could be arrested?"

"Probably not right now. The new governor has yet to sign the
orders."

"What about Pierre?"

"I told him. He shrugged and smiled. I don't think they will
catch him. But we must keep an eye on the Council. I'm trying to
contact the Governor's secretary."

This information had to be shared with Jean who did not appear
worried. With a handsome moustache he now had the air of *un
gentilhomme.* Blue-eyed Colette attended quietly to her husband's
needs. She was timid and not at ease with Jean's old friend. She
seemed pleased, however, to learn that his mother's name was
Colette.

Jean listened with interest to Remy's account of the voyage to
the mouth of the great river. Colette appeared astonished at this
strange story.

"Now what about you, Jean? You have not exactly been idle yourself. How did you move from Fort Frontenac and get started here?"

Jean had moved as chief woodworker to Fort Frontenac along with Brassart who was not comfortable there taking orders from the new commanding officer. When Brassart was offered a post as Associate Director of the new trading company in Quebec he agreed to take Jean with him.

"And how did you get started in business here?" Remy asked.

"You see, each year after the ships arrive from France new settlers in the area need lodging. Two years ago a great fire burned much of the Lower Town. This is taking a long time to restore. Many new buildings are now being constructed out of stone. Even so carpenters are always needed. I found work immediately and moved into a *pension*."

"Had you met Colette yet?"

"That comes later. I made some shelves and cabinets for an apothecary, André Marceaux, who liked my work. He encouraged me to go into business for myself.

Jean had gone to discuss that idea with Brassart, who offered him a loan of 30 pounds.

"Just when did Colette enter your life?" Remy asked.

"Well, about the same time. I still can't believe how all this came about."

"I'm listening."

"When *la Bonne Espérance* arrived from France last summer I was just finishing the cabinets for my apothecary friend."

Jean paused to refresh his memory. A ship's arrival was a major event. After a long winter when the first white sails hove into sight down-river, the village erupted into a rousing response to greet its reunion with the outside world.

"Everyone stopped work to watch *la Bonne Espérance* sail into port," Jean said. "As we hurried down to the riverside the church bells started ringing."

"You were all expecting it?"

"We knew a ship would be coming sometime but had no idea when. Since the arriving seamen don't like to remain on a crowded ship the village has newly built cabins to house ships' crews. I had helped with that."

"Did you meet Colette then?"

"I saw her. The men watched the women descending from the boat holding their skirts down against gusts of wind from the river.

There were two or three pretty girls, but I didn't think much more about it."

"Then how did you get to know her?"

"Colette was staying at *la grande maison* of Madame Anne Gasnier. Acting as hostess and chaperone she now lodges the *Filles du Roi*."

"So you saw Colette there?"

"No. She came to the apothecary shop on an errand for Madame Gasnier. While Monsieur Marceaux was looking for the medicine she watched me cut some boards."

"You recognized her as one you saw getting off the ship?"

"Oh, yes. She wanted to know why I was cutting the boards so short. I told her that I was making cabinets. Talking with her was most agreeable. I didn't realize then how lucky I was."

"What do you mean?"

"Well, after a week or so the eighteen girls were divided into three groups. Men came to look them over and select the one they desired."

"Like buying a cabbage in the market?" Remy asked.

Jean laughed. "I hadn't thought of it that way, but yes."

"What if a girl didn't like the man who chose her?"

"Colette told me that *Les Filles du Roi* had a right to refuse. However, there was an expectation they would marry quickly."

"And if there was some poor creature no man wanted?"

"That didn't happen. There were more men looking for wives than girls available. That is why the women actually did have some choice."

"How long were you courting Colette?"

"Less than a month. At my first visit Madame Gasnier questioned me, wanting to know about my family and what kind of work I do. Colette and I were permitted to sit and talk in the parlor for no more than one hour—never out of her sight."

"So you two didn't have much time to be alone."

"Not at first, but one day—evidently after convincing Mme. Gasnier I was serious in my intentions—we had permission to go for ride in a canoe. Colette had never before set foot in a tipsy craft and at first was terribly frightened. Even so she was willing to try something new and we had a happy day together. I fell in love."

"So you asked her to marry you?"

"Not right away. Living in a *pension* I had no idea how I could dare ask her to leave her shelter. Brassart suggested I rent a place. Very few are available. But I found the little house where we are now living."

"Any difficulties getting married?"

"On the contrary they even awarded us a sum of money."

"*Combien?*"

"They gave me twenty pounds."

"That's generous."

"You haven't heard it all. In addition they paid Colette fifty pounds and we will be rewarded for each child we produce. With a family of ten I could get three hundred pounds a year, enough to live on without working."

"*Bonne idée.* I can take over the shop while you care for the children. Colette would like that."

Jean laughed. "Colette wants a baby and so do I, but not ten."

"Just to save money for the *roi de France?*"

"*Bien sûr.*"

"I had no idea that getting married was so profitable."

"Brassart says the King wants many French settlers here without being obliged to pay their passage from France. This way costs less."

"And is an advantage for you."

"*Sans doute.* And I was able to pay back my loan to Brassart."

For the first few days Remy stayed with his friend, sleeping in Jean's workshop that was then a part of his residence. But Colette was timid, and Remy sensed her resentment at his coming unexpectedly into their lives. He moved to a *pension*.

In the meantime Jean's business was so successful that he purchased the shop in the *La Basse Ville* with money borrowed from *la Compagnie du Nord.* He accumulated orders for work that might take about a year to finish.

Remy had already inquired about Tika in the convent at Quebec. An Ursuline Sister replied there was nobody with that name. Wendats at Lorette had told them of the massacre but they could connect it with no residents of the convent. So he knew not where to turn. Colette encouraged Remy to make the acquaintance of one of the women who would come with the boats from France the following spring. Perhaps he would try.

As fall days contracted into nocturnal chill the streets of Quebec emptied. The Lower Town looked like a village modeled in snow. Everywhere piles of firewood rose like battlements. Houses closed their eyes as shuttered windows fought the cold. After a day at the atelier and dinner at the *pension* Remy started returning to the shop to continue his work by lamplight. Then he would stroll about in solitude, not knowing where to direct his steps or thoughts. The loss of his book and journal in Lake Huron had been a severe blow, leaving a nagging sense of Lenten sparseness in his mind. Now in his room he could take Father Bernard's advice and record entries in his new journal. One night he penned:

> Like bears hibernating in this wilderness, I feel that my real life is just sleeping. Where is my fascinating Tika?

Now in late spring with a sturdy Algonquin canoe he spent his leisure hours exploring the Saint Lawrence. About two leagues downriver with its multicolored gardens and patches of wheat and rye along the shore line the *Ile d'Orléans* invited a closer look. Here grapevines were beginning to display shiny new leaves. In season the rich black soil would produce some of the greens, peas, carrots, and grapes coming to their tables. From the southern point of the island Remy could view *La Haute Ville* Clinging to the Rock de Kébec.

Passing in mid-river, boatmen exchanged friendly salutations. Idly, Remy rather hoped to see a lovely lady floating by, but no such fortune had yet favored his travels.

Although their fur business was expanding Jean found the greatest pleasure in cabinetwork. Remy contributed to their enterprise the half bale of beaver pelts that Tonty had given him at Michilimackinac and the pay he had collected from the Sieur de La Salle. He spent time greeting red-sashed *voyageurs* as they came in to the docks, always making the same queries about the Wendat maiden.

One day Jean and Remy received a special request from *la Haute Ville*. Governor Denonville himself ordered a set of cabinets. They were elated. Jean hastened up to the Governor's chateau to take measurements. A draftsman had made sketches of the two pieces of furniture that Jean studied and returned with suggestions of his own. Once approved the two carpenters set to work.

Remy cut the planks while Jean did the trimming and fitting. Together they assembled the parts. They labored for weeks to complete the two precious *objets d'art*. The first was an *armoire* tall enough to hold the Governor's uniforms. The second one was a long desk with open vertical spaces for maps and large documents at one end.

Jean had been so nervous that he was constantly looking over Remy's shoulder as they were finishing their work with a coat of sun-bleached linseed oil. Yes, this was indeed the most beautiful furniture they had ever created. Before loading the pieces onto the cart for delivery they stopped to admire their work.

Secure on a *tombereau* (tip-cart) with wheels almost head high they realized that the cabinets were much too heavy for the two of them to transport. So they enlisted the help of three robust men.

The Château Saint-Louis in gray stone with its steep dormer roofs rested on level ground atop the Rock of Kébec. From this highest point of the Upper Town, Governor Denonville could look down upon the river and out toward the distant Laurentian Mountains. The two-story château was by far the largest building in the village. Jean and Remy counted more than thirty windows.

Passing a soldier guarding the grounds they halted the cart before the stone steps leading to a heavy wooden door. A servant directed them around the back to the tradesmen's entrance.

Just then a well-dressed gentleman came out. Introducing himself as Monsieur d'Ormonde, secretary to the Governor, he pointed them toward the main entrance that led to the Governor's office. He called out two more servants to help and supervised placement of the cabinets. He then turned and complimented them on the workmanship.

At this moment His Excellency the Marquis de Denonville, Governor of Quebec, came down the corridor from his office. He stopped to acknowledge the introduction by his secretary to Remy and Jean. Briefly he examined the new desk running his hand over the surface.

"*Bien fait, Messieurs,* a credit to French craftsmanship." He then hurried away accompanied by a soldier.

Although they spent little time in the château the two craftsmen peeked into rooms as they were leaving.

"Jean, look at those chairs, hand carved and cushioned in red velvet. Just like in a painting."

"They are magnificent. Is this a picture of something in Paris?" Jean pointed to a huge wall hanging.

"That is *la Sainte-Chapelle*. I have seen it up close. The bottom border of bright blue must be the Seine."

They both moved closer to see what appeared to be a golden *Fleur-de-lis in* each corner. As they left the building Jean paused to study the huge door sculpted in oak.

Jean paid the three townsmen who descended with the cart. At *La Place de la marché* the exuberant cabinetmakers purchased a bottle of fine red wine and returned to the shop to celebrate. With *Vive le Roi* for a start they toasted everybody they could think of, themselves included.

Recalling that Governor Denonville had not yet signed the arrest orders for illegal fur traders, Remy proposed a toast to him as their special customer.

"It's mid-afternoon." Jean looked at the empty wine bottle. "We can close the shop for today. I can't wait to tell Colette that the Governor had good words to say about our work."

"It's mostly your skill but I'll gladly share the compliment."

As Remy departed Jean reminded him that he was invited for dinner that evening.

"Jean, I come over often. That makes work for Colette, especially in the middle of the week. Perhaps we should wait."

"There may be a special reason. Anyway I would like you to come."

"Is that a secret?"

"You will find out."

Chapter 30

REVELATION

Why had Jean been so secretive about their dinner this evening? Having no idea Remy began to picture the smiling face of Odette on the ship coming over from France. Had Colette found for him a young woman like herself?

Remy headed toward his *pension* with an unusual lightness of heart. It was mid-afternoon. He and Jean had stopped work early after an extraordinary day. He was recalling their visit to the grand *Château Saint-Louis*. What good fortune they had to meet Governor Denonville himself.

Not accustomed to drinking wine during the day Remy entered his room and stretched out upon the bed before sinking into a profound slumber. When he awoke the obscurity of his windows reflected a darkening evening sky.

On his way to dinner he stopped at the bakery for *une miche de pain* for his hosts but Gabon had already closed his shop. When Remy arrived at their house Colette met him at the door and announced that she was serving venison and red wine.

No lovely stranger appeared. He kept waiting patiently for something to happen. Stirring the embers of the fire Jean looked up to say casually, "Armand Brassart is coming by for dessert."

"*Quel plaisir* " Remy said. "We can tell him about our adventure at the governor's residence."

They finished their dinner and Colette brought out a cornbread cake with dried blueberries and herbs. She was preparing to serve it when they heard a knock on the door.

Remy hurried to open and warmly embraced Brassart. "You would never guess where Jean and I were today."

"You took a holiday from the shop?"

"Not exactly. We delivered some cabinets to the *Château Saint-Louis* and the governor himself examined our cabinets and stroked the wood. Then he said, 'Well done, gentlemen, this is a credit to french craftsmanship.'"

"He did not recognize that you are an outlaw?"

"I did hold my breath for a moment when I was introduced."

"*Félicitations*." Brassart turned to greet Jean and Colette. "That should bring in many clients."

"We will have to tell Tonty about that when we see him."

"Would you believe it? I just received word from Tonty today."

Brassart appeared relaxed as he told them that Tonty was now establishing a new trading post down among the Arkansans.

"Any news about La Salle?"

"No," Brassart answered, "and Tonty is extremely worried. All we know is that La Salle was given four ships for his proposed colony. He sailed from France more than a year ago. We should have had word long since of his whereabouts."

Colette seated her guests at table and asked Brassart to say a blessing. He obliged and as they ate their dessert he jested with the young carpenters about getting a foothold into royal circles of government.

Jean stirred restlessly and finally said, "Remy, I think our guest has something to tell you."

All eyes turned to Brassart.

"Remy." He put down his wine glass. "I know where Tika is."

Remy sat there for a minute stunned. Then he jumped to his feet. "Where is she?"

"Sit down," Brassart commanded.

"Why didn't you bring her?"

"Sit down, *mon ami*, and let me tell you about it." He was speaking with irritating deliberation.

Remy seated himself.

Brassart went on softly, "Where is she? She is here in Quebec at the Ursuline convent with the Reverend Mother Angelica..."

"But that is where I inquired first of all and they knew nothing. What is she doing there? Did..."

"Please, Remy, kindly let me finish. I have not talked with her nor do I think she saw me. Yesterday I was delivering a trading company financial contribution to the Mother Superior of the convent..."

"Yesterday? Why didn't you..."

Brassart held up his hand. "Please allow me to tell my story. Yesterday I went up to the Ursuline convent. As you know, it is at the end of a little street called *la rue du Parloir* in la *La Haute Ville*. It was early in the day and as I drew near the board fence around the convent I saw a line of young women rounding the corner heading toward the front entrance. I held back waiting for them to go in. They were wearing *coiffes* so I did not see their faces. But just while I was watching one of the women turned toward me. She looked like Tika."

"My God! What did she say?"

"I'm certain she did not see me. I was partly behind the gate."

"And you didn't tell me then? Why?"

"Remy, you know I have really been looking for Tika. She was gone in an instant. I just could not trust my own eyes. I thought about it all day."

"You aren't certain it is Tika?"

"This morning I went up to the convent a little earlier. I told the *concierge* that the trading company wanted me to look at a fence that needs repair. She nodded and went inside. In the shelter of a large mountain ash where the young women could not see me I waited as they returned from their morning walk. There is absolutely no doubt in my mind that Tika was there amongst them."

"Why didn't you talk with her? We will go up there tomorrow morning. She can stay with me at my *pension* until we find a place."

"Remy, be patient. Most important, we do not know if she has taken vows. Then a man does not burst into an Ursuline convent to seize one of their women. I know nothing about the rules of the Ursulines. However there are favorable reports about the Reverend Mother Angelica. Let me make some inquiries."

"For God's sake, Brassart, have you no pity? For three years I have done nothing but look for her. I can't wait."

"Yes you can. And you must."

Chapter 31

VALLEY OF DECISION

"I can't believe that I'll be seeing Tika. Maybe we'll be together to-night. She can share my room at the pension."

"I wouldn't count on that if I were you. Let's slow our pace a bit." Brassart took hold of Remy's arm. "We must not get there before morning chapel is over."

"Do you think Mother Angelica will be difficult about this?" Remy shortened his steps.

"I believe she cares a great deal about all the young women in her charge."

They had reached the top of *la rue de la Montagne* and turned into *la rue du Parloir*.

"Look. The only reason she would allow this interview is that Tika has not yet taken her vows." Brassart pointed down the narrow street to a fenced courtyard on the left.

"Mon ami, I wish you well."

Brassart raised the latch to open the gate. A bell attached by a heavy rope announced their arrival. After a long moment the concierge in a gray robe came out. She led the two men toward the reception room where an elderly nun greeted them.

"Kindly be seated. I will inform the Mother that you have arrived."

A wooden bench, a chair, and a small table with a Bible furnished the reception room. The smell of candles permeated the air. Here in this building is where Tika spends her days. This must be what Monique's convent looks like inside, Remy was thinking. How dreary.

A grating noise like somebody dragging a table across the floor came from the other side of the wall. Muffled voices could be heard from adjoining rooms. Minutes passed. Semi-silence hung in the room as they waited for the door to open. Conscious of his own breathing Remy was trying to remember the smell of Tika's hair.

"Why does it take so long for Tika to come?"

"We are not in a trading post, *mon ami*." Brassart held up a warning hand. "Be grateful to these nuns for interrupting their established schedule to receive us."

Finally the sound of footsteps approaching the door held the visitors' attention. After the walkers stopped and rattled the door latch there was a silence and then voices too low to be understood.

They stepped forward into the room. Tika entered first followed closely by Mother Angelica. Tika, head down, was looking straight ahead. When at last she saw Remy she stood stock-still, speechless.

"Tika!" Remy held out his arms and took several quick steps toward the two women. Mother Angelica moved closer to her charge and put her hand on Tika's shoulder. Remy stopped. For a moment they all stood motionless.

"*Chérie.*" Remy looked at Tika. "Are you not glad to see me?"

Wide-eyed she nodded.

Remy turned to Mother Angelica, "Will you permit Tika to leave with me today?"

"I cannot, monsieur. Thérèse has obligations to her students and to her sisters here. And we must discuss what our final decision should be."

Brassart stepped forward. "Mother Angelica, I have known Monsieur Moisson for a long time. He has studied in a French monastery school and I know him to be a person of exceptional character. Would you permit me to participate in those discussions?"

"I see no reason why you should not, Monsieur Brassart. "

"Could these young people have a moment together in private?"

She paused for a time.

"Yes, but it must be brief. We have our schedule to keep."

She opened the door to a small parlor. In blessed privacy Remy and Tika were in each other's arms.

"Why you not come sooner?" Tika looked into his eyes.

"*Chérie,* for two years I have been searching for you."

He led her over to a bench and pulled her down on his lap. With her head on his shoulder Tika ran her fingers through his hair and closed her eyes. There was so much to be said but the sheer joy of being together held them in silence.

Out in the reception room Brassart and the Mother Superior were in earnest conversation.

"I must tell you, Monsieur Brassart, how grateful we are for the support of the trading company. You know that we rely on you to repair the building and maintain the grounds."

"Mother Angelica, with your Convent school and the hospital you and your Sisters are bringing a precious contribution of French culture to this New World. We are proud to support your work."

"Thank you. And we continue to depend upon your services. So much needs to be done and we are few."

She spoke of their desire for long straight timbers to construct flowerbeds on the convent grounds. The hospital lacked cabinets for supplies.

"I can send some workers over this week," Brassart said. "Now may we continue our discussions of Mademoiselle Tika's future tomorrow?"

"Mid morning after chapel would be possible," she answered.

Mother Angelica knocked and opened the door to the little parlor to summon Tika and Remy.

Brassart stood by the entrance. Remy, with backward glances at Tika, moved up beside his friend.

"Mother Angelica," Remy looked directly into her eyes, "for Tika you have been a gracious friend and protector. I hope we can agree about her future."

"May the blessings of God be our guide. Until tomorrow, *messieurs*."

After the two men passed through the gate of the convent into the *rue du Parloir* Remy stood looking back until Brassart nudged him with his elbow.

"What is there to discuss? Tika wants to leave the place." Remy's voice was strained. "Perhaps I will go up there and just take her away."

"Are you planning to line Mother Angelica and her nuns up at the point of your musket? Do you imagine she would hand over her precious charge to a rogue with a weapon? What would you tell her?"

The two walked in silence for a time.

"Brassart, *mon ami*, tomorrow will be the most crucial day of my life. Either the Convent will agree to release Tika or I shall become an outlaw in the forest. And I will not be alone."

Chapter 32

FATE OF L'AIMABLE

With Captain Beaujeu and Henri Joutel, his childhood friend, Robert Cavelier de La Salle stood at the bow of *le Joly* and scanned the shoreline.

"We should have spotted the mouth of the great river by now. I remember a wide delta where our canoe touched shore. Something is wrong"

Recovered from a month-long illness with tropical fever in Santo Domingo, the explorer had departed on *l'Aimable*, a small supply ship, into the rough waters of late summer storms. The loss to Spanish buccaneers of *le St. François*, their ship loaded with cattle and supplies, still rankled in his mind.

La Salle was on bad terms with *l'Aimable's* Captain Aigron who had refused to accept orders from anyone except Captain Beaujeu. In the Gulf of Mexico, after negotiating the channel between the *l'Isle de Cuba* and *la Péninsule de Yucatán*, they had sited *La Belle* and their command ship, *le Joly,* which La Salle promptly boarded.

Although their vessels were equipped to determine the latitude with an astrolabe, there was no way of accurately reckoning the longitude, to establish how far west they had come. They arrived finally in February of 1685 at a broad bay that La Salle at first believed to be near the outlet they were seeking. He named it *la Baie de Saint Louis.*

"We can use the wisdom and courage of the good Saint," La Salle remarked.

The surrounding prairie was sun-drenched and uninviting. But a river channel that lead to higher land protected the bay from the sea. There the French colonists unloaded their supplies and set about constructing a fort. After more than six months of perilous voyage from France it was reassuring to have solid earth beneath their feet.

Reckoning the sailing time from their initial entry into the *Golfe Du Mexique* until their landing on this bay, it seemed logical that they must have sailed too far west in the darkness of night thereby missing the mouth of the great river.

When La Salle came to this unhappy realization he confided to Henri Joutel, "There is but one thing to do, *mon ami*. We must explore eastward from this location to find the river's mouth. Then, God willing, we can enter *la Louisiane.*"

He promptly ordered that the channel into the bay be buoyed out so that *l'Aimable* could approach in safety. Almost immediately a band of Savages appeared along the shore. At first they seemed hostile and their language was completely unfamiliar to the ears of the newcomers.

"We must visit their village at once and offer our friendship," La Salle said.

As they headed for the native village, La Salle glanced over his shoulder toward the sea. The *Aimable* was sailing directly toward a shoal. Uneasy about the vessel's erratic course he nevertheless decided to continue on his way. Moments later a boom from the ship's cannon carried across the plains. The Indians ran away in fright. La Salle feared that he had heard a signal of distress and indeed it was. Rushing back to the channel he saw *l'Aimable* foundering on the shoal.

"Go aboard the *Aimable* and help bring it safely into the bay," La Salle had ordered Captain Tessier of *la Belle* before setting out for the native village.

L'Aimable's Captain Aigron absolutely refused any aid. As he maneuvered under full sail through the marked channel, the men on board shouted that he was steering off course. Aigron continued to head straight for the sand bar. It looked like a deliberate act but of course there was no proof. Nonetheless there was the ship's prow deep in the sand, grounded and leaning heavily to portside.

Evening descended upon the settlers as they waded into rough waters up to their shoulders. They rescued the gun carriages useful for their protection and for their wheels. They managed to retrieve certain precious supplies, including gunpowder, nails and meal. Thirty hogsheads of wine and brandy were saved to be loaded onto *la Belle*. Then they were obliged to stop, the day being so far spent that complete darkness was coming on.

They retired to their camp for the night with hopes of salvaging more cargo on the morrow. Once again good fortune eluded them. During the night the incoming tide split open the hull of the foundered ship. Morning revealed that all else had been lost---food, supplies, and remaining tools. While he was pacing the shore that night in a lonely vigil over the disintegrating vessel, what thoughts coursed through the head of the great explorer? He confided in no one.

In despair a number of colonists decided to return to France on *le Joly*. By delivering his passengers and cargo Captain Beaujeu's mission had been accomplished. Now he could return to his duties in the French navy. Having been reprimanded for his loss of *l'Aimable*, Captain Aigron would be a passenger on *le Joly*, heading for a hearing into his conduct by a French naval board of inquiry.

Le Joly sailed away after the crew shared their remaining supplies as generously as possible.

"Now our little frigate *La Belle* is our sole link with civilization," Joutel remarked.

La Salle sketched out plans for the stockade, the fort and residential buildings. They gathered and dried out driftwood logs thrown up along the shore by the sea. The men squared and used these logs to construct their colony. In October, eight months after their arrival, the explorer announced his plans.

"With forty able men I will set out along the shoreline to the east, searching for the great river."

Despite doubts expressed by Joutel that it would be wiser to complete the fort before departing, La Salle selected his search crew.

"You are becoming a part of your country's history," he told these men as they were leaving. "Together we will see proof of France's claim to *la Lousiane*."

He was remembering a glorious image of the plaques he had placed high on a hill overlooking the banks of the Mississippi.

As the company made their way overland *La Belle* was to accompany them by sea to assist in locating the river they sought.

La Salle's trusted aide Henri Joutel agreed to stay at the camp in charge of the shrinking community.

Those who remained on this desolate stretch of land continued to complete the buildings and hone their survival skills. The surrounding walls and the fort itself had been almost completed but the interior was still under construction. They had to seek additional lumber from a distant grove of trees.

"This is not fit work for man or beast. These cannon mountings from *l'Aimable* weigh more than the wood we are transporting."

The Sieur Duhaut wiped sweat from his face and sat down on the iron gun carriage. He was a *gentilhomme* who had contributed some portion of his own wealth to finance the expedition and he was not accustomed to hard labor.

Joutel looked at him.

"You are quite right, monsieur, but there's no other choice. These are the only wheels we have."

Duhaut replied quickly, "Now we could use the help of the men the Sieur de La Salle took with him."

La Salle's surgeon Liotot who had also invested money in the colony was accompanying the workers to be with his friend Duhaut. He had been pressed into service helping to pull the load of timbers. He looked at his hands.

"I feel uneasy that La Salle took *la Belle* along with him. If anything should happen to..."

"That ship," Duhaut continued, slipping down from his seat on the gun carriage, "we would have no way to escape from this hole in hell that he chooses to call Fort Saint Louis."

Several days later Joutel, on the parapet scanning the sky for signs of changing weather, caught sight of a dark blot approaching on the horizon.

"Barbier," he called out. "Something is coming toward us on the plains. Is it Indians from the village?"

"I don't know. But let's get the women and children into the log stockade. I'll tell the men to fetch their muskets."

They continued slowly across the eastern plain. The figures, too far distant to identify, were definitely heading their way. Joutel and his patrol stopped to watch the small body of men straggling across the prairie. Then they recognized La Salle and his party, first with joy and then with horror. All were in rags. The cassock of the Abbé Jean Cavelier was in tatters. His brother, the Sieur de La Salle, having long since lost his wide-brimmed hat, wore a battered cap. Remnants of shirts and breeches covered their bodies. Some were barefooted. But they were carrying fresh meat. Crossing the prairie they had killed two buffalo.

"What happened? Did you find the river?" The Frenchmen exchanged tearful embraces. "You have lost some men?"

"We did not have good fortune. Yes we did lose some comrades and failed to find the great river." La Salle looked around. "How about the three men who returned from our party? Did they arrive home safely? Where are they?"

Joutel looked puzzled. "Which men?"

They were Sieurs Clerc, Hurie and the young Duhaut brother. They found themselves unable to maintain the pace of the expedition, so they were given leave to return to the fort."

"You sent Dominick and the others back? How could you do that?" cried the older Duhaut.

"They were exhausted and chose to return," La Salle replied. "We were only ten days out and with a supply of dried meat and corn I thought they would have no difficulty finding the way back."

More than three months had elapsed. The colonists were forced to conclude that the three men had perished in the wilderness. Duhaut was devastated.

"This is a terrible misfortune." Liotot placed his hand on Duhaut's shoulder. "Your brother Dominick was one of our bravest young men. He will not soon be forgotten."

"I won't forget him." Duhaut gestured with a clenched fist. "There must be a day of reckoning for what La Salle has done. I will never forgive him."

Chapter 33

SETTLING IN

"Bon soir, ma Chérie."

Tika cuddled against Remy's cheek, clinging in a rapturous embrace.

"We had a busy day at the workshop," he told her, "and I'm ready for dinner."

"I was hungry, too. I just finished eating."

"It would be pleasant for us to dine together."

"Good idea. I like that."

She was not teasing. Why not eat when you are hungry?

Sometimes when Remy came home from his day at the atelier she would be out hiking along the river. Despite having observed regular hours for prayer and meals in the convent, Tika could see no reason to continue the practice.

They had found a place on *la rue De Meulles,* a new street that connected *La Basse Ville* via a steep flight of steps with *Cap Diamant* atop the Rock of Kébec. This dwelling had been left in a state of disrepair. The double walls, almost a pace thick, were filled with sawdust. Remy and Jean discovered an empty house when they pushed through a door half off its rusty hinges. An interior measured about ten by ten paces.

Jean studied the space. "We could divide this into two rooms, perhaps three."

He offered Remy a loan for its purchase. To Tika the idea of "owning" four walls on a little square of land made no sense. She could not understand the concept of using a sheet of paper to "purchase" a piece of the earth. Like taking possession of the air you breathe, beams of the sun or moon that shine upon Mother Earth.

Jean and Remy enclosed a chamber for sleeping, leaving an area for a parlor and space for eating— including a kitchen with a stone fireplace and brick oven. A handsome oak table was a wedding gift from Jean.

Their discussions with Mother Angelica had required only two morning meetings thanks to Brassart's diplomatic skills and Remy's reasoning.

"Tika has lost her family and her entire community," he reminded the Mother Superior. "Having a family of her own may help a little to make up for that loss."

"I am most reluctant to see her leave," the Mother Angelica said at the beginning. "Thérèse is a person of spiritual depth and she has a strong character. But for some time I have noticed a certain melancholy about her that has distressed me."

Finally Mother Angelica decided that it would be wiser for her to leave.

"She will always be welcome as a visitor but it may best for all concerned that she feel free to leave the Convent completely. We will miss her"

Tika quickly gathered up her meager belongings but took some time bidding farewell to the good Sisters. Then she accompanied Remy to his *pension* where she would be sharing his room until they found another domicile.

To her surprise Tika learned that both Remy and Brassart had inquired about her at the convent earlier. In good faith the nuns had denied any knowledge of a woman named Tikanaka whose people were victims of an Iroquois raid. The hospital nuns at the *Hôtel-Dieu* had found Tika's Wendat name difficult and registered her under the name Thérèse. At that time they knew nothing of a massacre, accepting her reluctance to say anything beyond the fact she had lost her parents.

The Ursuline nuns at the hospital and at the convent had appreciated her ability in the French language. They wondered how she learned it. She would say only that a religious person had helped her. So Tika's past remained a mystery to them.

Early in her residency she was asked to guide some of the native girls in their studies. This gave her a certain pleasure. But she felt imprisoned by the walls and inflexible rules.

Tika had chosen not to take vows. In the day school for natives she was treated as an unofficial novitiate. Her first months in the convent were days of loneliness, surrounded by high walls. One night she emerged sobbing from a dream in which Moon Cloud had chided her for wandering far into the forest. Sister Marie lighted a candle and hurried through the dark corridor to wipe away her tears and hold her hand while praying. Tika desperately wanted to put her arms around the nun and longed for an embrace in return. But the gentle sister resisted close contact.

Where then did Tika belong in this circle of life? And where was Remy at this moment? Weasel Tail had faithfully delivered Remy's message. She decided to wait for him if he would agree to stay with the tribe. Moon Cloud said if he really loved her he could find a happy life in the longhouse community. Why did he not come when he learned what had happened? As a Frenchman he had ways to find her now if he so desired.

A life of teaching native children might at least repay her debt to Father Laurent. It could be endured, she thought, if only she were free at times to walk in the woods, feel the wind on her face and leap from on high into the river. She would resist taking vows as long as possible.

Tika had started her third summer at the convent feeling a mounting sense of *ennui*. The Mother had observed the sadness of her young novitiate and worried about her future. When Remy appeared Tika pleaded with such ardor that Mother Angelica had found it difficult to refuse.

Now she was experiencing a renewed sense of freedom and moments of pure joy with Remy. But sometimes she would awaken in the night, wondering if marriage vows with him would be a betrayal of Father Laurent. What would he have thought of her choosing to live with a Frenchman instead of giving her heart to Jesus? Images of the good Father kept invading her memories.

Tika first visited the nearby Wendat village of Lorette to make arrangements for their wedding. At the ceremony in Lorette, although he found their marriage customs to be rather strange, Remy took part with an inner happiness. Tika had taught him some simple words to repeat. They stood on a mat holding opposite ends of a stick as was the custom. Then after the vows, dancing and drumming awakened a joyous sense of celebration.

The villagers welcomed any occasion for feasting. They did not appear to notice the white face. The newlyweds were then presented with the gift of a handsome beaded belt. The following day Brassart urged them to have a church marriage.

"Tika is considered a converted Catholic," he said to Remy, "but she has no papers to show for it. Married to you by a priest in a Catholic ceremony she becomes *une citoyenne de France* with the privileges that implies. You will never regret it."

Father Péletier at the Récollet Chapel officiated in a ceremony with only Brassart, Jean, and Colette as witnesses. Facing possible arrest for illegal fur trading, Remy did not want to call attention to his presence in Quebec.

As she settled into married life Tika had little interest in housekeeping. The table would be stacked high with squares of buckskin she was decorating with quills or lists of French words she was writing at the moment. Then she just pushed the pile back to make room for eating.

One night when Remy returned from the shop she was working with cracked dried corn in a bowl. She would put a handful in her mouth and chew it before spitting it out and adding it to a shaped ball of dough. The yellow ball glistened.

"What is that?" he asked.

"I bake for our dinner."

"You can't do that. *C'est dégoûtant.*"

"Why? This has good taste."

"*Chérie,* you cannot give someone food you have been chewing."

"That is the way animals and mothers feed their babies." she replied. "Moon Cloud did that with me. So what is wrong with my mouth?"

"Nothing. But people don't eat things somebody else has been chewing."

"You no like kissing me?"

"That is not the same thing, *Chérie.*"

"You no mind getting into my mouth when we are lying together. At first I no like that. Now I think you taste good."

"Well, we just don't do that with food."

"*Bien*. I bake this for me. What you going to eat?"

She smacked the ball of dough onto a hot stone in the fireplace.

For their sparsely furnished house Jean had made them a sturdy chest of drawers, *une petite commode*. They placed it in the bedroom, convenient for clothing and what few linens they possessed. When Remy came home the next day Tika was ready to show him how she had arranged their affairs. Neatly folded piles of clothing on deer hides had been shoved under the bed. In the drawers she had placed shoes, some tools, writing materials and a *pot-pourri* of small objects.

When Remy explained the use of this piece of furniture she pointed out that sheets and clothes would be easier to reach under the bed.

Remy thought, that in time, she would see the logic of good housekeeping. He was too happy at the moment to insist on having his way.

She often made corn cakes in the fireplace. When they bought bread from Gabon's bakery they usually just broke off chunks from *une miche de pain* to eat or dip into a sauce. But when Remy once bought *une tarte à la crème* for a special treat Tika broke it apart with her hands and the whole thing was a mass of dripping pastry.

"I never learn your ways." She wiped the sticky liquid from her hands.

"You are doing fine, *chérie*, and you are not afraid to try new things."

"If we live in Wendat village you learn new ways."

Fish was usually to be found in the market. One day she fried cod rubbed with lard and rolled in dried corn she had crushed into a powder. She had purchased some bread from the baker and they sipped *chopines* of cider.

"This is delicious, *Chérie*," he told her.

For the next five or six nights she presented the same repast.

"It would be *agréable* to eat something different," he finally remarked.

"But you say you like this fish?"

"I like it. Still, it would be pleasant to try another dish."

"We always eat what is there," was her response.

"You seemed to have a variety of meals at the longhouse when I visited."

"Was because you are there."

Colette was generous in giving Tika advice about cooking and she was quick to learn. But then Tika would remark that French people do strange things like putting salt and sugar in the same food. She would be happy to forget the salt.

Once when they invited Jean and Colette to dinner Remy carved a roasted chicken. He mangled the meat in an attempt to separate it from the bones.

"I'm not skillful at this." He loaded slivers of meat on their plates.

"That's all right. You have skill in bed."

When Tika talked like that Colette would blush and look at Jean. Remy wondered if she really shared his joy at finding Tika. Perhaps she would have preferred that he marry *Une Fille du Roi* more like herself.

There were times when Tika would be quiet for a long while. Her husband could sense a profound sadness and knowing that she missed her family, he worried. But she refused to burden others with her thoughts.

Remy speculated that she was uncertain about her friends the Catholics who had helped to rescue and care for her. He knew that she had great affection for Father Laurent and was perhaps deeply troubled because he was still missing. However she never mentioned him.

Tika was grateful to the Ursuline nuns. Twice she went down to visit at the convent and said nothing to him upon returning. Remy wondered if they had really welcomed her. He was beginning to believe Indians simply do not complain. Perhaps they think it cowardly unless you are suffering an illness.

One day Tika wanted Remy to walk with her past the *Hôtel-Dieu* built for the hospital nuns three years before. She had been in their care after fleeing to Quebec from the massacre. She read aloud a plaque over the door asking all who entered to pray for the souls of the Duchesse d'Aiguillon, *fondatrice de l'hôpital,* and her uncle Cardinal, le Duc de Richelieu."

Coming out of the door Sister Cécile recognized Tika. Saying *bonjour, mademoiselle* she hurried on.

"She was kind with me." Tika watched the departing figure. "I would like to embrace her."

Tika's French was flowing with greater ease, but her expressions were sometimes rather original. ("Remy likes selling his own skins.") With Tika's prompting he was acquiring more Wendat words.

Brassart enjoyed helping them both with language study. Tika admired him greatly and was certain he could answer any question.

She was looking at some manuscripts of French history Brassart had brought for her from the library of *la Compagnie du Nord*.

"What does 'discover' mean?" she wanted to know.

"It means to find something for the first time, something that you did not know exists," Remy told her.

"They write that Jacques Cartier discover *la Nouvelle France*. How could this be? We here all the time."

"Perhaps 'discover' means finding something new to us Europeans. We did not know about your country," Remy responded.

"So if I tell your mother you not exist before my people know you, how she feel about that?"

The belabored question made sense as he considered it. She would never be satisfied with a quick answer.

When first Remy questioned her about the Iroquois attack on her tribe she said simply, "I have no words for that."

He waited. "You don't want to tell me more."

"No."

He hoped that someday she would find the words.

She had the habit of telling the truth. No matter how damaging to her an admission of a mistake might be she never made excuses nor told a lie. He was aware that she swam in the river by herself in remote places and asked her not to do that. She shook her head. Later, while preparing supper her hair was wet.

"Have you been swimming?" He touched her head.

"*Oui.*"

"*Cherie*, I do not want you to do that. If you were drowning there would be no one to rescue you."

"You think I not know if it is safe?"

"You are wise, but not always."

"No like rules about swimming. Want to be free."

"Freedom" was a word she used frequently. For her, their life in a French village was bound by complicated rules. She would say no more. Silence was her natural defense.

She recalled a deer once straying into a tent at the tribe's hunting camp. In attempting to escape when the flap closed it charged against the soft sides, causing the wigwam to collapse. Struggling in panic the animal fell on its side completely enmeshed.

Her brother Naromaka and Little Eagle rushed to release the trapped creature. Head lowered the panting doe stood dazed, foaming breath gathering on her nose.

"We could sacrifice it for food," Little Eagle proposed.

"No." Moon Cloud led the trembling animal back into the forest.

Sometimes Tika remembered that incident and felt related to that trapped deer.

In Tika's tribe not telling the truth was one of the worst things you could do.

"So your people don't tell lies?"

"Well, sometimes. But if it's about something everyone needs to know that person no will be trusted again."

One day they went into the baker's shop after Gabon had burned a bake of bread. There was smoke in the air.

Tika sniffed. "Smell bad here."

Gabon glared at her.

"That was not a wise thing to say," Remy told her as they went out.

"Why?"

"Because sometimes it's better to be polite and not say something that may offend people, even if it's true."

"So I'm to be polite and not honest."

"No...Well, yes. Many people don't like to face the truth."

"You lie to me to be polite?" she asked.

"Probably I do."

"No do that. I want that you love me and not be polite."

Chapter 34

ALONE IN THE WILDERNESS

"We failed to find the great river," La Salle related to the waiting men and women at the fort when finally he returned from their terrible ordeal. "We had lost sight of *la Belle* as the ship followed us along the sea coast and sent out a search party of five men who are now making their way along the shoreline trying to locate the vessel."

A week after their return La Salle's brother, *l'Abbé Cavalier*, spied the five returning men, ragged and exhausted. They had found no trace of *la Belle*. La Salle and Joutel looked at each other.

"They probably deserted and sailed back to the West Indies or"—La Salle paused to slap at a mosquito—"they sailed back to France."

Never one to give up hope, La Salle conferred with Joutel, "The Illinois-Mississippi Rivers flow southeast. If we go in a north-eastern direction with say twenty men, we may come upon the Mississippi in a short time. I would recognize its course and we could find help for our colony."

The great explorer chose twenty of the men from his former crew. It was early March when they departed again.

"He has left us once again," the Sieur Duhaut told his friend Liotot. "I imagine that I'm not the only one losing patience."

Fears that *la Belle* had been lost were confirmed soon after La Salle's party had departed. One night in the darkness a *pirogue* scraped up on the shore. Six occupants climbed out of the over-crowded craft. The next day they related another tragic story.

Five men of their crew had lowered the only lifeboat from *la Belle* and started ashore one afternoon in search of fresh water. An instant squall moved in with violence and their comrades on *la Belle* watched in despair as the small craft capsized. Darkness closed in before they could reach the spot. The men were never found.

Back on board they had no fresh water and no lifeboats. But they were carrying a large store of wine and brandy from *l'Aimable*, enough to supply the entire colony. The master of *la Belle*, they recounted, drank himself into a state of stupor.

"We all decided to lift anchor and sail back to Fort Saint Louis" one of the survivors reccounted. "More bad luck. Continuing storms forced our ship onto a sandbar where it tipped and sank."

The six remaining passengers reached shore by clinging to boards roped together. They landed just east of the bay.

"Yesterday afternoon was our first good fortune. We found this boat beached in the sand and paddled along the shore to the fort. But we are *désolés* to bring you bad news of the loss of our only ship. *La Belle* is no more."

Now there was real fear and discontent among the settlers with remarks about their leader.

"Finding his precious river is more important to La Salle than our lives," were the words of Duhaut.

A trusted young man named Barbier hinted to Joutel that a small group was planning action.

"The Sieur Duhaut is leading them," he said, "They are collecting small arms."

Joutel sought out Duhaut. "Return the arms you gathered or I will have you in irons."

"If your friend La Salle no longer wishes to be the leader of this colony, some of us will have to take actions," Duhaut answered as he reluctantly complied.

La Salle returned in late June, three months after his departure, with only eight of the twenty men he took with him. Four had deserted. One man was eaten by an alligator. The others were presumably lost trying to return on their own initiative.

Joutel had waited for a time to inform La Salle of the discontent in the colony and the growing realization among the colonists after the loss of *la Belle* that they had no escape by sea. The two men were strolling through the stockade.

"Just look at that." Joutel pointed to grave markers in their cemetery. "Thirty of our people have died. We are now down to less than sixty. The men are in revolt. How can we make it through another year?"

"We will find a way."

Chapter 35

MARRIAGE RIGHTS

"My time of moon not come." Tika told Remy.

"What does that mean?"

"Perhaps something happens." She placed a hand on her stomach.

"Something?"

"Like little baby."

"*Pas possible.*" Clasping her in his arms he started to dance around the room. Then he stopped abruptly. "Are you certain about this?"

"I think so."

"You must be careful."

She laughed. "*Chéri*, no will be for long time. Colette wishes me see her midwife, Madame Joncheaux. I not go. She is three moons with baby."

"Madame Joncheaux?"

"No, Colette." Tika laughed.

"Colette is right. You must see the midwife."

"I have no need."

"*Chérie*, you cannot have a child without the help of a *sage-femme.*"

"I see many babies come from mama. Is like way of Earth Mother. Now I wish for Moon Cloud. I miss her always."

"You should not be alone," he told her. "I hear that Madame Joncheux is skilled."

"I try to find Wendat woman at Lorette."

The arrival of a child, Remy realized, might call attention to his outlaw status. He had almost forgotten about this. Because of

Tika's terrible losses in the massacre, he had wanted to keep her from worrying by not sharing this news. Now he had to tell her.

"I will never be taken away," he assured her. "I would resist with my musket and find refuge in the forest if necessary."

"I can show you place where they never find us." Tika brightened. "Would like that."

"This may be a problem for you," Remy told Jean that evening.

"I am worried, too." Jean paused in thought. "Colette goes to mass often. She was told that the new Bishop Saint-Vallier, who replaced Laval, is urging the governor to proceed with the pursuit of all illegal traders, past and present."

"That would not include you?"

"No," Jean replied, "Brassart had authorized me to trade with the company. But you and Pierre may be in danger. Colette is upset about all of this."

Tika and Colette had many differences. Remy hoped that being pregnant at the same time would bring them together. Colette had once given Tika a little cross made of burnished maple which the Wendat promptly fastened onto a piece of woven cloth decorated with quills.

"Is for spirit of house," she said. "For Earth Mother."

"Colette may not like that," Remy remarked.

"Why?"

"She believes the cross is sacred by itself. She considers you a Catholic."

"Catholics no believe in the spirit of nature?"

"They might call that an idol, a false image."

"Are quills from real porcupine."

"That's not what I mean. Catholics believe only images of Christ or the Virgin Mary or Saints are sacred."

"Christ no like things in nature?"

"Maybe He did but I'm only teasing. Don't be angry."

"Well, your God strange. Want to know more about how is different from Great Spirit."

She soon had an occasion to talk with another Wendat about that.

After work one day Remy came home to find her sitting at the table with an elderly man. He looked familiar. Was he the one who chanted at their wedding?

They stood to greet Remy.

"You remember, *Cheri*? Is Sondakwa, Shaman of Wendats at Lorette."

Sondakwa nodded and bowed as he took both of Remy's hands. Then he departed.

"Where did you find him, *Cherie*?"

"On *la rue de la Montagne* climbing up from river. He greet me in Wendat. Remember me from wedding at Lorette. I invite him to our house. Talk of many things. He wise."

At dinner Tika spoke with excitement.

"*Chéri*, Sondakwa learn that two of my Cord clan escape. Are at Georgia Bay north. Maybe we do Ceremony for Dead if more Wendats at *le lac Simcoe*."

"Excellent. We can have it here. Our house will be happy to receive them."

"You no understand. Feast of Dead must be there."

"Where?"

"At hunting camp. Where are the bones."

For a moment Remy could not speak.

"*Chérie*, you cannot go there and suffer once again. That will open old wounds. I do not want you to do that."

"Is most sacred ceremony for our people. Need to go."

"You said that the massacre was horrible. You cannot even talk about it."

"Is way to honor my people."

"You just cannot. Visiting that scene of death and destruction overwhelmed me. It must be even more agonizing for you."

Remembering the burn circle and grisly remains Remy felt a return of the nausea. The murder of Moon Cloud and Chief Owassoni and the burning of her village were too frightful to imagine. He loved Tika and wanted to protect her. This was their first serious argument.

Remy enlisted the counsel of Armand Brassart. His friend did not agree.

"Are you going to tell Tika she cannot go?"

"I'm considering that."

"You have the right?"

"Look, *mon ami*, I love her. I do not want her to suffer."

"Remy, your wife grew up with women who were in charge of the household. It is the man who must leave when Wendat couples separate. You are not in a French marriage."

"Are you saying I should agree to her going back to the place where almost all of her tribe were slaughtered? That will only recall the whole terrible scene. She has not even told me about it yet. It can do her great harm."

"To the contrary, this is something she needs to do."

"I think I can convince her otherwise."

Tika and Remy argued until finally she kept quiet. When he tried to discuss it again she just would not talk. Indians could be stubborn, he reasoned. In the following days she attended to housekeeping but became more withdrawn. Their happy and often mixed up conversations gave way to speaking only of everyday things. Sharing her bed was for Remy like sleeping with a totem pole.

His friendship with Brassart had also been strained. Usually a model of discretion, he talked again with Remy.

"Ask yourself if you are concerned about Tika or about your own anguish. I know what pain the site of that massacre caused you. I was there. Remember?"

"I know she has had terrible experiences and misses her people. But you saw that burn circle. Will it not be a terrible shock for her? I love Tika and you protect the people you love."

"Remy," he replied, "I know you and Tika love each other. But she is not asking *you* to choose between your parents, French customs and what you need to do. Just think about what you are asking of *her*."

"I don't think that is fair. Both of us have had to make choices. I still firmly believe it would be best for her to have the protection of a secure home life here in Quebec. Why should she open old wounds?"

Torn between his desire to respect Tika's traditions and a feeling that he needed to protect her from further pain Remy even talked with Jean about his problem.

"I wouldn't know what to do," Jean said, "but Colette thinks it would not be a good idea for Tika to go where her people were massacred."

Sondakwa would soon be back. Decisions had to be taken. Meanwhile Colette wanted to talk with Remy.

All Colette said was, "Remy, Tika is unhappy and this might not be good for her baby."

"It's my baby, too," he said.

But, unable to sleep, he woke Tika in the middle of that night. She struggled out of the covers and followed him into the other room. He lighted a lamp on the table and built a fire in the fireplace. By the lamp's dim glow they stared at each other.

Determined to be at the ceremony, Tika was feeling betrayed. If Remy would not help her, who could? Brassart? She had come to like and respect him, but he was Remy's friend and a whiteface. Maybe Sondakwa can come to her rescue.

Remy was remembering going as a child to sit beside his mother's grave in the churchyard. There he would vent his anger at God for taking her away. Yet, at the same time, he felt a strange comfort having her all to himself for a visit. When the villagers came to bring flowers on All Saints Day Remy resented them for invading his private place. Why would anybody want to celebrate a feast for dead people?

Tika broke the deep silence.

"Remember in my hut at the village? I say I would fear to go away with you?"

That remained the sum of their entire conversation for some time. Finally Remy spoke out, "*Cherie*, I'll be with you at the Feast of the Dead, wherever it is."

They went to bed. With his hand resting on her belly he wondered, as he fell asleep, if the movement he felt was their baby.

Chapter 36

FEAST OF THE DEAD

"I still fear that we're making a mistake with this death ceremony," Remy told Brassart.

"Patience, you may be in for a surprise," his friend replied.

Sondakwa, the Shaman of the Wendats, came again to plan the special occasion with Tika. They invited Armand Brassart to join them. Remy sensed that his friend felt honored.

Sondakwa suggested opening the ceremony with a day of mourning. At the winter campground, scene of the massacre, volunteer Wendats and Petuns would collect all the bones and carry them to the longhouse village site. There, these bones could blend with those already in the communal pit. A joyous reunion of spirits would thus be celebrated.

"Presumably the communal bone pit melds forever the spirits of all who had ever lived in the tribe," Brassart explained to Remy. He smiled. "This ceremony they call the Kettle."

Members of Sondakwa's clan were willing to help prepare the site in advance.

Although still reluctant to return to that grisly scene Remy wanted to encourage Tika's renewed liveliness as they prepared for the journey. It would be the first time they had traveled such a distance together.

As they were paddling up the St. Lawrence he asked, "Can you tell me more about the Feast of the Dead? I didn't understand all the planning."

"When I am little we move village to new place. Carry bones of ancestors with us."

"And when a person dies in between these events? You do nothing?"

"Oh, yes. We mourn for one year. Wrap body in beaver robes. Give precious gifts. Place person in bark box with gifts high on platform to protect from animals and birds."

"You grieve then at time of death and again for this ceremony?"

"Is one day of weeping but Feast of the Dead is joyous. Bring together for always the spirits, living and departed, all bones of clan. Take many days."

"Why not have the Feast of the Dead when people die?"

"For a time spirits of dead stay with us, share joys. We lonely for them. They lonely for us. We not say names for one year. Then, at Feast of Dead, we are again with all ancestors."

"So the spirits of people survive after death?"

She stopped paddling and looked around at him.

"We believe. I try to tell Father Laurent. I not know how explain what to call after you die. He teach me a word—moral, mortal..."

"Immortality?"

"That is what he say. So I believe we think like him. Except Father Laurent say punishment for sin after death. Why? How can change anything?"

"The Church believes that fear of punishment after death will encourage people to be honest and kind while living."

"You think that?"

"I do not. The priests are convinced that many of us don't follow the Bible and its teachings. So we must be punished sometimes even after death."

"I must think about. I like our way."

She resumed paddling in silence, turning them shoreward as they had drifted off course. Tika wielded a strong blade, so they covered much distance each day. Lines in her face revealed the strain of planning this ceremony. She was eager to reach the site. Remy was not.

As they arrived late one afternoon the sun lighted an area where ashes had been leveled and debris removed. Wild grasses had reclaimed patches of earth. Sondakwa and his friends together with dozens of the Tobacco Tribe (Petuns), had come to prepare the ceremonial site. Tika explained that neighboring villages often help each other and happily the Petuns spoke the Wendat tongue. The bones, many of them fire-darkened, had been cleaned and stacked up on skins.

Skeletons of blackened trees stood witness to the destruction. Few birds and insects disturbed the silence. Tika quickened her pace and called out when she spotted other survivors approaching across the burn circle. Old Katawitha with her scarred face, hobbled along. She reached Tika and the two fell into an embrace. The five survivors of the tribe gathered off to themselves. Their voices were heard late into the night. Tika made Katawitha comfortable on a bed of fir boughs in her shelter and rested with her until the old woman went to sleep.

Next day they arose at dawn to the sound of drumming. Ceremonial dancing started after a dried corn breakfast beside a rock-lined fire pit. Squash, corn cakes and bear meat were tossed into the flames, nourishment for the departed spirits. As dancing and drumming accompanied lamentations Remy saw Tika and Katawitha locked in embrace and chanting now on their knees oblivious to the world around them. He watched first in amazement and then in alarm.

Remy saw that Tika and her companions were in the throes of a grief like nothing he had ever seen. Gesturing with clenched fists, as was their custom, the tribesmen pranced to slow drumbeats. Remy started forward, calling on her to stop. Brassart grabbed his arm.

"This is something she must do." His friend held firm.

"She is carrying my child and I have to stop her. I can't watch her do this."

Brassart continued to hold him. They struggled for a moment.

"If you can't watch her," Brassart told him, "then go away."

Remy did just that. He turned his back on Brassart and stalked into the woods until he could no longer hear the drums.

That night he slept alone while Tika stayed with Katawitha in her hut. The next morning Katawitha had braided Tika's hair. Remy caught his breath when she appeared, as beautiful as the first time he saw her.

The following day they took the trail leading to the longhouses. The bones in skin-wrapped bundles were with their other ceremonial objects: beaver robes, beaded belts, and decorated pots that were to be placed along with the bones into the common grave.

The mourners completed their journey in one strenuous day, arriving in the dark.

Morning light revealed that nothing remained of the longhouse village. Where Remy and Tika had once gathered squash from around corn stalks wild grasses were breaking through ashes leaving in blackened soil ghostly footprints of a longhouse village.

The Petuns had prepared a feast for the second day at the beginning of ceremonies. The old burial ground had been opened into a pit with sides of about five paces in each direction. It was lined with skins overlapping the edges. Along one side stood a scaffolding of limbs. In the center of the pit were three large kettles filled with food for the souls on the journey to their final resting place.

From the scaffolding platform Petun Chief Kikasona, Kathawitha, and Sondakwa emptied the bags of bones and other artifacts into the pit. They were to be covered with skins and then bark before the cavity was finally filled with earth.

Meanwhile there were prayers and speeches at intervals amidst the dancing as the bones went into their final resting place. Watching the movement of people Remy marveled at their finery: women with decorated belts, and bands of beads around their necks and wrists; in their hair combs of animal figures carved in bone. A deerskin cape with bright red figures adorned one young squaw. A heavy necklace of bear claws moved with her dancing feet.

Pots of food were continuously carried to the feast as the celebrants paused for refreshment. Games and contests of skill with bows and arrows followed.

Tika pulled her reluctant mate into the festive circle. Raising high his knees Remy followed the drumbeats. The rhythm slowly invaded his senses. Sondakwa, having descended from the platform, maneuvered Remy along the circle of dancers. For the first time Remy began to experience the exhilaration of the dance.

He could feel drumbeats in his head and on his skin. Flowing around the circle reverberations from other dancers washed over him as if they and the ground beneath their feet were one, moving and breathing in the same rhythm. Remy felt he could go on forever.

Four days later when dancing stopped and the closed pit had been decorated with spruce sprigs and pinecones, his body was still hearing the drums.

As they walked toward the canoes Tika asked, "Would you like to be in the Kettle with my people one day?"

"I don't know."

The question at first seemed awkward. But as they made their way along the trail Remy found him self saying unexpectedly, "Chérie, I think I would like to have my bones someday mixed with those of the tribe."

"I no can say how I feel." Tika's voice was low as her moccasins crunched through layers of dry pine needles. "Moon Cloud will never hold our baby. I not know where I belong. Will our bones be with ancestors?"

"I think so. And you will be a wonderful mother." Remy put his arm around her shoulder.

The third night of their return trip along the north shore of Lake Ontario Remy and Tika made camp near the water. On the horizon shone a slice of light. Tika called it a "canoe moon". They sat around the fire late not talking much, listening to wind in the leaves.

In the dead of night Remy awoke with Tika shaking him.

"What is it? Are you sick?"

"No. I have dream. We must talk. Let us build fire."

Remembering what she had said about the future, a dread thought struck him. Maybe this whole Indian ceremony had been a mistake and Tika had changed. Would she leave him to follow her old life?

He had learned from Armand Brassart and Tika that Wendats take dreams more seriously than their waking thoughts, almost always acting out what they experienced in their sleep. He was so clumsy with the flint and steel that Tika had to light the fire. With flames blazing she sat by him on the ground and took his hand.

"Cheri," she said, "I have something to tell you."

Chapter 37

JESUIT LETTER

My Reverend Father Nicholas
The Peace of Our Lord
June 1687

I hope this letter finds you in good health and happy with your mission. You may not have heard that the first French ship this year carried a letter from the family of Father Maurice Laurent. Despite all the time that has passed they continue to believe that he may still be alive as a captive of the Indians. Sadly, we must now confirm for them his martyrdom at the hands of the Iroquois.

You inquired some time ago about a young woman convert of his. We do not know her fate. But her story inspires us. Despite its tragic end, progress made at that Huron mission gives us reason for optimism.

With no news of survivors we must now presume that all or almost all of the tribe at that Niagara location perished in the massacre. I know that you corresponded with Father Laurent. If some of his letters remain in your possession they could be included in a final report about his mission.

Father Drapeaux, our spiritual director, kindly consented to give me two letters. He will also recommend a memorial tribute to our beloved colleague. The martyrdom of so many Reverend Fathers, brothers in our noble mission, is the price of fulfilling our task. I fear that the King and His Holiness in the Vatican can never appreciate the immensity of this sacrifice.

We all know of the martyrdom of Fathers Jean de Brébeuf and Gabriel Lalemant, but only recently did I find in our Quebec archives a copy of the eyewitness accounts of their death that were sent to Rome.

What an unlikely pair they were. Father Brébeuf appears to have been a rugged giant of a man while Lalemant, his young assistant, was of frail body and failing health. They shared a zeal for missionary work with the Hurons and a genial gift for learning native languages.

Here is an excerpt of the report in our archives:

> "On March 16, 1649, near St. Ignace II, about one league from Sainte Marie in Huronia, Iroquois warriors, after destroying a Huron Village, captured Fathers Brébeuf and Lalemant. They dragged the two priests between long lines of Iroquois warriors where... a hailstorm of blows with sticks fell on the priests' shoulders, their loins, their legs, their breasts, their bellies, and their faces, there being no parts of their bodies that did not endure its torment... Iroquois braves gathered a couple of dozen iron trade hatchets that they placed in fires until they were white hot. Then stringing them on green withes, the fiendish savages draped them over Father Brébeuf's shoulders." "If he leaned forward the hatchets rested on his back searing the flesh to the bone. If he leaned back the hot iron hatchets ate into the flesh and muscles of his bare chest."

Witnesses attest to the fact that the Iroquois could elicit no cries of pain from Father Brébeuf even when they wrapped his live body in resinous bark and burned it. Father Gabriel Lalemant suffered a similar fate.

The recent death of Father Laurent is another occasion to reveal the nature of our martyrdom. Perhaps we can make our superiors in France realize the cost of promoting the commercial interests of France, not only in the lives of priests but also in the difficulties of building for the motherland a Christian nation.

You know of course that Bishop Laval has resigned so there is no one in the Quebec office at the present time to organize such a project.

When Governor La Barre replaced Count Frontenac we were all heartened. We had hoped that a new administration would insist upon the enforcement of laws restricting the trade in furs, guns and alcohol. This proved to be an illusion. La Barre wanted to build his own trading empire. He had less education and even fewer moral scruples than La Salle. It was a quarrel among thieves as to whom the greater profits from this terrible commerce would go.

Plus ça change, plus c'est la même chose.

That old adage retains its truth. The more things change, the more greed seems to surface. In the face of our sacrifices this is disheartening, but we must ever keep the promise of our faith. We can only pray that the advent of our new Governor Denonville will make our task easier.

The *Intendant* De Meulle has persuaded the Governing Council to approve arrest orders for a list of traders with whom La Salle has done business and those men who now or in the past were his employees.

These orders however cannot be executed without the signature of the governor. The Marquis de Denonville, recently arrived, has not yet activated these Council actions. We trust that he will proceed swiftly.

There is hope. The way our new *Intendant*, De Meulles, is carrying out the recent instructions of the French Court indicates that he may be more favorable to our cause.

We cannot sacrifice in vain the accomplishments of so many of our brothers. Maurice Laurent was a personal friend and his loss is painful for me.

We must preserve and cherish his memory by promoting the work for which he gave his life.

YOURS IN HOLY UNION
FATHER P. BUGUET, S.J.
QUEBEC

Chapter 38
RENDEZVOUS WITH DESTINY

The Sieur de La Salle hunched his shoulders and pulled a ragged cap down over his ears against a late autumn wind from the sea as he walked with his old school mate Henri Joutel along a strip of beach still spongy from the receding tide.

"My friend, Fort St. Louis cannot make it through the winter without help." Henri Joutel looked hard at La Salle. "After two years of effort we cannot produce enough food for a winter season that is not good for Buffalo hunting."

La Salle was silent then finally admitted, "Some of us must head northward to seek help, from Quebec or perhaps even from France."

He invited the male colonists to help devise a strategy for salvaging their settlement. Obviously the women and children could never undertake such a hazardous journey through the wilderness. How many should go and how many remain?

Finally they selected seventeen men to accompany La Salle, leaving—they hoped—enough skilled people to maintain the colony.

La Salle called a meeting of the whole group to announce this plan.

"How can you do that?" The women were weeping. "Why cannot all of us leave this terrible place?"

"You have the resources, my dears, to keep the fort until we bring more men and supplies," La Salle answered them.

The others sat as if stunned. Henri Joutel was among those chosen to go. He felt both relieved and a little guilty about leaving the companions with whom he had shared such hardships.

With five horses recently acquired from the Indians, seventeen men departed in late January of 1687. There were few dry eyes as they clasped each other in long embraces before their party headed out across the prairie.

With horses carrying most of the load they made good time for the first few weeks over relatively flat plains. Then they were instantly entrapped in a marshy canebrake like flies in a spider web. The mud sucked at their moccasins. All seventeen men were hungry and footsore.

Joutel began to hear grumbling behind La Salle's back. The men resented his urging them on like a man possessed.

The Sieur Duhaut was thinking of his fortune sunk in this colonial enterprise. Of course it was the fault of La Salle.

"We are getting into spring and must pick up our pace. If we miss the first boats we cannot possibly get an answer from Versailles before winter," La Salle told the men.

The Sieur Duhaut eyed his leader across the fire that evening. "Do not push us too hard. It was your blunder that got us into this predicament."

La Salle replied. "Recall, *cher monsieur*, that I am the one who discovered the mouth of the great river. One day all of this will belong to *la France*. That is our mission."

Duhaut was still grumbling when they loaded the pack animals the next morning. "We should stop a while and butcher one of these horses for a proper meal or two."

La Salle appeared not to hear his remark while Duhaut continued to question the wisdom of this entire journey.

"We left too few people at Fort St. Louis to maintain the colony. They will probably perish. Spending three entire months seeking the river's mouth was a foolish mistake."

"Please understand, Sieur Duhaut. We had no way of judging the distance back to the great river's mouth."

"You, Sieur, were responsible for the death of my brother on that march."

"That is hardly fair, Sieur Duhaut. He could not support the rigors of the journey. I deeply regret the loss of Dominick. He was a brave young man, but I can take no personal responsibility. He chose to go back. Each one was a volunteer."

Later that evening Joutel overheard Duhaut saying to Liotot, "Not up to the rigors. That villain takes the credit for everything and the blame for nothing."

"The men are in an ugly mood." Joutel reported to La Salle.

Passing into more pleasant country along the Illinois River their leader believed he recognized an area where he had previously hidden a supply of Indian wheat and beans in some hollow trees. The travelers were by now half starved. Salle dispatched several men out to search for it. The Shawnee hunter Nika, Hiens, Duhaut, and La Salle's Footman named Saget set out to explore.

Confirming La Salle's good memory Nika did indeed discover the precious cache of food.

"Here it is," he called out falling to his knees by a hollowed out tree.

Eagerly Saget poked his fingers into the dark moldy substance and held it to his nose. He looked around at his companions. "Just smell that. It is rotten."

The despondent men were heading back to their campsite when Nika spied at some distance two buffalo crossing a small stream. The others held back while the Indian crept forward with his musket and shot the animals as they emerged from the water. There were shouts of joy.

"We can butcher them here," said Duhaut quickly, "We'll need to return to camp for some horses."

Nika and the faithful Saget volunteered to go back. When they arrived at the main camp, news of the kill was received with a great cheer. The next day La Salle sent two horses with Nika, Saget, De Marle and his nephew Morganet to the site of the kill.

Arriving at the hunter's encampment they found that the men had already skinned and carved up the meat laying it on a rack of limbs for smoking. The men had carefully set aside for themselves the succulent marrowbones and tender portions of flesh to broil.

Young Morganet strode up to the drying rack. "I suppose you planned to eat the choice parts before bringing the rest back to camp."

"Indeed we intend to eat some of it," Duhaut replied. "We made the kill and by woodland custom it is our right."

"My uncle, the Sieur Robert Cavelier de La Salle, has placed me in command. Nobody will touch this meat without my permission."

Infuriated, the hunters withdrew behind some trees to agree upon a plan of action. Duhaut asked Morganet, Nika and Saget to take the first *tour de garde* of camp. De Marle, who had accompanied Nika, knew nothing of their intentions. When each of the three unsuspecting victims had served a tour of duty and had fallen asleep the plot was carried out.

While Duhaut and Hiens kept watch, the Surgeon Liotot arose. With an axe he crept toward the three sleepers. He struck a blow at the head of each in turn. Nika and Saget apparently died immediately without a sound. But Morganet, his head gushing blood, cried out and tried to sit up. This caused a surprised Sieur de Marle— now awake and not in the plot—to reach for his musket giving Morganet a *coup de grâce* as an act of mercy.

Liotot tossed down his axe. "What shall we do now?"

"We will wait until our great leader comes looking for us," said Duhaut. "We will then do what is necessary."

They knew that to escape with their lives they must rid themselves of La Salle, three leagues away at the main camp with the other men.

Meanwhile at the main camp the hours passed and the hunters did not return with the horses and the kill. The hungry men became restless. Finally, on a clear March morning La Salle set out with one of his Indian guides and Father Anastasius Douay, leaving Joutel to guard the camp. As they approached the hunters' encampment on the far side of a small stream La Salle pointed out two eagles circling above as if they might swoop down on some prey.

The priest shook his head. "That is not a good omen."

"I pray nothing has happened to our comrades." La Salle drew his pistol. Fearing for the safety of his hunters he fired a warning into the air. The plotters, awaiting their victim, heard his shot. A worried La Salle was striding along ahead of Father Anastasius and their Indian guide. Out of the bushes Larchevêque appeared.

"What brings you here to our territory?" he asked.

Surprised, La Salle demanded, "Where is my nephew?"

"He may not want to see you." Larchevêque stepped backward keeping his distance. In a rage La Salle rushed forward. From the bushes a shot rang out. The ball struck him in the forehead. Robert Cavelier de La Salle dropped to the ground.

As the plotters ran out of their hiding place in the tall, reed-like grass, Father Anastasius Douay and the Indian fell to their knees in terror.

"Don't be afraid. We wish you no harm," Duhaut assured them.

The killers hurried over to the body of La Salle.

"Never again will you give us orders," came the voice of Duhaut as they threw their lifeless leader into the bushes.

Father Anastasius Douay and his Indian companion drew away in horror, then turned and ran back to the main camp to announce that their leader had just been killed. The plotters now led by Duhaut were not far behind, bringing the horses laden with meat. An unarmed Henri Joutel, the Abbé Cavalier, and the others stood there in astonishment. Having no alternative, they all yielded the command to Duhaut.

The next two days as they made their way along together the plotters behaved as if nothing unusual had happened. Then they came upon a village of the Cenis people where the travelers were received in a friendly manner.

Joutel remained with the Cenis tribe to arrange a trade for corn while the others moved on to an advanced location. Here he encountered an individual named Rutter, a deserter from La Salle's previous expedition. So completely had he adopted a native mode of life with painted body and Indian robes that Joutel did not recognize him as a fellow Frenchman until he spoke.

Heins, the German, arrived to pick up the corn Joutel had purchased. Leading two horses laden with the grain they arrived at the new encampment to discover that all was in disarray. Hiens was now in a rage because Duhaut and the surgeon Liotot had already taken most of the plundered goods for themselves. The remaining nine unarmed men were terrified that they would never be permitted to return alive.

The following day Hiens, who had gone back to trade with the Indians for more horses, returned with the deserter Rutter and a man named Groller, another French deserter turned Savage. Hiens had encountered them near the Cenis village.

Heins immediately approached Duhaut, pistol in hand. "I want my part of the goods taken from La Salle. We should all share alike."

"The goods are mine. I have a personal investment in La Salle's colony."

Hiens shot twice into the body of Duhaut, killing him instantly. At about the same time as the surgeon Liotot drew his pistol, the deserter Rutter fired and mortally wounded him.

Although afraid of the possible testimony of the witnesses to these murders, Hiens finally allowed the men to continue their journey toward Quebec upon a promise that the Abbé Cavelier would give him a signed certificate declaring that he, Heins, was innocent in the murder of Robert Cavelier de La Salle. The Abbé quickly complied.

Heins departed early the next day with the French deserters and the horses, leaving the survivors one musket with ammunition and side arms.

Joutel turned to the tiny group "What will we do now? How can we save ourselves?"

The leaderless group now reduced to six persons stood in silence looking first to Joutel and then to the Abbé Jean Cavelier.

"If the natives in the north learn of my brother's death they will not hesitate to kill us. So we must move with great caution. On open plains we can travel by night to avoid Savage attacks." The Abbé had knelt in prayer.

"It will take us a long time to reach Quebec if we travel that way," said Father Anastasius.

"That is how we must try to survive."

The Abbé stood and picked up his pack. He started walking slowly into the forest. As he followed along, Henri Joutel began to fully experience for the first time his private grief at the death of his boyhood friend and to realize the enormity of his loss. With an unexpected pang his thoughts turned to the sad little party of colonists on the southern sea waiting to be rescued by Robert Cavelier de La Salle.

Chapter 39

DELIVERANCE

"What must you tell me, *Cherie*?"

Sitting close to the fire on the beach of Lake Ontario Remy studied Tika's face. Had she decided to leave him and have the baby among her own people? Had the Feast of the Dead been a horrible mistake?

Tika's low voice broke into his thoughts.

"When you want to know of Father Laurent and the massacre, I no talk."

"I remember well. I thought that in time that you would..."

"I decide never tell nobody, even you. But this night in my sleep he come to me in black robes. Before I give you my dream I say what happen." Her voice trembled. Remy moved closer.

"We know Iroquois is coming. All day they in woods around camp. As darkness make them hard to see our warriors go meet them. *Papa* and Moon Cloud with Father Laurent and me stay in my hut. Papa waiting for answer from Iroquois for parley. They say no. But they know is Black Robe here and no want to harm him. Say he can leave if he go now."

"Did Father Laurent understand what was happening?"

"I interpret but he know. He say to us, 'You my people. I will not leave.'"

Tika paused to collect her memories.

"Ready to join battle *Papa* stops," she continued. "We look at each other. Then Father Laurent start to take off robes. He say to me. 'Put this on. You go. You young. Can do more for work of God than Black Robe. Go. I beg you.'"

"I saying no. Moon Cloud and *Papa* beg me with eyes but no speak. Father Laurent start to pull robe over my head. Mama help. We hear attackers coming. Arrows make fire to next hut. Father Laurent pull me across floor and push me into dark. I look back and see Moon Cloud putting blanket around him. When I hear Iroquois warriors come into camp. I run."

She was weeping. Remy waited.

"In Black Robe I run from Iroquois. Now I think they all around camp and let me go. I see nobody. I run fast, then fall, tired. Again I run more before I stop for sleep."

She hesitated. The only sound was the crackling of their fire and the lapping of waves against the beach.

"Next morning," she continued, "I see two Algonquin warriors who hunt in woods. They surprised at blood on my face and torn robe. Help me escape."

"Where did they take you?"

"To their village. I afraid."

"Why?"

"One older warrior with a scar on face. Other young hunter not kind. When we walk to canoe he take my arm and pull me."

"Did they ask you what happened?"

"They not talk much. When we get to canoe the young man push me into center. Old warrior tell him be careful. I not move until we arrive at village."

"What happened then?"

"People come around. Start talking about me. A warrior bring out slave band. I cannot breathe. Their dialect like ours. I understand."

"They wanted to make a slave out of you?"

"Like I am enemy. I look at scar-faced man. His name is Manetera. People call him *nibwaka* (wise one) like in Council of Elders. After a time he speak. He say they see village burning."

"This was near your village?"

"I think far. We see smoke in sky."

Tika then related how the scar-faced Manetera described the burning camp in early morning after the raid. There were still Iroquois warriors about. The two hunters hid in the woods before resuming the hunt as they returned to their canoe by a river.

"Did he not talk about you?"

"People listen. Manetera tell them, 'Her village burned. We must let her go. She may be the only one who live.'"

"So he wanted to help you?"

"*Oui*. Next day he tell two young warriors take me to Quebec."

"That was a long way. Were they friendly?"

"They not talk much but are kind. Make bark shelter each night. Give me corn to eat. But they are strange."

"How so?"

"They act afraid. Looked at black robe and talked so I cannot hear."

"Why was that?"

"Maybe afraid somebody think we steal it from a Black Robe. I do not wear over deerskin after first day but keep for cover to sleep. They want me to burn it."

"Perhaps they were right."

"They start a fire. We burn robes. They cover ashes. Give prayer to Great Spirit."

"You did not mind?"

"Maybe that help me forget. I have trouble to think. They never ask me where I want to go. I not know."

"How far were you from Quebec?"

She paused. "I count eight days. By water at the docks they help me from canoe. I say thank you. They wave and start back."

"Where did you go then?"

"People on the landing. I go to woman and say I need help. She surprised I speak French. She and husband take me to Ursulines in *l'Hôtel Dieu*. Is hospital."

Remy looked for branches to feed the fire and waited for her to continue, dreading where her story might lead.

"Each day in my head I talk with Moon Cloud... want to know... ask myself... Is better I stay with my people, with Papa and Moon Cloud? Am I coward?"

"You chose the wisest thing, *ma Chérie*. What did you tell the nuns?" Remy spoke slowly. She did not seem to want his arm around her just then.

"I not tell them what happen, only that I not know where are my *Papa* and *Maman*. They called me word like orphant."

"An orphan?"

"*Oui*. That is it."

"Why did you not tell them?"

"I no want to talk about, no think about what happen. No want to say I leave my people."

"And your French speaking?"

"I tell them a priest helped me learn French and I do not know where he is. They are kind not to ask."

She was no longer crying but he could feel the rapid heart beats as he moved closer and tried to hold her.

"I am afraid to talk about dream. Father Laurent give me so much. Want me to be nun. Then I run away."

Remy waited in silence.

"In dream tonight Father Laurent speak to me, so real, *Chéri*, just like I see you now. He tell me serve God like you think best. 'Help children know Jesus.'"

Streaks of dawn appeared in the sky as they sat by their campfire.

"He give his life for me." She dug in the fire with a stick. "Is that right? This will not go away from my mind."

Tika chose not to fully share with Remy her distress. How could she do what the priest had requested in her dream without taking vows in a convent? Her thoughts continued to grapple with the question as she sank into sleep.

They awoke late to load their canoe and departed about noon in calm water. While Tika dozed Remy puzzled over whether to be relieved or more concerned. Once rested Tika began to think about how Cord clan survivors could see each other again.

"I wish Katawitha live in Quebec village," she mused, "Think she no will come."

"She might come to Lorette. Talk with Sondakwa about that. All the same we have some happy prospects. Just think, Tika. Our baby will arrive early next spring."

She sat for a time trailing her paddle in the water.

"Maybe he come with first flowers."

Chapter 40
DAYS OF WAITING

Autumn lavished brilliant colors upon a season that always seemed surprisingly short and subject to many moods. When a thick *brume de mer* descended upon Quebec, the village transformed into a fleet of rooftops sailing upon a sea of fog.

At home once again from the Feast of the Dead, Remy worried that he might be jailed for illegal trading and increasingly concerned about hearing no news of La Salle. Tika began to read French stories with Remy and to practice her writing. She took long walks along the river and did what she could to prepare for the baby.

Then cold weather arrived. On wintry days Tika felt restricted by village life. Fresh vegetables did not exist except in a few cold frames. Shop bins were bare. The outdoor market in *la Basse Ville* was closed. She was developing a taste for different kinds of food but preferred other activities to food preparation. Meals for her were of minor importance. She told Remy, "*Chéri*, when you talk about eating I wonder what you love first, food or me?"

Tika drank wine only on special occasions. Once Remy teased her about fur traders using alcohol to get Indian women enthusiastic for love.

"They do that?" Her eyes flashed.

"Some of them."

"And you do?"

"Never."

He thought she believed him but was never certain about her silence.

Tika wondered what the baby was doing inside her and if it liked some of the strange French food she was eating. If she could dive into a river, would the child enjoy the thrill of falling? Her curiosity about all aspects of having a baby often shocked Colette, who was already seven months into her pregnancy. She disapproved of Tika's refusal to consult a *sage-femme*.

Business increased. Since Armand Brassart had influence in *la Compagnie du Nord* their fur trading was legal and had prospered.

Jean did the most skilled cabinetwork. Remy assembled and finished. He also kept the books and ordered materials. Because he was under possible surveillance, official records were in his partner's name.

"You must continue to be careful," Brassart told Remy. "I am becoming more concerned about those arrest orders."

The Governing Council's arrest warrants for Remy and Pierre, along with other unpopular business regulations, had lain dormant since the arrival of Governor Denonville.

"I have been unable to learn more about the governor's intentions," Brassart told Remy and Jean. "That gives me reason to worry."

"However, Brassart thinks the governor is being advised by some merchants not to pursue the traders," Jean told Remy. "Local business would suffer."

Jean would do everything possible to support his friend and partner. He was happy in his marriage with Colette and looking forward to becoming a father.

Tika and Remy were each trying to decide on a name for their child, which he predicted would be a girl. Tika was preparing for a boy.

"We could give her a name both Wendat and French,"Remy said.

"Him."

"*Très Bien*, him. But we want our *bébé* to be proud of her heritage on both sides. "You know what Sondakwa tell me?"

"I'm listening."

"He say few Wendat tribe now at Lorette. Only five members of Cord clan. Our baby have nobody of his mother's blood."

In fact, their child would enter the world without living grandparents. Remy had corresponded once each season with his papa through Father Foignet until last year when no letter arrived from France. The past summer came a letter from a new village priest to say that both Martin Moisson and Father Foignet were no longer living. Remy knew that his sister Monique would never leave her convent.

They had to plan for the arrival of their child. Scheduling for meals, shopping and cleaning was strange to Tika. Her tribe thought in terms of generations. The idea of their child one day having no place to mingle her bones with her people would not have given Remy concern. One evening, while visiting with Jean and Colette, they amused themselves talking of things they would like to have or do.

Jean wished for a bigger residence on the heights of *la Haute Ville*. Colette hoped to take her children to see the French orphanage near Paris where she grew up. Remy pictured a *chaloupe* to sail with Tika and family around the great inland seas.

Tika was reluctant to get into this conversation. They did not urge her. At home Remy observed that she had been silent all evening.

"I no understand this wishing," she said. "It has no sense."

"It's like a pleasant dream about new possessions or adventures that change your life."

"I do not wish for that," she said.

"Not even to have a baby?"

"I have pleasure to be a mama. Our baby come even if we no wish for it."

"So there's nothing you desire?"

"I am happy if you love me for many moons. Will happen or no."

"Think about things that will not happen," he challenged her, "and imagine how you might have what would most please you."

"Would be sad."

"Why?"

"The way I wish to change my life cannot come true. Our baby will not know Moon Cloud or my papa. No Cord clan here to teach him."

"*Chérie*, our child won't know my ancestors either."

"No is the same."

"Why?"

"The homeland of your *Papa* and *Maman* is far. Nobody try to take it away."

"We'll both make our child proud of her people and your nation. The Sieur de La Salle said your Canada is vaster in territory and richer than all of France."

"Even before the words of Sondakwa I know I never have a country. More of us will disappear. From France will keep coming your people, always with better fire sticks."

"You and Sondakwa are too gloomy," he told her. "The great forests are truly home to your kinfolk. All of you can teach us about nature. Our child will live in a land with a rich heritage."

"No. For him will be new land of square houses. No place for Sacred Circle."

She was right. The French did make better weapons. And to survive the massacre of her entire family and Black Robe friend. What could Remy say about such a loss?

Word had been spreading around that the Sieur de La Salle's expedition was not successful. More than two years had passed since he left La Rochelle with four ships.

They knew the vessel that carried him across the Atlantic, *le Joly*, had returned to France. There were rumors that he had failed to locate the mouth of the Mississippi and landed far to the west. Could that be true?

Although he had never been a personal friend, the explorer was a hero who had changed Remy's life. After all he would never have encountered Tika. Despite a resentment of La Salle's haughty manner, Remy admired his determination and his indomitable courage. Nor would he ever forget that magic moment of discovery, that endless *Mer de Mexique*

Remy had told Tika of his dispute with La Salle over the treatment of the Indian women captives. Thinking of Moon Cloud Remy had been furious and confronted his leader who had promptly deprived him of his honored assignment as a scribe.

Many an evening had been passed recounting stories of the great expedition. And Brassart enjoyed listening, along with Tika, to Remy's account of his historic journey.

One night Brassart told them that he had encountered recently a fascinating gentleman who was visiting in Quebec.

"He is the Baron de Lahontan who is writing a book about French Canada and is reported to have said scandalous things about French policy in this country. He will want to know all about La Salle's explorations. That interests me a great deal."

"Maybe you could invite the Baron to our house. He could then write about that," Tika said. "I like to hear these stories of the great river, especially about tribe of Taensas."

She had taken great interest in Remy's description of that village. Their lake would be a splendid place to swim and the houses would probably have earthen floors.

He told her that both the Sieur de La Salle and Tonty had mentioned the possibility of a parcel of land for him along the great river. He asked if she would be willing to live there in a French settlement.

Tika's face brightened and she nodded. "If they invite us, living with Taensas more interesting, close to Mother Earth and a place to swim with our child. Would have stories of ancestors."

"*Chérie*, we can keep the legends of your people." Remy assured her. "Our child will be excited to hear the story of the Great Turtle. And he can tell it when he is an old man." Finally they talked about the fate of Father Laurent. She owed him a debt of gratitude. And for her people this obligation was sacred. He had opened her life to the joy of the written word. She liked the magic in his stories of Jesus. Could she make his spirit happy by teaching native children?

"That no would be easy in convent school," she said.

"Why?" Remy asked.

"Nuns good people and kind to me. But they take children away from Mother Earth. They not know the excitement of drumming and dancing around a fire."

Remy smiled as he pictured the gentle ladies in black robes stamping around to drum beats.

"How would you teach Indian boys and girls?"

"I would teach some French. They could learn letters to write some words in their own language. Sister Marie de Saint Joseph started a dictionary of Wendat. Is never used."

"You are working on a written list of Wendat words?"

"I owe my people. Brassart help. I like more than prepare food."

Remy suggested an excursion to the Ile d'Orléans where they camped and hiked for two days. She wanted to walk all around the island but Remy worried that it might be too fatiguing.

"I miss five times of the moon," counting with her fingers. "I swim but you not like."

"Tika, you cannot be serious. You would not take our child into ice water would you?"

She laughed. "He would be warm inside me. We have babies in the woods when we scrape hides."

They had celebrated the Feast of the Dead and were anticipating the birth of their child. But Remy's joy was now tempered by a sense of foreboding about the Sieur de La Salle and his colony.

Remy wrote in his journal:

June 1685
Two great men have come into my life: Tonty, the man with an iron hand, as a friend, and the Sieur de La Salle, the man with an iron will.

Chapter 41

THE BARON DE LAHONTAN

Remy was worried.

"Tika, what is it you don't like about our village?"

"Houses square. Everything square."

"Why is that bad? We build our homes that way to make them stronger."

"You remember story of Mokanoa?"

"A little."

Mokanoa and Onendo teach us world is Sacred Circle of Life. Birds build nest in circle, foxes dig round dens in earth. Look at trunks of trees and the moon. Show me square flowers."

Then too Tika could think only how their new wood floor separated them from Mother Earth but remained silent. She did find consolation in sharing Remy's friendship with Brassart to whom both of them turned for his wise counsel.

From the library of *la Compagnie du Nord* Brassart would bring them books. He was searching for Horace's *Ars Poetica* to replace the one Remy lost in Lake Huron. At the moment Tika and Remy were reading *Garguantua* by François Rabelais.

Tika admired *l'abbaye de Thélème* where the young men and women residents dressed in lively colors, lived and studied together, and were free to think for themselves.

"He say follow own pleasure, not prayer bells and rules. Father Laurent tell me follow Bible for good life. Was Rabelais really priest like Black Robe? How can be? He make me laugh."

"He was a Benedictine brother who later studied medicine but the church feared his writings."

"He would be happy Wendat."

She was excited by reading words written many moons ago.

"Is like speaking with bones of ancestors."

"What an imaginative way of thinking," Brassart told Remy. "She must meet the Sieur de La Salle when he returns. She will probably like him and perhaps charm him. He's always eager to learn about native customs and to master local dialects."

Remy brightened, "*Bonne idée*. Of course he's never seen her."

Nonetheless, Tika did have an opportunity to speak with another nobleman, the Baron de Lahontan, whom Brassart had mentioned. She and Remy urged Brassart to invite him to their home.

The Baron de Lahontan was writing a book about his travels in Canada and was eager to meet the man who had journeyed south with La Salle.

Young and handsome, the nobleman arrived one evening carrying a bottle of vintage Burgundy. When he was introduced to Tika the Baron made a deep bow and kissed her hand, holding it for a moment. So obviously startled was she by this unexpected greeting that he laughed.

"I am sorry, Madame, if I've offended you."

"Not offended. I feared you bite me."

"Madame, we don't have the habit of attacking our hostess, *surtout une femme aussi séduisante*." The Baron turned to Remy. "And you, monsieur, accompanied the Sieur de La Salle to the mouth of the great river? You were present at the moment of discovery?"

"That was my good fortune."

"Please tell me the whole story. You traveled all of the way to *la Mer de Mexique* by water?"

"It seemed an impossible mission, monsieur, but without the determination of our leader and the courage of our *compagnons* we would never have succeeded. This started in bitter winter weather. We were obliged to build solid sledges to make our way across frozen waterways. We encountered hostile natives and had several portages. From the river of the Illinois we made the entire journey by canoe."

"Streams were navigable all the way?"

"Yes, in sturdy Algonquin canoes. Then too the Sieur de La Salle had explored some of this country before and he knew it would not take big sailing ships."

"There were native tribes along the way? How did you speak with them?"

"La Salle is clever with language and diplomacy. He speaks local dialects and his manner of dealing with people gains him respect. Then too he has no fear."

Recounting his trip to the mouth of the Mississippi Remy could not avoid reflecting on some of La Salle's resentment of the Jesuits' opposition to his plans.

"We shall speak more about the Jesuits," said the Baron, "but first I must ask Madame Moisson..."

"I am called Tika."

"Tika, my greeting startled you. Tell me, Madame. May I apologize?"

"What mean apologize?"

"A way of saying I would regret making you angry or unhappy."

"No, is all right." She paused to think. "You study native ways. Maybe I help."

The Baron stared at her in amazement. "You speak French very well."

"*Oui.* You speak my language?"

Baron de Lahontan turned his complete attention to Tika.

"Where did you learn to speak our language with such ease? Is there a school for natives that I know nothing about? I can speak some native dialect, Tika. *Tani tichinika*?""

"*Nindijnikatan Tikanaka*," she answered. "So you speak Algonquin. I understand a little. I am Wendat. I practice with Father Laurent and at Ursuline Convent. Sounds not easy but most difficult is writing."

"Forgive my curiosity," the Baron replied, "but I must learn more about you."

Tika served one of Gabon's apple tarts. Over glasses of wine they began to learn about each other.

"I understand you were a volunteer officer in the Marine." Brassart, who had just arrived, joined the conversation. " May I ask why you left the service so soon?"

"The short answer, Monsieur Brassart, is that I came to believe that certain policies of our French government for controlling the natives are stupid and dangerous. But I will not burden you with that."

"I want to hear more." Tika broke in almost before he finished.

"*Bien, madame.* I fought in three campaigns against the Iroquois. In the last one we were under the command of Monsieur de Champigni."

"The *Intendant* of Canada." Brassart added.

"Yes, serving with *le Gouverneur Denonville*," the Baron replied. "With about three hundred French troops and native allies we surprised the Iroquois villages of Kent and Ganeoussé near Fort Frontenac. This is not a pleasant after-dinner conversation." The Baron paused and looked at Tika. "I fear you might find this displeasing."

"I wish to know. Tell me what happen."

"*Bien.* We attacked early in the evening and captured all of the young men. Before their eyes most of the women and elder males were massacred."

"Is possible?" Tika drew back her chair.

"Sadly yes, Madame." The Baron looked at Tika. She motioned him to continue. "We took our prisoners to the nearest fort. There we bound them with cords to stakes driven into the ground. They were stretched out in such a way that it was not possible for them to escape."

"How long were they kept like that?" Brassart inquired.

"About one week. An Iroquois hunter who once supplied us with venison was among the prisoners. I recognized him because we had talked together in Algonquin when he provided prime morsels of game. I promised to bring him water and food. He wanted no treatment better than his comrades. I will never forget the profound sadness and the look in his eyes when he related the details of seeing his family killed before his eyes. I could hear him weeping as I left."

"What you do?" Tika asked.

"Twice a day for five days I brought him food and water. I slipped him a letter stating he had helped supply us and requested that he be accorded the best treatment possible. On the sixth day as I approached him Huron allies from Quebec spied me. They were so angered that they went to get their muskets and threatened to shoot me. They told my superiors they would leave if I were not punished for helping the enemy."

"What happened then?" Remy asked.

"Monsieur de Champigni placed me under arrest in my tent. The Hurons kept guard to see that I had no food or water for two days until the Iroquois were led away to work in French galleys. At the insistence of our Huron allies Champigni punished me but did not press formal charges. However, he was not at all pleased. I was so distressed with our abuse of the natives and disenchanted with the whole military operation that I took a leave of absence."

"Any difficulty with getting permission?" Brassart asked.

"No, I was a volunteer officer and free to leave. In fact I later came back into the service on my own terms as a scout and explorer."

"What did you do in that service?" Remy replenished the Baron's wine.

"I set out to seriously study native customs and language, which I have only begun to do. For almost two years I traveled west past the great inland seas and to the north visiting different tribes."

Brassart intervened. "I would be interested in your reflections on that."

"*Bien*, but I have done much talking. Now I must learn something about you, Madame." The Baron looked at Tika. "Tell me about your people. Can you arrange for me to meet with them?"

"That no is possible." She choked back tears. "One night Iroquois attack our camp. They kill all but five of us."

"Madame, I'm so sorry." The Baron reached out to touch her shoulder. "I'm constantly shocked how we can be so cruel to one another. Please accept my sympathy."

They sat in silence while Tika regained her composure.

"Near here is small village of Wendats at Lorette. Maybe can meet my friend Sondakwa. Is wise Shaman. My own Cord clan has four survivors. And me."

"With your husband's permission I would be pleased to go with you to visit your friend's village."

Remy nodded his assent.

"Let us arrange this soon. You were asking me, Tika, something before we talked about your Cord clan."

"Yes. Do you think of us as like wild animal? Not real people?"

"Of course not, but human beings are different from one another. Your people can learn from us about making tools, raising crops."

"So we should know to live like you? Is better?"

"Not at all. We have much to learn from the way you live. You are kinder and gentle with your children. In a native village I am always pleased to hear shouts and laughter as the young ones play. Were you free, Tika, to do what you wished as a child?"

"*Oui.* I liked to go far into woods when Moon Cloud did not know."

"In France wealthy parents dress their children as little adults and teach them good manners. Peasants on the other hand are forced to place their young to work in the fields at an early age. Their only education is in the Church. I have observed that you are much freer to make choices in your lives."

"What that mean?"

"You can marry and change mates as you desire. In France, ancestral noble family heads decide whom one will marry. You can honor your Great Spirits and nature gods in many ways. There is no Bible to teach you all to worship only one God."

It was past midnight and they had long since finished the wine.

"The hour is late," the Baron said. "This has been a charming evening. I must ask you, Tika, if you have more questions before I leave."

"Most important what you think about my people?"

"I find inspiring your friendship with nature, believing yourselves as part of the circle of life you described. If I were a native I would have a new freedom."

"Freedom for what?" Brassart asked.

"From Cardinals and Kings. In France the church and the government try to control how we think and act." The Baron paused. "I must see you again, Monsieur and Madame Moisson. We have much to discuss. I wish to know of the tribes along the great river to the south and I am also eager to make the acquaintance of your Sieur de La Salle."

"You know we have been without news of his colony for two years. We fear for its safety."

"I must tell you that I recently met some countrymen from his southern French settlement," said the Baron.

At this astonishing information Brassart sat upright.

"Where was that, pray tell?"

"A few months ago when I was back on military duty I relieved a certain Lieutenant Henri de Tonty for a time as commander of Fort

Saint-Joseph. This is located at the mouth of the Saint Clair River near Lake Huron."

"We didn't know you had seen Tonty." Brassart looked at Tika and Remy. "We have been expecting him in Quebec. Was he going south to search for La Salle?"

"He told me only that he was going into the country of the Ilinois," the Baron replied. "Then about three weeks ago, just before I left Fort Saint-Joseph, there were some tired and ragged men from the Louisiana colony who wandered into our camp."

"Who were they?" Remy asked.

"Let me think. There was Abbé Cavelier, his nephew Colin Cavelier, *Récollet* Father Anastasius Douay, a man whom they called Sieur Joutel and several others all headed toward Montreal. They said they were from the Sieur de La Salle's colony carrying dispatches from him for the governor in Quebec and for the King."

"What about La Salle?" Remy asked.

"They were there only two days and did not seem eager to give information. I spent little time with them and was at once suspicious. They hardly looked like emissaries from a thriving colony."

"I cannot understand why we have had no news of this. They should have reached Quebec by now." Brassart's face betrayed his dismay.

"I myself was puzzled," Lahontan replied. "If the Sieur de La Salle had important dispatches for the King why would he not bring them himself?"

Brassart shook his head. "I can't understand why we have not been contacted."

"I'm pleased that you are willing to help me learn more about this country. And I pray there is nothing amiss with your friend," the Baron said as he departed.

When he took up her hand, Tika accepted the gesture graciously.

"How could the Baron take part in a massacre at Ganeoussé, like at my village? Such a polite man."

"He was young and new in the country at that time. At least he learned from such an experience," Brassart told Tika.

"But what about his seeing La Salle's men?" Remy asked.

Far into the night they discussed this surprising news. Remy slept late so he worked longer hours at the shop. He had scarcely arrived home the next evening when an exhausted Tonty appeared at their door. Remy hastened to embrace him and helped him into a chair. "Are you ill?"

"No, Remy. I have come a great distance today and I just need to rest and collect my thoughts."

Walking in from the kitchen Tika stopped and stared at the stranger.

"Tika this is my dear friend the Sieur de Tonty."

Tonty pushed himself to his feet and pressed her hand. *"Enchanté, madame.* I have been wanting to know you, Tika."

She offered him an earthen cup of fresh water and he emptied it as they settled down around the table. It was several moments before he was ready to speak.

"Remy and Tika, let me tell you my story. I gathered together a small group of loyal comrades to search for our lost leader. We made our way back to the mouth of the Mississippi and found no trace of the Sieur de La Salle and his colony."

"The Baron de Lahontan said he saw you recently. You were on your way then?"

"No, I was going back to Fort Saint Louis when he saw me. Our search for the colony was almost a year ago."

"You saw no tribes who knew about his colony?" Remy asked.

"No, but just now I learned that the Sieur Henri Joutel will be in Quebec tomorrow. He had sent a message to inform the governor that the Sieur de La Salle is dead. He was murdered by his own men, by fellow Frenchmen."

Chapter 42

THE RECKONING

Under a sky covered with rain clouds Tonty set a brisk pace for his companion as they descended *rue de la Montagne*. They were en route to a meeting with Henri Joutel in *la Basse Ville*.

"You know, Remy, Sieur Joutel lied to me when I talked with him in Illinois country. I just cannot believe it. I arrived yesterday too late to see him. Now I want to hear his explanation of that story he invented."

Remy had never seen Tonty so angry.

"Where in Illinois country?"

"Fort Saint Louis at Starved Rock on the Illinois River. They were returning from Sieur de La Salle's southern seacoast colony that they told me was also called Fort Saint Louis. Before leaving they informed me that La Salle and his party were on the way. We kept watching for them to appear on the horizon."

"What a horrible deception. Why would he have done such a thing?"

Before Tonty could reply they had reached the entrance to *la Compagnie du Nord*. Brassart and his guest were waiting. With a cool nod Tonty acknowledged the presence of Henri Joutel. Brassart then presented Remy to the newcomer.

Haggard and clad in ill-fitting buckskin, Henri Joutel still displayed the bearing of a soldier. He had arrived at Montreal a few days earlier in remnants of clothing worn all the way from the colony on the *Golfe du Mexique*. At Brassart's invitation the men sat down and waited for Joutel to shuffle through his papers.

"I have only scattered notes and will speak from memory," he began. "But first I must offer my apologies to you, Sieur de Tonty. When we met at Fort Lewis on our return we willfully deceived you. We would have you believe that the Sieur de La Salle was still alive. Frankly, we were concerned with our own survival. So great is their respect for our leader we feared that the natives would kill us on the spot if they learned of his death. Being a stranger to this country and new to the wilderness I myself was filled with terror. I dared not forswear the story of my companions."

"I see." Tonty's face showed no expression.

"I must tell you first of all," Sieur Joutel continued, "that Robert de La Salle and I were both born at Rouen and were close friends. He was a classmate of exceptional intelligence. His family expected him to succeed his father, who had become wealthy by importing textiles."

"And just how did you first learn of his proposed colony in New France?"

"It was quite by chance, monsieur Tonty. Having recently completed sixteen years of military service I encountered my old friend in the streets of Rouen. He was visiting his family and recruiting colonists before sailing to the Louisiana territory. He persuaded me to join his expedition."

Brassart leaned forward. "The Sieur de La Salle was a most private person. I am curious to know what he was like as a boy."

Joutel took a moment to reply. *"Bien. C'était un garçon impatient, franc, plein d'amour-propre.* Indeed this self-pride got him into trouble at times even with his teachers. Then too, as a boy he was already quite handsome. At school I remember that he dressed with elegance."

Joutel hastened to remind them that it was from Rouen that the Norsemen first departed across the Atlantic. Centuries later a brilliant Jesuit series of public reports, *Les Relations de la Nouvelle France,* were published continuously after the 1630s describing the exploits of the early priests in the New World. No doubt Robert's imagination was inflamed by reading these accounts. And the local Jesuit College was organized to train missionaries who would evangelize Savages in the New World.

Joutel was certain that La Salle shared that longing for travel and adventure.

"Why did the Sieur de La Salle not continue as a Jesuit?" Remy asked.

"Well, after ordination and teaching in the Jesuit *Collège royal de La Flèche,* at age twenty-four he was still considered too young to be assigned overseas. When his superiors refused him a mission in Canada La Salle promptly quit the Order. For that they have never forgiven him."

"Were you in contact with Robert de La Salle most of those intervening years and had he changed much from the friend you knew as a schoolboy?"

"I had seen him only on two occasions in all that time, monsieur Brassart. At La Rochelle I found him to be quite different from the young man I had known. He was of course still brilliant but he seemed obsessed with thoughts of all that his enemies had done to thwart his plans."

Then Brassart invited Henri Joutel to recount the complete story of Robert Cavelier de La Salle and his companions. Joutel, pausing frequently to refresh his memory, gave his account of leaving Fort Saint Louis along the great southern sea in Louisiana Territory. He related how some of the men became progressively more discontented and that a certain Sieur Duhaut had actually challenged his leader's authority.

Joutel was breathing heavily and moving around on his seat. Brassart took notice of his friend's discomfort.

"Let us bring Sieur Joutel a cup of tea and allow him a few moments alone."

Tonty and Remy followed Brassart to his bureau near the building's entrance. They sipped tea while studying the rude sketches of the Louisiana territory attempting to trace Joutel's route.

When they returned the visitor appeared composed and continued his story:

"The Sieur de La Salle was in desperate haste to reach Quebec and seek reinforcement for his pitiful colony of women, children and a few men faithfully waiting back at Fort Saint Louis on the Sea of Mexico. That is why he kept such a grueling pace." We had shared such hardships that I myself had a heavy heart in so deserting the colony."

When Joutel, relying upon the eyewitness report of Father Anastasius Douay, finally told of the fatal shot from the bushes striking La Salle in the head, Tonty cried out, "Oh no!"

There was a silence while Tonty tried to calm his nerves.

Joutel concluded with the tale of their promise to exonerate Heins in exchange for their freedom.

"I will not burden you with the story of our return which I have no pleasure in recalling."

"All of you are here now in Quebec?" Brassart asked.

"Yes. Father Anastasius, still exhausted, is resting at the house of the *Récollects.* I invited him to come with me today but he felt quite unable to hear again the events he witnessed. He was terribly affected. It was only in honor of our fallen leader he had the courage to push on."

"You are there with him?"

"Yes, Monsieur Brassart, and I share his anguish about what has happened. The people we left behind in the little colony of Fort St. Louis haunt my dreams. It is possible that they're still alive. We must find a way to reach them."

"That will not be easy." Tonty rose to press his hand. "Sieur Joutel, we have both lost a precious friend. I believe you have given us an honest account of the Sieur de La Salle's passing and I thank you."

"This lightens my heart, Sieur Tonty. I feel fortunate to have had the chance to relate this story to you in person."

Tonty and Remy walked out into the failing light. A drizzling rain was falling on streets darkening under a dull sky. Tonty declined Remy's invitation to dine with them, saying he would like to be alone for a while.

"Will you come along with me to my canoe?"

Remy nodded, wondering what his friend might have to say about Joutel's story. But Tonty was silent as they descended to the pier.

After putting his craft into the water he embraced Remy. Then he maneuvered the boat alongside.

"When will we see you again?"

"Next year perhaps."

Remy steadied the canoe as Tonty positioned himself. His parting words were, "Remy, once at Michilimackinac you asked me if I had ever loved a woman and we talked of your future. I see now that you can be happy with your decision. Bid farewell to my dear Tika."

He pushed off against the current. Turning away, Remy hurried up the street to his house. Tika had just returned from a walk on the heights.

"Will Monsieur Tonty have dinner with us?"

"He prefers to get back to his forest. Losing his best friend is a terrible shock, just as their dream seemed to be coming true."

"Will he look for the spirit of his friend in the woodlands as Dehndek chases his Mahohrah through the sky?"

"I think he will follow the dream they shared. Some day perhaps the story of Tonty and La Salle will also be told to children by parents who will by then know how it ended."

"How will it end?"

"On earth, not in the sky like Dehndek and Mahohrah. La Salle and Tonty wanted to open up the fur trade with tribes along the great river."

"Great Spirit maybe have other purpose for Mother Earth. What do you think?"

Remy paused. "I don't know. Tonty has been one of my truest friends. He certainly wants to help your people. I believe now that we should stop the fur trade and take no more of your people's land."

Tika prepared their meal in silence. While they were eating Remy recounted Henri Joutel's story of Robert Cavelier de La Salle and his ill-fated colony.

In her bed that night, reflecting upon this tale of death, Tika became aware of the life stirring within her. Would she and her child be facing an eternal search among all these strange houses for wild places to be with the spirits of their ancestors? Will Remy understand?

Giving back to the Sacred Circle of Life but one tiny baby seemed a small exchange for Little Blossom, her brother Naromaka, her Papa and Moon Cloud, Little Eagle and for an entire village. Now if she betrayed the spirit of Father Laurent could her bones go one day into the ancestral pit without shame at the Feast of the Dead? Sleep would not come to her.

Taking care not to awaken Remy she slipped from her covers and out into the night. A west wind blew wet against her face as she climbed the hill, rejoicing in the touch of her bare feet on Mother Earth. Patches of sky began to appear through the clouds.

On the plains above the *Château Saint Louis* she mounted a projection of rock. Below her the sleeping village was a mass of indistinct shapes. The Saint Lawrence was a silver serpent making its way across the land toward the sea. Tika sat there deep in thought.

Why, she wondered, did a white man's God decide to make the world in his work- shop. Was his *atelier* outside the world? Did he make the whitefaces first? Then why did he make Tika's people, so different from Himself? And why were her people not told sooner about God's magic? Father Laurent had said that all this happened more moons ago than anyone could count.

Through morning twilight her mother came into Tika's thoughts. Moon Cloud was leading a trapped doe from their hunting camp back to freedom in the forest.

With caution Tika descended from her rocky perch and started home to prepare breakfast for Remy who would be hungry. She also needed to feed the child she carried within. And how could she nourish his spirit? She knew now that the whitefaces would always be a part of his world.

The wet breeze and the smell of rain awakened childhood memories of hunting camp. Little Eagle was teasing her by holding her arms so she couldn't move out of the rain. She broke away in rage crying as she ran past Onendo.

"Why are you crying?" The medicine man held out his arms to block her way.

"I'm not crying." She tried to wipe away her tears as she looked him in the eye.

He returned her gaze in silence.

"Well, I *was* crying. Little Eagle was teasing me."

"Do not be ashamed. Sometimes it's good to cry." He gently held her at arm's length. "Mother Earth cries to clear the air and feed the forest. Tears can freshen the spirit and make it grow. Without tears there can be no rainbows."

Walking down the trail Tika silently vowed to help her child follow the wisdom of his ancestors.

Epilogue

"*Chérie*, I wish you would not take Onowa out so far away into the wild."

"But the forest is the home of my people. I want that our son no have fear of woods and animals."

Tika dropped her pack. Onowa grabbed his father's leg demanding a hug.

"Onowa had such joy to explore we stay long time." Tika was glowing. "You will do ceremony?"

"Of course and we need you to work with us."

"I will help."

After La Salle's death Brassart had tried twice to arrange with the Governing Council a memorial for the great explorer. Each time the Jesuits opposed such a celebration.

Disappointed, Brassart and Remy supported by the *Récollets*, decided that a private ceremony was better than none. At that moment Tika had slipped away to her *asile de forêt* where she would go with Onowa from time to time. Her son, lacking living grandparents, must learn that he is related to all things born of Mother Earth. Moon Cloud's spirit would be waiting there.

"In woodland Onowa already talk to wild animals. When fawn come near he not move."

"The ceremony and dinner will be in two days. You must speak with Colette. She has many ideas for a feast. She is excited about it."

"I wonder what I do before I must think so much about eating." Tika viewed the lightly laden shelves.

"Do you worry about food?"

"Is a big part of your life. Not for me." She paused. "Perhaps I should be nun after all. Meals at Convent not important or tasty. Always same."

"Don't complain. You would be eating only dried corn and dog if I had not found you."

"You find me? Not how I remember. I walk along the river. See white-faced man in water with clothes on."

"*Vilaine.* You tricked me. I have not forgotten."

"Ha. You are angry." She was beginning to cheer up.

"Anyway we must now think about the memorial service."

Hearing a noise near the fireplace Tika called out in Wendat, "Robert Onowa, keep away from the fire."

"*Chérie*, Onowa is three. We should be teaching him French."

"I want him to know his own language."

"My language is also his. And you speak it quite well."

"For me Wendat is more easy. Later he can learn French."

"To make his way in the world he will need writing," Remy told her. "That is not possible in Wendat."

"You always get best words in conversation like this."

"We are not in competition, *Cherie.*"

"May be."

Remy looked at her in surprise. When troubled she kept quiet. Most of the time she did not seem angry, but he had no way of knowing.

He felt a special kinship with his son, having assisted in bringing him into the world. The Wendat woman who was to help Tika did not appear. Remy was comforted throughout the birth by Tika, who calmly told him what to do.

"You think Onowa finds his parents different because of language and skin color?"

She remained silent while unloading their packs. Remy had forgotten what he asked when she resumed the conversation.

"I do not know. Other people act like we are different. In shops clerk serve me last when I am there first."

"*Défends-toi.* Tell them about it. I would do that."

"You would have no need. Why must I defend myself in the land of my ancestors?"

Their eyes met. He searched into the depths of her silences, a world he could never know.

He was still pondering when a sharp knocking was heard at the door. There stood Pierre Chandavoine. It was a complete surprise.

"Mind if I join you? The word came from far upriver. Angus told me about your party."

"Magnificent." Remy felt a surge of joy at seeing his old friend.

"And Tonty? How did he receive the news of his friend's death?"

"You will see for yourself his suffering. He arrived *en ville* yesterday. I know he will be glad to see you."

On that bright May afternoon of the ceremony Remy accompanied Pierre toward *la Haute Ville*. He reminded his friend that they were no longer in danger of arrest for illegal trading in furs.

"*Zut alors*, I was beginning to enjoy the honor of being an outlaw. Still I'm curious. How did that happen?"

"*Alors* some time after he took office Governor Denonville unexpectedly cancelled the arrest orders. Brassart suspects that he just wishes to gain popularity."

"That message never reached us upriver but I have no objections." Pierre chuckled as they reached *La Haute Ville*.

At the small *Récollet* Chapel they joined Henri de Tonty and a host of others who had known René-Robert Cavalier de La Salle. Missing were the charming Baron de Lahontan, who had returned to Europe, and Father Hennepin. This courageous priest was now back in Belgium after his perilous rescue from Sioux captivity on the upper Mississippi.

Father Mercier in gray robe and sandals opened the memorial ceremony with a prayer. Then he turned and addressed the gathering: "There will come a day when René-Robert Cavelier de La Salle will be recognized as the greatest explorer in the history of our nation. It is our good fortune to have with us a man who knew most intimately the person we honor today, Sieur Henri de Tonty."

Tonty walked to the front of the chapel. His drawn face made a thick brush of moustache look even darker.

"First, I wish to thank Father Mercier for his eulogy, an eloquent tribute to our revered friend. The Sieur de La Salle has been like a father to me. I will devote the rest of my life in carrying out his plans as I imagine he would wish. Were they impossible dreams? I think not. Through many perilous adventures I came to admire and to care for him. I loved him more deeply than anybody I have ever known. And I will mourn his loss and the terrible circumstances of his death as long as I live."

After the service Remy stopped to talk with the apothecary Marceau, the baker Gabon and others at the chapel. Tika, who had brought Robert Onowa, hurried back to the house accompanied by Pierre. Tika and Pierre had taken an instant liking of each other. Pierre had swept Onowa up into his arms and the child laughed in delight.

Remy and Tonty returned to find the table arranged with blue and purple irises and gleaming yellow buttercups along with sprigs of fragrant spruce that Tika and Onowa had gathered. Brassart had provided a keg of fine Spanish wine from the cellars of the trading company.

They all sat down to revel in a feast of leek soup, *tête de veau*, a specialty of Colette, and a dessert of cornmeal pudding with pine nuts and maple sugar.

They raised their glasses to René-Robert Cavelier, Sieur de La Salle, the greatest of all explorers (*le plus grand explorateur qui fût*). Did those who knew him feel his presence in that small gathering?

Next they honored Moon Cloud and Chief Owassoni, Tika's Cord clan, and Henri de Tonty.

Tonty raised his glass. "To Colette and Tika, mothers of *la Nouvelle France.*"

To everyone's surprise Tika rose to her feet. "We must not forget my friend and teacher, Father Maurice Laurent, someone most special to me who is not here tonight." She stared into the distance. "I hope that you hear my words, dear Father. May God, your Great Spirit, bless your bones together forever in Mother Earth with those of my people."

As the dinner progressed, old friends and new fell into relaxed conversation. Colette and Jean, having left petit Jean Paul in the care of Madame Joncheaux, were enjoying a rare leisure. Colette had been quite angry at Remy when he persuaded Jean that they should stop their fur trading. This night, however, she seemed proud of her role in such a grand occasion.

Tika took her still lively son around to embrace each guest before she placed him into his small bed. She had seated Tonty at the head of the table and complimented him for his skill with Wendat dialect.

"My dear Tika, I take pleasure in speaking your language." He gripped her hand for a long moment.

There were stories about building the *Griffin*, the storm on the inland sea and then Tika in her forthright way asked Pierre why he did not admire La Salle.

Pierre looked surprised. "That is not true. I just do not believe in heroes. The Sieur de La Salle was promoting his own good as well as that of France. There's nothing wrong with that. We each look out for ourselves as we contribute to *La Nouvelle France*, but in a less imperious way."

Tonty frowned.

"But I salute a man of his age," Pierre hastened to add, "a nobleman at that who became a better woodsman than I will ever be. The great explorer learned Indian dialects and the natives respected him. They were also impressed by his large brimmed hat and flowing red robe."

Late into the night they talked, each recalling perils of their journey into the New World and rare happy moments with the Sieur de La Salle as he sought the mouth of the great Mississippi.

As they left the table Tika, who in Wendat was having one of her teasing conversations with Brassart, said so all could hear, "Remy told me, Monsieur Brassart, something that you said about Indian women a long time ago."

He looked uncomfortable.

"You told him," she continued, "that Indian women become fat squaws after they have babies so men do not think they are worth much wampum."

Brassart laughed. "I probably said that."

"You see I am not fat." Tika put her hand on his." But perhaps you are right. Remy has given me no wampum for many moons."

After their last guests had departed Remy and Tika piled dishes by the kitchen fireplace before climbing into bed, happy about the time with old friends honoring people who had been important in their lives.

Stirring restlessly in his *berceau de bois* Onowa started to cry.

Tika struggled from her covers to pick him up and carry him into the next room. Remy stirred the coals of the fire and lit a lamp at the table. Wide-awake now with eyes glowing in lamplight Onowa asked a question in Wendat.

"What did he say?" his father asked.

"He asked who is the man we talk about today?"

Remy looked at his son. "When he is old enough to understand I will tell Onowa how I went to the southern sea with Robert Cavelier de La Salle and Henri de Tonty, without maps and with enemies along the way, never hesitating to follow the great river through the wilderness until we reached the sea of Mexico. He will read about it in my journal."

"My precious little warrior." As she held Onowa tight Tika crooned, "I love you. (*YU, NOWNOI,E*). Your great river of life is un-explored wilderness. No clan or tribal elders to map your way. Someday I write for you the Wendat story to make you understand the magic of words. Little pictures can help you keep free spirit of your mother's people. Maybe like our tribesman Deganawidah you will teach them about peace."

Notes on *The Circle Broken*

Some of the earliest Europeans to live amongst Native Americans, French Jesuit Missionaries sent reports to their superiors in the Vatican at Rome. Collected by Reuban Gold Thwaites, American historian in Madison, Wisconsin, these accounts were published (1896-1901) in seventy-three volumes. They are a rich source of information about their work that the priests called the "harvesting of souls" and about their daily life as missionaries in the 17ᵗʰ century. It is available in French or English on the Internet ([http://puf-fin.creighton.edu/jesuit/relations/](http://puffin.creighton.edu/jesuit/relations/)) and in many libraries.

Certain time sequences in my story have been altered for purposes of the plot. However the expedition led by Robert Cavelier de La Salle to the mouth of the Mississippi, the dates of his momentous discovery, and his subsequent assassination by his own men are historically verifiable.

The writings of Louis-Armand de Lom d'Arc, (the Baron de Lahontan) were republished in a two-volume work recounting his experiences in *La Nouvelle France* (1683-1693). They include descriptions of the natives along with lists of words (as he heard them) from tribal dialects. (*La Hontan Oeuvres Completes, Vols. 1 & II, Les Presses de l'Université de Montréal (Québec)*, 1990. The Baron could well have been in Québec Village at the time of his fictional meeting with Remy described in Chapter 41. Written accounts of 17ᵗʰ century French Canada at this time include those of Father Hennepin, Henri Joutel, le Père Charlevoix and others. Studies of La Salle's activities in Canada can be found in the writings of historians including: Francis Parkman (American), Benjamin Sulte (Canadian) and André Bonne (French). An excellent account of Wendat culture can be found in the writing of Georges E. Sioui. (Canadian).

A virtual museum (*Musée virtuel de la Nouvelle France*) of the 17th century with relevant maps, documents and writings can also be found on the Internet at http://www.civilisations.ca)

René-Robert Cavalier de La Salle, his nephew Morganet, Louis de Buade (Count Frontenac), Governor of New France in Canada, his successors, le Febvre de La Barre, and the Marquis de Denonville were real living players in the history of Quebec along with Lieutenant Henri de Tonti, Father Hennepin of the Franciscan Order who first came to Canada on the same ship with La Salle, Bishop (François Montmorency) Laval, his successor Bishop Saint-Vallier, Jacques Cartier, Henri Joutel and several others, including the men named in La Salle's murder.

Martyred Jesuit Fathers Brébeuf and Lalement actually died in the manner described [by historic documents] in this novel. Fathers Laurent, Nicholas and Buguet are fictional characters.

Although many of the words, descriptions and expressions of opinion in this story can be found in the original manuscripts and established reports of these historic characters, all conversations and La Salle's prayer on the Griffin are constructed from the imagination of the author.

About the Author

Richard Johnston, Ed.D.,Teachers College, Columbia University, is Professor Emeritus of History and Education, University of Illinois, Springfield, and author of a novel, *The Big Lie* (AuthorHouse, 2007). Richard has been fascinated by Native American life ever since his family lived close to the Coeur d'Alene Tribe Reservation near the Idaho city and lake that bears their name. He has frequently visited Pueblos in New Mexico and participated in a workshop re-pairing and helping to preserve adobe structures of an 11th century Anasazi village site near Santa Fe, NM in the Kit Carson National Forest. He has talked with natives at historic Amerindian sites in the setting of this novel while enjoying the hospitality of Quebec City and the surrounding area.

Johnston researched this novel in the Springfield, Illinois, Historical Library, la *Bibliothèque Nationale,* and *les Archives Nationales de France* in Paris, the old *Reading Room* of the British Museum Library in London, and the archives of *l'Université de Lavale, Cité universitaire, Sainte-Foy (Québec) Canada,* where he took a course on French exploration in North America. See his web site: www.thecirclebroken.com. Richard welcomes responces to his writing.

The Circle Broken, A Story of Love, Death and Discovery by Richard Johnston